Tears
Of
Chios

Tears
Of
Chios

K. PEARSON BRADLEY

Lawson Press, LLC

ISBN: 9798985915105 (paperback)
ISBN: 9798985915129 (hardcover)
ISBN: 9798985915112 (ebook)

"First say to yourself what you would be; and then do what you have to do."

Epictetus

ACKNOWLEDGMENTS

I would not, and could not, have birthed this book without the help of many people. Mrs. Morrissey, who let my high school creative writing class get in touch with our muses by lying on the floor in the dark while she fed us writing prompts. Marilyn, Jesse, Ginger, and Natalie, my familial cheerleaders. Annabel, Audrey, Joelle, Kathie, Lisa L., Lisa M., and Stephanie, whose love of books and encouragement over the years helped make this possible. My soul sisters, Terri, Debby, Melanie, and Preetika, who have been there for me since we were kids. Dougall Fraser, who helped me rediscover my passion for writing and the color red. My editor, Emily Tamayo Maher, who provided eagle-eyed critical feedback with love, patience, and lots of Columbian coffee. Rachael and Christa for being my very first beta readers and sharing their keen insights on what I thought was my final draft. DejaVu for the art and cover design that brought Seba to life.

And finally, to my husband Dave, daughter Jane, and daughter/story consultant Kate, who endured the writing process with grace, compassion, and only a few raised eyebrows. I love you!

1 ISLAND OF SNAKES

Chios, Greece 1759

Sebastian Krizomatis had often seen Ottoman vipers slithering in the hills above his village. From a young age, he had worked the groves with his family and all the other inhabitants of Sessera. Now, at the age of eight, he carried a long olivewood stick to clear the area around the *skinos* trees, the most valuable resource on the island of Chios. Seba (as most in the village called him), lived on the only island in the world where the mastiha tree, or skinos, could grow. At certain times of the year, the gnarled trees dripped sap from their branches, which hardened into sparkling translucent tears reputed to hold unique magical healing properties. Everyone on earth clamored for the Tears of Chios; they were a treasured commodity more valuable than gold—and one which belonged to Mustafa III, sultan of the Ottoman Empire.

Life was hard for Greek families under Ottoman rule, but

Seba and his family were very lucky. They were keepers and cultivators of the mastic tears, carrying a legacy of skill and tradition passed down for hundreds of generations. The precious tears were tiny white-hued gems, tasting of mint, pine, musk, and green herbs—an enticing flavor that defied description. In order to protect his monopoly over the Tears of Chios, the sultan created a special government district within the Ottoman Empire, overseen by his mother, the Sultana Vidala. The district encompassed Seba's village of Sessera and the other twenty mastic villages that dotted Chios's southern region. In exchange for cultivating the Tears of Chios, the sultan protected the Greek villagers behind thick-walled cities made of stone, hidden in the valleys of the *mastichochoria*.

On this rosy morning in May, as they did most mornings, Seba and the other villagers of Sessera had left the safety of their stone-walled enclave to walk the dirt path to the skinos trees. The growing season was almost upon them, one of the busiest times of the year. The sun shone bright and warm, but a cool breeze flowed down from the mountains into the wide valley that bore Sessera's sacred skinos terraces. Seba was carrying his newly acquired olivewood walking stick, swinging it around as if he were training a donkey. He had recently attempted to use it on his family's donkey, Matilde, to little effect. Despite her keen sense of curiosity, she was not impressed with Seba's twirling baton, and had made her position known with a snort and a kick that sent him flying into a pile of dung. Now he only used the stick to pretend to train a donkey, and later to clear away the branches pruned from the skinos. He was kicking up earth from the dusty trail, which swirled behind him in an opaque brown cloud. The other children were laughing and playing tag as they ambled up the hill toward the hallowed trees.

A girl, a year older than Seba, skipped ahead, her tight brown braids bouncing as she talked nonstop to her older sister. The girls were carrying baskets of bread and figs for the midday meal, and chattered like little birds without a care. In all of his eight years of life on earth, Seba had never spoken a word to the girl, whose name was Xenia. He wouldn't have been able to anyway, because she was not the kind of girl who allowed interruptions. Her older sister, Demetria, was ten years old, but barely spoke a word, especially when Xenia was near. Demetria seemed perfectly content to smile, listen, and be entertained by her effusive little sister, whose free hand and lips were moving at a breakneck speed.

Seba had been in awe of Xenia since he was three or four years old. She was brave in a way that he wasn't. She seemed to know exactly what to say and do in every situation. While Seba would hang back in the shadows, silently observing, Xenia was in the middle of the fray, singing and dancing—but mostly talking. Seba could tell the adults in the village adored her, oohing and ahhing over her expansive vocabulary and her sweet confidence. He imagined her as some kind of exotic creature from a distant land. What must it feel like, he wondered, to be carefree and outspoken?

Ambling up the path, watching Xenia's mouth move at dizzying speed, Seba dropped his stubby stick. He had been thinking about what it would feel like to have everyone looking at him. He thought it would be excruciatingly embarrassing. And just as he bent down to pick up the stick, thinking that he *never* wanted anyone to look at him, he felt a shock of electricity bolt through his body.

"Sebastian, *stop!*" The sound of his mother's voice—she was the only one who ever called him by his full Christian name—struck him like a dagger in the back of his head. He held his breath. Xenia stopped talking and turned around; she and Demetria stared at Seba, terrified, as if he were an evil monster oozing venom from his very pores. What had he done?

"Sebastian, *don't move!*"

Slowly focusing past his dirty fingernails, he saw what had struck fear into his mother. An Ottoman viper was ensconced between two rocks, its head just ten inches from Seba's face as he bent down to grab his stick. The snake's brown-and-gray mottled head was raised and drawn back, as if it had been about to strike when his mother screamed. Seba was so close that he could see the black slits in the viper's eyes and the bumps on its skin. His first thought was that the hair-raising screech from his mother, like the cry of a vicious harpy, was so hideous that it worked on poisonous snakes. The viper and Seba were both frozen in time.

He knew if the snake bit him, he would probably die from the poison. Seba had heard the story of his sister countless times, though she had died years before he was born; he thought of it every time he visited her grave on the hillside above the village. She had only been three years old, playing in the skinos groves as Mama was pruning the trees, when the deadly Ottoman viper had struck. Maria had died almost instantly.

"As God is my witness, I will not lose another child to this evil serpent," he heard his mother whisper. "Mary, Mother of God, protect my son and deliver him from evil." Agnete Krizomatis often invoked the Virgin Mary. When she did, she always made the sign of the cross; but not today. She was absolutely still.

Seba stared directly into the viper's wide black nostrils, paralyzed by fear. They were at a stalemate. If he attempted to move, Seba would feel two fangs of searing pain in his cheek, or hand, or ankle—wherever the viper chose to strike. Even if he remained still, the snake might attack anyway; Ottoman vipers didn't need a reason to kill.

The earth stopped spinning for both Seba and his mother. It was as if they could feel each other's presence, but were unable to act.

Seba's grandfather, whom he called Papouli, was already far ahead on the path, and oblivious to the drama unfolding down the hill. "What's going on?" he yelled impatiently. "What are you waiting for? These trees aren't going to prune themselves!" He raised his shoulders and stretched out his hands, looking down for Agnete. When he saw her rigid with fear, he ran a few steps down the path, then stopped cold. Seeing the viper coiled up in the rocks, his grandson's face just a few inches away, he stood stock-still. A horrified expression seeped into the grooves of his wrinkled face.

Immobilized, Seba heard the sounds of his friends Thaddeus and Nikos making their way up from the village. He could hear them laughing, shoving each other in the ribs, teasing and taunting. They were older than Seba—ten years old, the same age as Demetria, though they had not matured as much as she had, and were so caught up in their roughhousing that they never saw Seba's standoff with the viper. Seba's mother was gesticulating with tiny flicks of her head for the two of them to stop and quiet down, but they were utterly unaware.

"You are so stupid that the donkeys feel sorry for you!" Nikos hooted, shoving Thaddeus in the chest with both hands.

"Well, you're so mean that the donkeys want to use your head for kicking practice!" Thaddeus, the larger of the two boys, donkey-kicked Nikos in the shoulder.

"You blockhead, are you trying to kill me?" Nikos swung wildly at Thaddeus.

"I could break you in half if I wanted to!" Thaddeus reached for Nikos's arm, but missed. Nikos, using Thaddeus's momentum, grabbed his shoulder and pushed him forward with all his might. Thaddeus went flying face-first in Seba's direction.

Seba saw a flash of light, inside of which Papa, Mama, Papouli, Thaddeus, Xenia, Demetria, and Nikos appeared and then vanished. He wondered if he had just died. But as Thaddeus put his arms out in front of him to break his fall, his right elbow sideswiped a palm-sized rock that skipped over the path, directly toward the viper. The rock missed the snake by an inch, and the viper instantaneously recoiled behind a jagged rock. It happened so quickly that Seba didn't even see it move. It was simply no longer there.

Seba instinctively jumped back and his mother ran to him, squeezing him so hard that the breath he had been holding was forced out in a grunt. Agnete stepped back and put both hands on Seba's face. "Sebastian, thanks be to God, you are safe!" Then she wheeled on Thaddeus. "You foolish boy, you saved his life!"

Thaddeus looked stunned to be chastised and congratulated at the same time.

Xenia came running down the path, braids flying behind her. "Mrs. Krizomatis, wasn't it just awful? It was as if we were all turned to stone! It felt like ages and ages! What if that snake had bitten Seba? I can't even imagine it! Thaddeus is a hero, isn't he? He's like Heracles!"

Seba cringed. Mama did not like any talk of gods, goddesses, or demigods like Heracles. Seba thought Xenia might earn herself a slap, as he often did for mentioning the heroes of the ancient stories. But he was shocked when Mama only smiled, wiped a tear from her cheek, and said "Yes, dear, Thaddeus is a hero, isn't he?"

Seba was dumbfounded. He would have been less surprised if his mother had turned Xenia over her knee and spanked her for blaspheming the Lord.

The spell was broken by Nikos's drawling voice. "Well, really, *I'm* the hero," he said churlishly. "If I hadn't pushed Thaddeus, the viper would still be there."

Xenia didn't miss a beat; she ran to Nikos and put her hand on his arm. "Oh, yes, Nikos, you're a hero, too! Isn't he, Mrs. Krizomatis?"

As Xenia and Mama fawned over Thaddeus and Nikos, Seba felt a warm and familiar grip on his shoulder. It was his grandfather, Papouli.

"You gave us a scare, young man. Are you all right?"

Seba looked into his grandfather's chocolate-brown eyes and nodded. His heartbeat was slowly returning to normal. Papouli reached into his pocket and pulled out one small mastic tear. Seba's eyes grew wide. The sultan allotted only a few tiny nuggets to each villager after the harvest. Anyone seen with mastic tears outside of their homes in the village were usually arrested for stealing, and the Ottoman enforcers were not merciful. Seba knew of several men in Sessera who had only one hand—the other cut off at the wrist as punishment. It was a constant reminder that the mastic tears belonged to the Ottoman Empire, not the villagers.

The fact that Papouli carried a mastic tear in his pocket was dangerous. He must have saved one of the few tears he had been given from last year's harvest. He handed it to Seba. "You almost died today, my grandson. If anyone needs the healing powers of the Tears of Chios, it is you.

Quickly, put it in your mouth and chew. It will bring you comfort all day."

Seba didn't question his grandfather. He took the little piece of mastiha; it looked like a hard white pebble, no larger than the knuckle of his smallest finger. He could smell the distinctive aroma—a mix of pine, sweet mint, cedar, and crisp green herbs. Wild edible plants grew all over Chios, but nothing came close to the ambrosial scent of mastiha. Seba popped the little tidbit into his mouth and bit down. There was a crunching sound as his teeth broke through the exterior. An explosion of flavor enveloped his mouth and worked its way down his body. His shoulders, which had been hunched with tension, dropped with relief. Seba released an audible sigh.

Papouli's face brightened and he said, "Keep chewing— mastiha is the food of the gods. That's why you can chew the gum of those tears for hours and it will never lose its flavor or potency."

Seba chewed slowly, savoring the minty herbal flavor; he imagined its healing power mixing with his saliva. He felt like everything was right with the world, a world where the Ottoman viper did not exist.

Papouli clapped Seba on the back and said, "Let's get moving. I don't want your Uncle Phillip to scold us for a late start in the groves today." He turned toward the terraces of trees in the distance.

Seba's grandfather was right to be worried. The Ottomans gave the villages of the *mastichochoria* many privileges, but they expected much in return. The mastic villagers did not pay land taxes, trade taxes, or personal taxes to the sultan, even though everyone else on Chios did. Sessera paid only a tithe of their mastic production. Most importantly for Seba, the mastic villagers did not have to provide their oldest sons to the Ottoman military as tribute. Other Christian families all over Greece were required to send their oldest sons to convert to Islam and be trained in the Ottoman fleet or the cavalry. The mastic villagers understood that their privileged position was a blessing bestowed on them by God. Instead of military oppression, taxes, loss of their sons, and violence, the mastic villages in the south of Chios had their own councilmen, judges, tax collectors, watchmen, and managers. By permitting the local Greek families in the *mastichochoria* to manage their own affairs, the Ottoman government reduced its administrative costs and maintained a level of peace and prosperity. In return, the villagers worked long hours in the skinos groves, and were penned inside the walls of the villages at night.

Pirates from Spain, Italy, England, the Maldives, Egypt, and Constantinople patrolled the Aegean Sea, for the island's mastiha was a coveted commodity. The mastic villages were always in danger of attack. As a result, the villages of the *mastichochoria* were nestled in the low valleys of Chios, surrounded by mountains and fortified with stone walls as thick as three men standing side by side. Each village had a central watchtower, or *viglia*, inaccessible from the ground. The watchtower stood above the stone rooftops of the village, with small trapezoidal windows at the top so the guards could view the sea and raise the alarm if pirates were in the area. The only way into or out of the watchtower was by a rope ladder thrown from the high narrow windows, almost thirty feet above the ground.

After the months-long process of harvesting, the tears were cleaned, dried, separated, and packed into storage crates until tax time. There was no private market for mastiha—the sultan had a monopoly. For anyone who attempted to smuggle or sell mastiha without the sultan's seal, which was only added to the crates after payment of taxes, the punishment was death. The sultan's enforcers were merciless. Any guard of the watchtower who failed to spot a pirate ship before an Ottoman overseer learned of it would be beaten—a hundred strokes with a bamboo stick—on the bottoms of his bare feet.

Seba turned to follow his grandfather, but was stopped in his tracks. Xenia, who had been hugging and congratulating Thaddeus and Nikos, broke free and grabbed both of Seba's hands in hers. "To think we almost lost you!" she said. "You must be more careful!" With that, she turned on her heel, and ran back up the path toward the others. "You'll never believe it, everyone! Seba was almost killed by a poisonous Ottoman viper. And Nikos and Thaddeus saved him!" Her voice trailed off as she flew up the path toward the mastiha grove, her sister following closely behind.

Seba's face flooded red with shame. Xenia made it sound as if he had purposely put himself in mortal danger. He wished that she would stop talking. Soon every Chian villager for fifty miles around would know the story of the boy from Sessera who stumbled blindly into the lair of an Ottoman viper. Uncle Phillip might even blame him for the late start to the workday, and everyone would stare and whisper about the idiot boy of Sessera. Why couldn't Xenia keep her mouth shut?

Seba glared after her—no longer an exotic beauty with sweet confidence, but rather an evil droning demon who talked her victims to shame and death. Like snow melting in the sun, Seba's admiration for Xenia disappeared, evaporating into the ether. He started up the path, vowing never to pick up another stupid olive stick.

2 LEMON SOUP

A near-death experience was nothing to the skinos trees; their branches needed to be pruned, and new saplings planted for the next generation. Seba, Mama, and Papouli worked until near sundown in the groves, and—as they did each day—arrived weary and dust-covered to their home in Sessera. It was a cozy dwelling of stone, just like all the other houses in the village. The animals were housed on the ground floor, while the family lived on the floor above it, kept warm by a huge stone hearth. As they climbed the ladder to the family's living space, Agnete, Papouli, and Seba were surprised to find Seba's father, Kostas, stirring a pot of delicious-smelling *avgolemono* over a roaring fire. The cast-iron pot hung from an iron bar on a hinge mounted inside the hearth. Although the late spring days were warm, the cold fell quickly with the setting sun, especially in a stone home with small windows. A bubbling warm pot of egg-and-lemon soup was a welcome treat for the whole family.

"Kostas Krizomatis, what are you doing home from the shipyard so early? And whatever on earth possessed you to cook?" Mama's tone was somewhat scolding, but her smile was so tender and the look of love she gave her husband so genuine that Seba knew she was secretly pleased with Papa.

Seba's grandfather, eyes twinkling, asked, "Do my eyes deceive me, or is that Hestia herself, goddess of the hearth, bending over the avgolemono?"

Seba's head jerked around to look at Mama, to see if she would reprimand Papouli for his mention of the pagan daughter of Rhea and Kronos, but Mama was so happy to see Papa that she hadn't even heard Papouli's voice. As the grandfather in the home, Papouli sometimes got away with stories of the Greek gods and goddesses in the house by saying they were part of the family's heritage—no different from Jesus, the disciples, Saint Luke, Socrates, Plato, olive oil, and lemons. Seba loved the stories of the ancient Greeks: Odysseus, Jason and the Argonauts, Heracles, and Perseus were his favorites. However, he knew not to appear too excited about them around Mama, lest he be punished for worshiping a false god or blaspheming the Lord.

Papa held his arms wide and Seba ran to him, giving him a huge hug around the waist, smelling the salty ocean air on him and the faint smell of exotic spices. His father wore a linen shirt, the blue color of the Aegean Sea, with canvas trousers tucked into his dark brown leather boots. His head was uncovered, and his black curly hair fell over his ears. Seba drank in the scent of his father, feeling warm and secure. Papa's calming energy fell like a cozy blanket over the whole house. Mama forgot to worry and scold when Papa was around, and Papouli was even more ready for a joke than usual. Papa's presence was like the sun's golden glow in May.

"I realize it must be a surprise for you to see me here at this early hour, egg and lemon soup at hand," Papa said. "But there are some interesting happenings at the shipyard, and Mesich let us all go home early today. He wants us to get a good night's sleep so we can be on our best behavior tomorrow. That's when one of the new ships from the Levant Company arrives for repairs. Now, go wash up. I'll tell all of you the news when we sit down."

Seba changed out of his dirty cotton shirt, dipped out some water from the stone amphora into a small basin for washing, and scrubbed his hands faster than he had ever done in his life, his mouth watering all the while. Avgolemono was his favorite dinner, and one of the first foods he had ever eaten after he was weaned from his mother's milk. It was made with chicken broth and barley, thickened with eggs and, most importantly, flavored with lemons; the combination was heavenly—both comforting and uplifting.

When Seba returned from washing up, his mother had ladled heaping portions of avgolemono into four large olivewood bowls, with pieces of chicken and *koulouria*— Greek bread formed into rings and copiously covered in sesame seeds—for dipping into the soup. His father was in his usual seat at the head of their small rectangular table, flanked by Mama on the left and Seba on his right, with Papouli sitting directly opposite. They all said the mealtime prayer together, which Seba had learned to recite not long after he could string three words together:

"The poor shall eat and be satisfied, and they who seek the Lord shall praise Him; their hearts shall live to the ages of ages.

"Glory to the Father and the Son and the Holy Spirit, now and forever and to the ages of ages. Amen.

"Lord, have mercy.

"Lord, have mercy.

"Lord, have mercy.

"Christ our God, bless the food and drink of Your servants, for You are holy always, now and forever and to the ages of ages.

"Amen."

Seba wondered if Papouli also said a silent thank you to Demeter, the goddess of agriculture, and Dionysus, the god of food and wine. If he did, he certainly didn't let Mama know it.

Seba raised the spoon to his mouth and inhaled the bright lemony aroma mixed with the satisfying scent of roasted chicken. The taste on his tongue was even better: silky, smooth, and just as comforting as his father. Most everyone in Sessera, probably everyone on the entire island of Chios, had a recipe for avgolemono. Some added wheat berries instead of barley, and the truly wealthy on the island added white rice imported from Anatolia.

Seba was lost in a world of egg, chicken, and lemon, when his father said, "Son, I'm guessing you like this version?"

"Yes, Papa!"

"As God has blessed our table, I would also like to offer a prayer of thanks to the wife of Mesich, who works with me at the shipyard, who has been blessed with so many chickens this spring that she roasted several and sent them to work to share with all of us." Papa pointed to the shelf where Mama kept the spices, where sat a stoneware bowl full of fresh brown eggs. "Apparently, she also has so many hens laying eggs that she can't keep up with the supply. Given those ingredients, the avgolemono was begging to be made."

Mama softly patted Papa's hand. "It's delicious, Kostas. Thank you—and please thank Mesich for us. I have some herbs I've dried over the winter. Shall I send them to work with you, to thank Mesich's wife for this bounty?"

"Yes, I think he would appreciate it. You can dry fennel and dill more perfectly than anyone I know, Agnete. Somehow the fronds stay green and fragrant, even through the cold winter months. And we have some long days ahead of us at the shipyard, so it would be a welcome treat for Mesich and his wife."

After they finished the meal, Mama said, "Would anyone like some coffee? Or are you men going to the village square tonight?"

"I'd love some of your delicious Turkish coffee, Agnete," Papa said. "Do we have any sweets—other than you, my sweet?"

Papouli groaned. "On that nauseating note, I'll be going to the village square to hear the news of the day. No coffee for me, Agnete. I'll get mine from Sotirios's *kafenion*. And thank you, Kostas, for the wonderful meal. *Kalispera!*"

Mama laughed and shook her head at Papouli. How different they were, father and daughter—Papouli so lively and happy, always telling stories and humming songs, tapping his fingers and toes or whittling little figures from the branches of olive trees; Mama pulsing with a frenetic kind of energy, more intense and alarming, like those Ottoman whirling dervishes of Papouli's bedtime stories. It was easier to see that Mama and Papouli were blood when Papa was around; he tamed his wife's ferocious energy and redirected it, making her seem like Seba's lively and entertaining grandfather.

"I have some yogurt from the goats we milked a few days ago, and the honey Mrs. Lampros gave us last fall.

Interested?"

"I couldn't ask for a more perfect ending to this meal! Thank you, *agape mou*."

Mama smiled and busied herself with cleaning up the dinner dishes, preparing the yogurt and honey, and making coffee in the *briki* over the fire. The hammered-copper coffee pot with its long wooden handle held a place of pride in Seba's home; it had been passed down by Papouli's grandmother.

"Would you like some yogurt, Sebastian?" she asked. Seba's head bobbed up and down vigorously. This meal and the time with his family had erased the fear and embarrassment of the day's events.

The yogurt was cold and tangy, thick with a hint of sourness on Seba's tongue. The golden honey smelled of citrus and oregano, balancing out the tartness of the yogurt. As he savored his dessert, watching his parents talk quietly, Seba thought about the two of them. Mama, like the yogurt, was often acidic and not too sweet. Papa, like the honey, was warm and soothing. Both pairs seemed to be made for each other. He couldn't think of a more perfect combination.

Seba knew he was fortunate to be from a mastic village; his Mama had told him so often that it could not be denied. However, it was his father's vocation and freedom that gave him butterflies in his stomach: the promise of the unknown, and the lure of the sea. Looking down at his feet, still covered in the dust of the mastic groves, he wondered if he would be lucky enough to work with his father someday, beside the wide expanse of water and the ocean breezes.

That evening, as he climbed the stone stairs to his straw mattress on the roof, he was so grateful for his family that he thanked everyone he could remember—God, Jesus, Mary, the Holy Spirit, Saint Paul, Saint Peter, Zeus, Hestia,

Demeter, Poseidon, and all the others.

#

The summer months rolled by and a very warm day in August arrived. The Krizomatis family was finishing a pre-dawn breakfast of sheep's milk cheese, fresh-baked herb bread, wild strawberries, and—of course—Turkish coffee. Papouli was tapping his toes and humming the tune to a *tripatos,* one of his favorite Greek dances. The name meant "three steps," and Papouli's feet were doing the three steps' dance under the table.

Papa said, "Honestly, Vaios, why didn't you ever learn to play an instrument? You've got the talent."

"Kostas, I ask myself that question sometimes, but then I realize if I were the musician, I'd have to keep these feet planted, and they would not be happy!" He did a few extra steps under the table for effect, and Seba laughed. He also couldn't picture his grandfather sitting still long enough to practice the *kithara* or *santouri.*

Mama said, "Then we three are lucky—the only ones blessed with a private concert by the great Vaios Georgelous!"

Papouli stood up and took a bow as if he were Apollo himself, the god of music and dance.

Mama looked at Seba. Did she know he was envisioning Apollo? He thought she was about to cross herself and accuse him of blasphemy, but instead she said, "Sebastian, your grandfather brings to my mind a verse from the Bible. Do you know which one I'm thinking of?"

He thought he did. "Is it Psalm 149? 'Let them praise His name in the dance'?"

"Good, Sebastian! Yes, it is! Why don't you recite it for us?"

Seba's face turned red. Why did Mama always test him?

He looked at his father, and his father winked, saying, "My son could recite the entire Book of Psalms if necessary. Go on, Seba, just the first few verses, I know you can do it."

Seba swallowed the strawberry he had been chewing and said,

Alleluia. Sing to the Lord a new song: his praise is in the assembly of the saints.

Let Israel rejoice in him that made him; and let the children of Zion exult in their King.

Let them praise his name in the dance: let them sing praises to him with timbrel and psaltery.

For the Lord takes pleasure in his people; and will exalt the meek with salvation.

Mama beamed and Papa nodded as if to say, "See, I told you so."

Papouli looked dramatically glum and said, "Well, if I have to be shown up by someone, I guess it should be my grandson."

Papa stood up and struck an uncharacteristically officious pose. "Seba, I was debating whether to ask you this, but now that you've shown how much you've learned at the young age of eight years, I think you are more than ready. Would you like to join me at the shipyard today? I believe there is another ship arriving from England for repairs, and it will be a sight to behold. It's called a clipper, and it's supposed to be one of the fastest ships on the sea. This one was caught in a storm, and we are told it is limping its way to Chios for repair of the main mast. This would be a fine learning experience for you. That is, if your mother does not object." He smiled warmly at Mama, knowing she would never refuse him anything.

Mama, her face still luminous in response to Seba's Bible recitation, placed her hand on his shoulder. "Of course,

Kostas. That would be a very special treat for Sebastian."

"Yes, Papa, yes!"

Papouli asked, "What have they got you doing now, Kostas? Aren't you already the best shipbuilders in all the empire? I can't imagine they can ask more of you than you have already given."

"That's very kind of you, Vaios, and we love what we do. Apparently, our reputation is growing. They say the sultan himself has learned of the work we've done to increase the speed and efficiency of his merchant fleet. The English are increasing trade with the Ottomans, and are proposing that we become the exclusive shipyard for repairs of their trading fleet, this 'Levant Company.'"

"Now it's to be Englishmen on Chios?" cried Papouli. "God preserve us, we're being overrun with foreigners!"

"We already repair ships from all over the world," Papa smiled. "And the English are men like any other. Pale, perhaps, and tending toward fat in the middle—"

"That's a nice way to talk of your fellow man," said Mama with a little frown.

"Quite right, my dear," Papa said. "I mustn't be unkind. England is a Christian empire, at least." He stroked his chin. "Although with the way they curse and swear—"

"You were *telling* us about the Levant Company," she said with a smile.

"Ah, yes. It's a trading concern, you see. Many ships. They've been using Smyrna as their port for repairs. But Ahmed has convinced them to stop here instead, rather than get caught up in the backlog of ships calling on Smyrna. He says the sultan has put great faith in the significance of Chios, and wants to make a good impression on these Englishmen. It is an immense honor, and it will bring much more work for us in the shipyard."

"More work?" Mama pouted. "We hardly see you as it is! I miss my husband."

"I know, my dear. And I miss all of you every day. But it won't be forever. The sultan is consolidating his ships in Constantinople, so eventually the bigger ships will be built and repaired there. From what Mesich and Ahmed tell me, this English company is changing trade practices all around the Mediterranean."

Papouli said, "Who is this Ahmed? I haven't heard you mention him before."

Papa looked pensive, then replied, "He's Mesich's boss, very high in the chain of command. I believe he may even be related to Sultan Mustafa III himself. His manner is overbearing, but it appears his bark is more fierce than his bite."

"Let's hope so. I don't trust any of those Ottoman vipers, not even Mesich."

Papa frowned. "I won't hear you speak ill of my friend, Vaios. We've worked together for many years, and his supervision is part of the reason our shipyard is gaining prominence in the empire."

"He's a Muslim," Papouli grumbled.

"He is," Papa said. "And he's my best friend."

Papouli looked unconvinced, but let it lie. Seba had never seen him argue with Papa, and today was no different. "Fine, but I bet his dancing doesn't compare to mine." He did a couple of dance steps, which had the desired effect of defusing the tension. Even Mama laughed, and smacked him with the towel she used to dry the breakfast dishes.

Papa changed the subject away from Ahmed, and as he described the sail-swept vessels, Seba imagined the beautiful ships' sleek wooden hulls and billowing canvas sheets. He yearned to see them with his eyes rather than solely in his imagination.

Conversation turned to that day with the Ottoman viper. Seba tried to blot out that morning from his memory, and he wished his family would stop bringing it up, but Papouli couldn't help himself. He would laugh out loud, slap his leg, and say, "Those boys, Thaddeus and Nikos!" Seba knew Papouli was envisioning them tussling on the path, which had ultimately saved him from a deadly snake attack, but he hated the feelings of shame and nausea that welled up every time anyone mentioned the incident.

"They remind me of Heracles and Hades!" Papouli often made that comparison because Thaddeus was big and strong like Heracles, and Nikos was thin and dark like Hades.

Mama frowned and bristled, and Seba couldn't tell if it was because of the mention of pagan gods or because of Thaddeus and Nikos themselves.

"Those boys need a good beating, both of them!" she said. "They are always causing trouble, and they never learn. I don't care if Thaddeus's father has a broken back, he should still be able to discipline his son. And Nikos's father, on Sessera's mastic council—he must be terribly embarrassed by his son's behavior. To think that a councilman's son would be so irresponsible! A thorough whipping would bring those boys in line."

Mama made a fist, as if she'd be happy to whip them both at the same time. Seba believed she could do it. Papouli had nicknamed her "five feet of fury," and Seba agreed it was an accurate description.

"No, no, Agnete," said Papa. "If advice will not improve them, neither will the rod."

"As if either one of those bull-headed boys would listen

to advice!"

"Agnete, I was once a headstrong boy, and yet you married me."

Mama laughed and held her hand up to Papa's cheek. "Very true, my sweet husband, very true. You are the heart and soul of good character and honor. Our family is blessed by your virtue, and I am pleased that our Sebastian has the wits to keep his mouth closed and his hands to himself. Not like Thaddeus and Nikos, those unruly heathens. Sebastian, I am proud to call you my son."

Seba was surprised to hear Mama say that, because he had thought for months that she might be angry at him—that she might blame him for tempting death with an Ottoman viper, even though he hadn't done it on purpose. Looking around the table, he realized that more than anything, it was Papa's influence. He made everyone around him feel safe, and he could even smooth Mama's rough edges and fiery temper. Thinking of Thaddeus's father with his broken back, and Nikos's high-and-mighty father, Seba felt very lucky to be the son of Kostas Krizomatis, the famous shipbuilder of Sessera.

3 THE SHIPYARD

Sessera was three miles inland, and the shipyard where Kostas worked was on the east coast of Chios, overlooking the Aegean Sea that separated the island from Anatolia. Seba had heard his father speak of the Silk Road, an ancient route by which caravans brought silks from China to Ephesus and Smyrna, where they were transported by ship to people all over the world. This trade had gone on for thousands of years, and Chios's location on one of the trade routes between Egypt and Constantinople made it an important part of the Ottoman Empire, even without the production of mastiha.

The three-mile walk to the shipyard opened a whole new world for Seba. It was as if they were walking toward the thrill of the unknown. Unlike each day in the skinos groves, where everything happened according to a plan and a schedule established by the Ottoman overseers, the shipyard was full of new and intriguing stories from the far corners of the globe. The smells of fennel, almythria, chamomile, and olive seemed so much sweeter and crisper.

"Papa, what are these smells? The skinos groves don't smell like this."

His father laughed. "You notice it, too? It is the breeze from the sea. It carries all the scents from the ships that travel throughout the world. It smells like adventure, doesn't it? There's a whole wide world of things we've never seen, Seba. I've heard stories from the men who have worked on ships that sail to places where the land is covered in ice all year round, and other places where the trees are so thick that it feels like night even at midday."

Seba looked up at the huge pine trees dotting the landscape, surrounded by stands of olive trees and lots of scrubby bushes. The pines provided plenty of welcome shade, but were not so serried as to obscure the sun, whose rays beamed between the trees and onto his father's head. With the sun's glow illuminating the outline of his head, Papa looked like one of the saints depicted in the icons in Sessera's church. Seba was filled with gratitude and love for his father.

Kostas stopped walking and put his hand on Seba's shoulder. "Did you know that we are descended from the best shipbuilders in all of Greece, since before the time of Homer? In fact, in ancient times, six hundred years before our Lord Jesus Christ walked on earth, the naval power of Chios was the pride of the Aegean and Ionian Seas. We supplied the largest fleet—one hundred ships, if you can imagine it—at the battle of Lade against the Persians."

Seba looked into his father's deep gray eyes and envisioned him as an ancient shipbuilder. It gave Seba chills to know that this was his family legacy.

"And later, when the Athenians formed the Delian

League, Chios was not required to pay monetary tribute to join. Instead, the Athenians requested that Chios supply them with ships for the alliance. Our Greek engineering is unsurpassed! In fact, in ancient Greece, even right here on this island, young students were only taught three subjects." Papa ceremoniously raised one finger and said dramatically, "Mathematics—to sharpen the young mind's use of logic." He raised another finger. "Music—to bathe the soul in gentleness. And athletics—to care for the vessels that carry our souls through this blessed life." He clapped his hands over his head for emphasis. "And that, my son, is why Greece has the best shipbuilders in the world, with the best songs!"

Seba nodded, and his heart expanded, filling with pride at his Greek heritage.

"Of course, I'd rather build the ship than sail it—I'll leave that kind of adventure to the mariners. Do you think you might like to build ships with your father one day?"

Seba nodded and jumped up and down, as if his soul's most fervent wish had just been granted.

"Well, maybe when you are older, I can teach you. For right now, however, we are a mastic family, cultivating the skinos trees, and you must learn the ways of the land from Papouli and Uncle Phillip. In fact, if your mother's ancestors had not been a mastic-growing family, you would be shipped off to the Ottoman military. You should feel very fortunate to have this position in the world. That is also your heritage, and we are blessed to live in a time where mastic is sought after by every country on earth. There is plenty of time to learn the ways of the sea."

As they approached the shipyard, they could hear the sound of hammers on wood and saws ripping through the enormous pine logs which would soon become ships' hulls.

At least forty men worked at the shipyard, many of whom had sleeping quarters there and worked long before daylight and long after nightfall. Merchant ships docked here from all across the globe for repairs. The workers charged these merchants a hefty fee for repairs and they were always busy. Trade with Europe was booming and it was the speedy merchant ships the sultan needed to exert the Ottoman Empire's strength in the world.

The shipyard was buzzing with activity, and yet Seba could still hear the waves crashing against the rocks beyond the jetty protecting the shipyard's small cove. Overwhelmed yet curious, he slowed his step and slid behind his father as they entered the workplace.

"A good morning to you, Mesich," Papa called. "This is my son, Sebastian. He is here to help me with some difficult mathematical calculations related to the angle of the hull as it rises up from the keel. This so-called clipper ship is said to have the sharpest angle, but I don't know if that's based on the block coefficient of fineness or the prismatic coefficient, and I'd like to see how this engineering marvel stays afloat."

His father reached behind, and touching Seba's shoulder, brought him to face Mesich. The Ottoman supervisor towered imposingly over the boy, his thin mustache dipping down into a thick, short beard, framing a perpetual scowl. "Sebastian here is a true mathematician in the Pythagorean mold, you know," Papa continued.

Seba froze, holding his breath, and tried to pull back. What was his father saying? Why hadn't Papa told him they were working on mathematics today? He liked math, and was slightly better than the other children in the village school, but he was not Pythagoras by any means. He had learned some mathematical formulas from his teacher, a priest named Brother Timotheos, but he knew absolutely nothing about hulls or keels. Then Papa winked at Seba, who realized it was a joke. He exhaled, sending a wave of relief down his spine.

Mesich appeared to take Papa at his word, but his scowl did not diminish. "Fine, Kostas, but you must keep an eye on your mathematical genius. We have much to do today, and I will not tolerate distractions. If I see him disturbing anything or anyone, I must report him to Ahmed." Looking down through narrowed eyes at Seba, Mesich said, "Enjoy yourself, young man, but do not get in the way."

Papa stepped between them. "Understood, Mesich. And don't worry about Ahmed. I know how to handle him. He values my work, and we do not like to antagonize our Ottoman governors, do we?"

Papa smiled, but Mesich continued to look unhappy. "Just keep me out of it. If anyone asks me, I've not seen a pint-sized mathematical savant today or any day. Now get to work—the English ship will be arriving before noon. I've heard there's more sail yardage on these clippers than any other ships on the sea. We should be able to view its arrival from a long way off, so keep a watchful eye."

As they walked through the shipyard, Seba's head was snapping from right to left, trying to absorb the varied sights. Men were bending and piecing slats of wood together, stitching sails, smelting iron, and sanding the huge straight trees which would become the ships' masts. Everyone was doing a different job, yet all of the pieces fit together perfectly. Men seemed to be enjoying the work, calling to each other, laughing, taunting each other with rude jokes, but jumping in to assist each other if needed. It reminded Seba of the way the villagers worked together to cultivate the mastiha of the skinos trees.

As they walked to a small wooden building at the edge of the yard, Papa put his hands on Seba's shoulders. "Seba, make sure you heed Mesich. As you know, the Ottomans direct our work, and we have a heavy schedule of ships to provide for their fleet. Although we are descended from the great Greek culture of ancient times, Chios is part of the Ottoman Empire now, and our masters do not tolerate laziness, incompetence, or distractions. You are a good boy, and quiet, so they will give you no trouble. Stay by my side and you will be fine."

"Mesich is your friend, right? The one whose chickens lay all the eggs?"

"Yes, Mesich is my friend. He was one of the first people I met when I began working here, and we have worked together for more than fifteen years. You could even say we grew up together here at the shipyard, even though I am Christian and he is Muslim. I consider him not just a boss, but a colleague—although he would probably have to deny it to his Ottoman superiors. He is a good man, and has helped me in my career many times over. However, the sultan has placed very strict demands on this shipyard. And because Mesich is in charge, all the responsibility falls on his shoulders. It is a difficult job, and he handles it well. We will not cause Ahmed any trouble, and he will be proud to see my son here with me today. You will meet him, don't worry."

Seba worried just the same.

He listened to the men talking about wind speeds, tides, the best substances for waterproofing and sealing a ship— even about how to keep worms from destroying a wooden hull. He overheard a heated argument about the flexibility of the pinewood of Chios, which shocked Seba; the skinos trees were not flexible at all, and he could not imagine these gargantuan pine trees of Chios having any give to them. Every so often throughout the morning, the men would look out toward the sea, trying to spot the white sails of the clipper. The excitement mounted with every hour that passed, and the whole shipyard had a palpable atmosphere of anticipation as the men laughed and joked, poking fun at each other and telling stories of their childhoods, until shortly before noon.

A booming voice came calling across the shipyard. "Do I see a new method of construction in the production of the Ottoman merchant fleet?" A tall man wearing an enormous and lavishly decorated silk bashlyk had emerged from the building and was striding imperiously toward the workmen. "I did not know that ships were built by the wagging of tongues. My cousin, the Most High Sultan Mustafa III, will be anxious to learn this enigmatic manufacturing method—especially in light of the amount he pays you from his sacred treasury."

The newcomer's trousers, loose and draped down to his ankles, were a deep shade of red, matching his pointed leather boots, upon which intricate designs of tulips and scrollwork were embroidered in gold. A pale pink and white striped cotton vest topped the red trousers, held in place by a wide sash of gold silk that shimmered like the sun on the sea. Most magnificent, however, was the long silk indigo robe that fell from his shoulders to the tops of his boots and covered the full length of his arms. Seba had never seen anyone dressed so extravagantly, and had only viewed that shade of blue a few times in the twilight sky. It was mesmerizing; the power radiating from the tall man was unmistakable.

Papa put down his tools, stood, and walked confidently across the shipyard to greet the imposing man. Seba stayed where he was and shrunk into the log he was using as a seat.

"Just a bit of fun, Ahmed. We can't help but show our pride in shipbuilding, and once we get our hands on this so-called clipper ship, there will be no stopping the sultan's fleet. You know we are the best shipwrights in the world—better than Athens, Rhodes, Alexandria, and Crete combined. The men were simply showing their pride."

"Yes, Kostas, I never fail to tell the sultan, whenever I am at court, that Chios boasts the best shipbuilders in the Ottoman Empire." Ahmed sniffed. "However, I'd prefer this buffoonery not be on display when the English ship arrives. England is working hard to develop a relationship with the sultan, and I will not let anything get in the way."

Mesich's workers needed no further prodding. Their reputation was secure, and they intended to show Ahmed how they had earned it. The men quietly and quickly resumed their work.

Throughout the morning, Seba remembered his father's words, "Mesich is my friend." Seba could see that despite his gruff demeanor and glowering face, Mesich took pride in the work of his shipyard. The silk-dressed Ahmed, though—the cousin of the sultan—gave Seba a bad feeling.

Word came that the clipper ship had been delayed by weather; and so Papa was permitted to come home to Sessera with Seba that evening. Seba was disappointed that he hadn't seen the clipper; but he had managed to spend the whole day at the shipyard without incident, which meant that he would be invited back another time. Many nights his father had to sleep at the shipyard, so he was happy to have him at home this evening.

As Seba and his father entered the large wooden gates of Sessera, Xenia and her sister Demetria were filling their family's amphorae with water at the village well. Xenia jumped up when she saw Seba, almost knocking the amphora onto her sister.

"*Kalimera*, Mr. Krizomatis! *Kalimera*, Seba! Did you build any beautiful ships today?"

Seba shrunk behind his father. Ever since his confrontation with the snake, he had tried to avoid Xenia. In school and in church, he made sure not to sit anywhere near her. If he left his home and saw her in one of the narrow alleys of the village, he went back inside to wait a few minutes until she was gone. She talked too much, and always embarrassed him.

"No, we didn't finish any ships today," Papa smiled. "But we have several in the works, and one gorgeous clipper ship from the west will be visiting the shipyard for repairs very soon. I, for one, am excited to see it—and I think Seba is, too."

Papa put his arm around Seba's shoulder and brought him to stand at his side, elbowing him in the ribs.

"*Kalimera*, Xenia." Seba said it with as much enthusiasm as a dead slug, but that's how he felt at the moment.

"Seba, would you like to help Demetria and me fill our water jugs? They're going to be really heavy, and it would be so perfect if you would help us carry them home to our mother."

Seba's eyes pleaded with his father to make an excuse for him, but Papa was smiling broadly; Seba knew he could not escape. "Seba would love to assist you young ladies with your chore. Wouldn't you, Seba?"

Seba stifled his urge to groan. "Yes, Papa."

Xenia jumped up and down and clapped her hands. Then she grabbed Seba's hand and led him over to the village well. "Demetria and I were just talking about the cutest boys in the village. For some reason, she thinks

Thaddeus is the cutest, but I told her you were the most handsome boy in Sessera."

Seba felt his neck and face grow warm and he knew that he was flushing from pink to red. Demetria looked knowingly at Seba, as if she empathized with his plight, but she said nothing; she continued to pump water from the well into a large stone amphora.

Seba was dragging his feet as Xenia pulled him toward the source of water. He looked back at his father for salvation, but his father was laughing and walking in the other direction. Was Xenia destined to be the bane of his existence for the rest of his life?

She grabbed his hand and coiled it around her own, her tight brown braids bouncing and a smile lighting up her whole face. "In fact, I told Demetria that you and I were going to get married one day."

4 SCHOOL DAYS

At harvest time, the island of Chios brought forth every kind of fruit, vegetable, herb, and flower. The olive and fig trees hung heavy with fruit, and the villagers worked in the hot sun every day. Summer had turned to autumn, and the villagers of Sessera harvested the glistening tears from the skinos trees. When the harvest was over and Seba could see the first patches of snow on the tops of Chios's highest mountains, the village children attended school, taught by Brother Timotheos in a space adjacent to Sessera's central church.

On this early November day, Seba stepped outside the threshold of his warm home to see Xenia and Demetria walking to school. Brother Timotheos taught all ages at the same time in the village's school building. Seba had been on his way to school as well, but seeing Xenia, he retreated inside and silently latched the door.

"What are you doing, young man?"

Seba jumped out of his skin, his chalk and slate tumbling

to the floor. Papouli had climbed the ladder down from the living area to the animal pen, wearing his wool coat and boots; he was ready for his second morning coffee, this one in the village square. Seba tried to look nonchalant, but he knew he'd been caught in an act of cowardice, a near-sin for any self-respecting Greek boy. To make matters worse, his own grandfather was the one who saw it all play out.

"Not afraid of a couple of girls, are you?" Papouli couldn't help but grin at his grandson.

"No," Seba said indignantly, trying to preserve a tiny shred of manhood. "I just don't want to walk to school with them. Xenia talks too much."

Papouli put his hands on his hips, a sure sign that he was about to dispense a dose of ancient Greek wisdom. "Some people say I talk too much, Seba, so don't judge her solely on that basis. Quiet ones like you should enjoy having the talkers around. They take the pressure off."

"But she's a gossip."

Papouli nodded knowingly. "Ah, yes, the gossip. She's not the only one in Sessera. What do you think the men in the village square do every evening? They're mostly harmless once you realize they merely want a little attention. It reminds me of one of my favorite stories about Socrates. Have I ever told you the story of Socrates's three rules for discerning gossip?"

Seba had heard this story more times than he could count. Papouli preferred Socrates over the other ancient Greek philosophers, often spouting heuristic wisdom in a flowing fountain of epigrams. Seba could almost envision Papouli in an ancient Greek student's chiton and cloak, learning at the feet of the master.

However, Seba needed to put some distance between him and Xenia, so he leaned up against Matilde's pen and shook his head no.

Papouli continued, "Well, when Socrates was asked whether he wanted to hear a piece of gossip, he replied, 'Only if it passes this three-part test: One, Is it true? Two, Is it good or kind? And three, Will it benefit me to hear it?'" Papouli held up three wrinkled and slightly crooked fingers for effect.

"Socrates's friend considered the three rules. After a moment, he hung his head and left, realizing that he didn't know if it was true or whether it would benefit Socrates to hear it. What he did know was that it was not kind.

"I apply Socrates's three rules whenever someone in the village wants to gossip with me, and you can, too. When your friend Xenia offers to tell you something, ask her if it is absolutely, unquestionably true, if it is good and kind and helpful, and then ask her if it is something that will benefit you to hear it. Chances are, one of the answers to those questions will be 'no,' and then you can send her on her merry way."

"I don't think anything Xenia says is useful, good, or true, but that's not going to stop her from talking."

"Well, the next time you talk to her, why don't you mention Socrates's three rules, and see what she does?"

Seba wasn't planning on talking to her any time soon, so he didn't think he'd have a chance to find out. However, he wisely held his tongue, and smiled to himself, thinking he was the one putting Socratic wisdom to use.

"Now get to school, and don't ever let me catch you backing away from a conversation with a girl." Papouli winked and opened the door.

Xenia and Demetria were out of sight, and Seba was able to walk to school in peace. The school was a stone structure, just like all of the buildings in Sessera, connected by shared walls and divided by narrow streets and alleys of no discernible pattern. The narrow winding ways, many leading abruptly to dead ends, were another form of defense against pirates and raiders. If mastiha thieves somehow managed to penetrate Sessera's thick stone walls, they would be lost in a maze of twisting alleys leading nowhere. It was one of the many features of the village that made Seba feel safe. The school building was on the opposite side of the village square from Seba's house, about a ten-minute walk. As he entered the classroom, the children were buzzing with excitement.

Brother Timotheos was dressed in a peculiar fashion, with an apron over his monk's robes. He looked something like an ancient Greek philosopher himself, similar to the busts of Socrates and Plato that Seba had seen in the school's picture books. Brother Tim had a large head—probably to house his enormous brain, Seba thought—and a circle of dark curls that fell past his ears and wove seamlessly into his untamed beard. He was endlessly fascinating to Seba, and could expound on everything from the muscles of the Ottoman horses to the names of the constellations in the night sky to the thousands of medicinal uses for the Tears of Chios.

There was not an ounce of erudition that was outside Brother Tim's purview, and his enthusiasm was unlimited. He taught school all day in late autumn and winter, and then talked into the evenings with the men drinking in the village square. Being a monk, Brother Tim never drank alcohol (aside from the Eucharist). He was up hours before dawn in his little house behind the village church, reading and conducting experiments to share with the children during their lessons. Seba wondered if he ever slept, and imagined that he had been given some kind of divine energetic appointment from God. That's probably why he became a priest, along with all the others who were trained at the mountaintop monastery at Nea Moni. The monastery was as sacred to the people of Chios as the tears of the skinos trees, and its place in their world was no less cherished.

The story of Nea Moni was known to everyone on the island. Papouli's version was one of Seba's favorites, on par with the stories of Odysseus and Achilles. Mama never interrupted Papouli when he told this tale, and she assured Seba it was true. Papouli's story went something like this:

"Once there were three pious monks—Nikolas, John, and Joseph—who, forsaking a distracted life in the port of Chora, chose to live humbly near Mount Provateio in a small cave. One night, they saw a shimmering orange and yellow light slowly rise over the tree-lined slopes of the mountain. The brothers were terrified, but the Holy Spirit told them not to be afraid, because the Lord had a mission for them. Nikolas, John, and Joseph were led by the Holy Spirit to set fire to the area surrounding the mysterious glowing light. They understood that God used fire to purify and refine; they didn't know why, but they believed the Lord had asked them to purge and sanctify the ground surrounding Mount Provateio. Being good servants of the Lord, they obliged.

"Immense flames erupted high into the sky and engulfed the hills, moving higher and higher to the peak, filling the entire valley with intense glowing orange light as bright as the eastern sun. As the monks gazed into the inferno, it suddenly disappeared. Everything was charred and scorched the darkest black, the few remaining stumps of trees and bushes still smoldering. A grey and hazy smoke rose up from every inch of the mountainside, a burnt offering to God. Through the misty brume, our three friends spied a lone myrtle tree, on whose branches hung an icon of the Virgin Mary, unscathed and welcoming the monks with outstretched arms.

"As they drew closer to the myrtle tree, the Virgin Mary showed them a vision of the exiled Constantine Monomachos. He was an enemy of the state, but in the vision he became emperor of the Byzantine Empire. The monks were perplexed—Constantine had been accused of plotting against the current emperor and was living in exile on the island of Lesvos, ninety miles north of Chios. Nevertheless, the devoted and dumbstruck monks immediately made arrangements to travel by ship to Lesvos. It was a hazardous journey fraught with danger, but they knew they had to communicate the vision to Constantine in exile.

"They found the banished Constantine and shared their holy vision with him. He was amazed and gladdened to hear their story and the Virgin's prophecy. He promised Nikolas, John, and Joseph that if their vision came true, he would build a monastery on Chios at the site of the miracle.

"And, as we all know, Constantine IX did in fact become emperor of the Byzantine Empire in 1042, and fulfilled his promise to the monks by sending his best architects and artists to build Nea Moni, which was completed in the year 1054, more than 720 years ago."

#

A few of Nea Moni's monks, such as Brother Tim, were assigned to the village churches as priests and teachers. Seba couldn't imagine that any of the other mastic villages had a teacher as interesting or engaging as Brother Tim, who was trying to quiet his students as they entered the school.

"Settle down, children," the monk called. "I know it's cold, but we will be on the roof of the school today, making our own *clepsydra*, based on the fully automated water clock of the ancient Greek inventor Ctesibius!"

This was why Seba loved school—Brother Tim was always opening their eyes to new ideas and explaining how the old ideas worked. Whereas Mama often argued with Papouli, saying the ways of Jesus left no room for Papouli's ancient wisdom, Brother Tim never seemed to have that problem with Christianity. He often said, "Everything is of God, even the scientists and mathematicians."

Once the students had arrived, they followed Brother Tim up the narrow carved stone steps to the schoolhouse roof. The roofs were the best part of Sessera. The entire valley lay spread out before them, the rocky mountains creating a ring of safety around the small stone-walled community. To the east was the Aegean Sea, and further east in the distance, the Anatolian coast.

Brother Tim had a clepsydra already constructed; it consisted of three colored glass cylinders, a siphon, and an unending supply of water that he had created with the help of another Ctesibius invention, the water pump. He spent the day explaining to them how it was made, taking it apart and showing how each component worked with the others. It was extremely accurate, and ingeniously made of materials which were available to any ancient Greek sailor or craftsman. "Isn't it amazing?" Brother Tim was delighted with his clepsydra, and his exuberance was contagious. Even Thaddeus, who was not the best student, appeared to be mesmerized by the workings of the water clock.

Sometimes Seba stayed after school to help Thaddeus with subjects that gave him the most trouble, which were usually science and math. Thaddeus's father had been crippled the previous summer when a cart full of mastiha had broken loose from its hitch and gone careening down the skinos terraces. He jumped in front of the cart thinking he could slow it down, but it hit a mound of dirt and tipped over just as he grabbed the side of the cart. Thaddeus's father lost his balance, and the cart's weight almost split him in two. He had survived, but the village physician said that he would never walk again. Thaddeus, as the oldest boy, shouldered most of his father's family responsibilities after the accident. He worked so much that between chores and school, he almost never saw his father. Seba empathized, explaining to Thaddeus that he often went weeks without seeing his father because he was working long hours at the shipyard.

This science lesson seemed to appeal not only to Seba and Thaddeus, but to all of Brother Tim's students. It was unfathomable that a system of differently sized containers, each holding various amounts of water, could create an accurate clock. It looked like a series of water jugs structured like a pretty fountain. The container on top had a hole in its base, and the water drained into the other containers from that hole. Thaddeus said, "Are you sure that's really a clock?" He wasn't convinced, but he was definitely intrigued.

Brother Tim smiled warmly. "I understand your skepticism, Thaddeus. It is a tradition that dates back to our ancient Greek ancestors, and hallmark of an inquisitive mind."

Nikos snickered and Thaddeus whipped around, fists clenched and right elbow drawn back, ready to strike. Brother Tim cleared his throat loudly, signaling that he would not let the boys' fighting disrupt his class: "My friends, after the invention of the clepsydra, our ancient

Greek ancestors were not dependent on the sun to tell time. Ctesibius was a genius who revolutionized the world of navigation! Sea captains and crew members could tell time on their ships in the middle of a storm, which would help them find their bearings when the sun finally reappeared."

As if by magic, the water flowed through the containers and moved a lever attached to the bottom container. The lever pointed to various lines that equated to minutes. Brother Tim removed a mechanical watch from his pocket and held it up for his students to see. "Students, this small watch—a gift to me from my brother Stavros—will test the accuracy of the clepsydra. Demetria, will you please assist me?"

Demetria shyly stood and took the round brass watch in her hands. Brother Tim said in a loud, theatrical voice, "What time is showing on our clepsydra?"

Seba looked at the lever, which was pointing to a line that said 2:59. Xenia said loudly, "2:59!"

Brother Tim continued in the same voice, "Demetria, please tell me what time shows on my watch?"

Demetria smiled and said softly, "2:59." The students erupted into laughter and shouts of surprise and amazement. As if on cue, as the clepsydra's lever moved to the line pointing to 3:00, the village church bells rang out three times. The clepsydra worked!

Brother Tim was so pleased with himself that he actually took a bow, and the students clapped enthusiastically, as if he had performed a miracle. Everyone crowded around him asking questions and taking turns looking at his mechanical watch, and Demetria withdrew to the back of the group. Seba understood how she felt; he didn't like being the center of attention, either. Out of the corner of his eye, Seba saw that Thaddeus had a strange dreamy look on his face.

Following his friend's gaze, he saw that he was staring at Demetria, his hand cupped under his chin. Seba wondered if Demetria was the reason why Thaddeus had trouble in school; his thoughts were not entirely on Brother Tim's lessons. Seba, for his part, was much more interested in the water clock. This was by far the best lesson Brother Tim had ever taught.

Seba lingered in the classroom as the other children filed out at the end of the day. He noticed a spyglass on Brother Tim's desk that looked exactly like one his father had shown him at the shipyard. *Where did Brother Tim get one of these?* Brother Tim returned his brass watch to his pocket and said, "Seba, did you enjoy our lesson today?"

"Yes, sir, very much!"

"I'm sure the children are wondering how a monk trained at the monastery of Nea Moni knows anything about ships and clepsydras." His eyes were gleaming mischievously under his bushy eyebrows, as if he had a secret.

Seba knew Brother Tim wanted to share something, so he gamely took the bait. "How *do* you know so much about ships and sailing, sir?"

"I was hoping you would ask that, Seba. Did you know that Nea Moni's monastery owns its own ship and travels the Aegean Sea doing the work of the Lord our Savior?" Seba's mouth gaped open, clearly betraying his surprise. Brother Tim laughed. "I didn't think so."

"Have you been on the ship?"

"Oh yes, many times. It often travels to Smyrna. That's where my older brother Stavros lives, so I try to visit when the Lord's work calls me there."

"I'd like to sail on a ship one day." Seba couldn't believe those words had escaped his lips. He had never said them out loud to anyone, not even Papa.

Brother Tim nodded, a smile peeking through his bushy beard. "I know your father works on sailing ships; I've heard he's quite the engineer. Have you ever seen a real ship's clepsydra?"

"No, Papa is always so busy with work—he doesn't spend as much time with us as he'd like. I've visited the shipyard before, but I didn't get to go on board. Mostly I just had to stay out of the way. I know he would show me one if I could visit again."

As Seba was speaking, Brother Tim closed his eyes and clasped his hands together in front of his heart. It appeared as if he was praying; Seba thought it was an odd time for that, right in the middle of their conversation. Maybe this was how monks interacted with each other, or with God and the Holy Spirit. In any case, it made Seba uncomfortable.

Just as Seba was about to turn and slip out the door, though, Brother Tim opened his eyes and said, "I think you will have the opportunity to see a clepsydra in the near future. The Holy Spirit tells me that you have a strong connection to the sea, just like our Savior, Jesus Christ, who was raised by the Sea of Galilee." Then he winked and said, "Have a good evening, Seba!"

Seba walked home in the gathering cold, lost in thoughts of the Holy Spirit, water, clocks, sun, wind, and tide.

5 THE *DELIGHT*

A few weeks later, Seba was wrapped in his heavy coat against the late November chill, standing with Papa on the hill above the shipyard, watching a massive English clipper ship sail into the cove. It was just after mid-day. The ship, the *Delight*, loomed so large that it seemed it might not fit into the slip. She was 120 tons in the water, and her main mast was badly damaged.

The workers leaped from their jobs and ran to bring the ship to anchor inside the shipyard's protective jetty. Even without any sails on the main mast, the *Delight* looked to Seba like a giant group of billowy clouds moving just above the water. He thought he had never seen anything so massive—or so beautiful. Even with the broken mast, she looked like a sleek dark dragon, a creature lifted directly from Papouli's stories of the ancient Greek heroes.

As they walked down the hill into the shipyard proper, Seba saw that there were at least fifty men on board the clipper, all speaking a bizarre stunted language he did not understand. Whereas his native Greek tongue was sonorous and melodic, this language was rough and choppy, as if the speakers disliked the words they were saying so much that they cut them off before they were finished.

Mesich emerged from the office to greet them; unlike the first time Seba had met him, this time Mesich was wearing a genuine smile, and looking pleased with himself that his shipyard on his island was chosen as the place for this speedy vessel to be repaired. Seba was glad to learn that Mesich's scowl was not a permanent fixture after all.

Papa grabbed Seba's shoulder and said, "Son, stay back and do not speak to anyone. I don't want them to think you are an errand boy looking for work on a ship. They'd grab you in a second and put you to work without pay. You would be at the opposite end of the world in a matter of months. Do not leave my sight. If anything happened to you, I don't think your Mama would be able to survive it."

Seba wasn't so sure, as Mama's "five feet of fury" was often directed at him, but he simply nodded and stayed behind Papa.

To Seba, the sailors looked just as extraordinary as Ahmed, the silk-adorned and terrifying Ottoman he had met on his first day at the shipyard. These men were dressed in a completely different costume, and barely gave the impression that they lived on the same earth as Seba and his family. The only similarity was the tone they used when speaking to each other. It was very much like the shipyard workers just before Ahmed had rebuked them.

"Get out of the crow's nest! Remember what happened when we left the Rock of Gibraltar, you imbecile!"

"Shove off and mind your own business, you French molly!"

"Shut up, the both of you and get to work—or I'll tan

your hides so you'll never sit again!"

"I'd like to see you try, you English sea crab!"

Seba had no idea what they were saying, but he could tell they were slights and slurs, and he could tell they all loved it.

Papa put his hand on Seba's shoulder. "Pay them no attention, son. They're so happy to be at anchor that they can't contain their enthusiasm. We've got work to do, so stay with me and keep quiet. I'm not sure you will be allowed on the ship, but once I know it's safe for you, I'll try to bring you aboard. Would you like that?"

"More than anything!"

Seba climbed into one of the unfinished ships that was situated on wooden blocks about fifty yards from the shoreline. He stepped down between the slats, hidden behind the rib-like boards of the unfinished ship's hull. From his vantage point, he could peer through the spaces between the strips of wood and watch the men, unnoticed. He heard his father asking questions in Greek, and one of the crew of the ship acted as a translator, explaining the design of the ship to Papa and his coworkers. Seba thought he had the perfect spot until he felt a boot on his head.

"Oh, for the love of Allah, you irksome math genius! Must you always be under my feet? Hasn't your father taught you anything?"

Seba couldn't understand why he was being scolded when Mesich was stepping on him while he sat perfectly still, so he said nothing.

"More like oracle than genius, I'd say! Will you emerge from your trance to speak your words of wisdom?"

The back of Seba's neck was throbbing where Mesich had just thrust his heel, and he snapped at Mesich, "When I came before you told me not to speak."

"And insolent, too!"

Seba was still irritated, and no longer afraid of Mesich. "Why were you climbing in this boat, anyway?"

"Well, you ungrateful boy, I told your father I would look for you, and I was climbing into this boat to get a better look around the shipyard."

"Why did my father want you to look for me?"

Mesich huffed. "Just keep your mouth shut and come with me."

Seba hesitated; his father had told him to stay out of the way, and he wasn't sure if Mesich was taking him somewhere to punish him.

Mesich said impatiently, "Come on, we're boarding the ship. Your father asked me to find you. Lucky for you, your father is a good friend, because I wouldn't do this for just anyone."

With that, Seba jumped up and followed Mesich across the shipyard and up the plank to the clipper ship's main deck. Some of the workers were helping the crew untie the rigging from the broken mast, and it appeared the others were in the hold, looking at the design of the ship's hull. Seba didn't see his father anywhere, but he was so happy to be on the ship that he didn't even mind Mesich's grouchiness. He noted with relief that everyone appeared too busy to try to kidnap him and put him to work as a slave boy.

"Don't let this go to your head," Mesich growled, "but your father asked me to show you around the ship. I have to wait for Ahmed to finish with the ship's captain before I can put together the invoice for this work, so I've agreed—on one condition."

Seba waited.

"You have to do exactly what I say, stay behind me, don't

ask questions, and act invisible."

Seba started to object that those were four conditions, but he looked at Mesich's self-righteous expression and decided against it.

Mesich squinted his eyes and leaned toward Seba. "Do you think you can manage that?"

Seba nodded yes, and Mesich led him to the bow. As soon as they were on the ship, Mesich seemed to forget that he was giving Seba a tour, and he adopted a more accommodating tone, as if he were promoting the shipyard to a visiting merchant.

"This ship is part of an English trade alliance called the Levant Company. Not unlike the East India Trading Company, but they focus on goods and resources from the Silk Road, brought to Anatolia through China, India, and Arabia. Silks, tanned leather, velvet *çatma* panels, spices, citrus, and exotic fruits are just a few of the many treasures bringing these rough-speaking westerners to our island. The faster the ships, the more money we make for the sultan. If these ships can get our resources to Europe in half the time, it doubles the amount of money we make in trade. This is why we need to see how these ships are able to move so quickly. If we can build the Ottoman merchant fleet in this way, we will be unsurpassed on the sea. Shall we see what's being carried on this ship?"

Seba remembered he was told not to speak, so he shook his head yes. He could tell that Mesich loved talking of the merchant trades on the sea. His dour demeanor softened, and his eyes lit up as he described the workings of the world's economy.

They climbed down a thick wooden ladder into the vessel's hold just behind the ship's wheel near the front of the main deck. Seba and Mesich found themselves in an enormous space, loaded to the rafters with every kind of goatskin, sheepskin, cinnamon, currants, ginger, and even mastic originally shipped from Chios to Smyrna, for export to England. Unfortunately, because a storm had crippled the ship on its way west, these supplies would be delayed while Papa and the other workers repaired the mast. All the better for Seba, though, who was able to see the astounding wealth and diversity of resources moving in the east-west trade.

As they walked through the hold, Mesich explained the origins of the intricately designed Ottoman fabrics.

"Did you know in Smyrna and Bursa, the Ottoman designs are so extravagant that they are prepared for royalty all over the world? This ship was bound for London, and these fabrics—these gold- and silver-threaded silk and velvet designs—are intended for King George III and his royal court, and any other nobleman who can afford them. Of course, their wealth is nothing compared to Sultan Mustafa. Have you ever seen indigo fabric?"

"Like Ahmed's long robe?"

Mesich looked at Seba. "You're not entirely unobservant after all, then," he said. "These Englishmen cannot get enough of the deep dark blue. It is extremely difficult to make and expensive to buy." He peeled back a covering of brown linen to reveal layers of silk that looked like liquid sky in late evening. It was at once dark blue and deep purple, shimmering in the low light of the ship's hold.

Mesich returned the covering and pointed to the brown linen on each stack of fabrics. The sultan's seal was in the center of every one, showing that the quality had been approved by, and the taxes paid to, the Ottoman Empire before these costly products were released for trade. He pulled back the corner of the brown cloth from another stack, revealing a gorgeous silk textile bearing a pattern of golden tulips on a background of deep red, bordered in indigo.

"What is this for?" Seba had long forgotten Mesich's four conditions.

"It could be the cushion for a king's ass, for all I know," said Mesich. Apparently he had forgotten his conditions as well. "Can you imagine having the money to buy something so frivolous? This tulip design is one I've seen before. The English and the Dutch love their tulips. Fortunately for us, our Ottoman textile workers are the best in the world, the only ones who can create these intricate designs. Smyrna and Bursa boast the most talented textile artists on earth. The quality of their products is unsurpassed. The only thing more popular these days is mastiha from right here on Chios. That, or maybe opium from China."

"What's opium?" Seba asked innocently.

Mesich suddenly seemed flustered. "Oh, it's nothing important," he said. "Forget I ever mentioned it. And you needn't tell your father. Or your mother. Er, you do have a mother, right?"

Seba, just now remembering he was not supposed to speak, nodded yes.

"Of course you do. Well, definitely don't tell her. In fact, don't tell anyone I said anything about opium." He walked to a corner of the hold where the familiar herbaceous and pine-cedar-mint smell of mastiha emanated. There were wooden crates filled with thousands of the tiny, brilliant Tears of Chios. They looked like white pebbles, hard and shiny, each about the size of Mesich's thumbnail. Seba knew that once he bit through the crunchy shell of one of those little pebbles, they would soften as they released their intense flavor and healing properties. His mouth watered with the memory of the herbaceous gum.

Papouli had once told him Homer was known to have chewed a single piece of mastiha for six months, just to see what would happen. According to Homer, the mastiha's intoxicating flavor never diminished.

Mesich opened the top of one of the crates, which was stamped with the same seal of Sultan Mustafa III. "Can you imagine how much one crate of this precious mastiha costs?"

Seba shook his head. No one from the village was allowed to get near the mastiha after it had been harvested and cleaned, except maybe Uncle Phillip and the council members. If a villager was caught stealing even one minuscule tear, the punishment was severe—loss of a hand, cut off at the wrist by the Ottoman gatekeepers of the village. If a larger quantity was stolen, it could mean the loss of two hands. Fortunately, no one in Sessera had ever stolen enough to lose two hands. Seba was tempted to reach in and grab a tear, but he was afraid of Mesich's reaction. The Tears of Chios were so tiny that no one would even notice one was missing, just like Papouli said. But Seba didn't think he could snatch one without Mesich seeing it.

Mesich was staring at the crates full of mastic tears. "I bet that English King George III eats mastiha pastries every day, and chews a tear every morning for medicinal purposes. It's the most valuable resource on the planet for a very good reason. Fortunately, Sultan Mustafa III knows how to protect the mastiha and bring the best prices for the empire."

Seba looked at Mesich inquisitively. "What, you think your village councils are in charge of the mastiha trade?" Mesich chuckled. "You have much to learn about the ways of the world." He looked over his shoulder and quickly returned the wooden lid to the crate of translucent tears. "Let's get out of here before someone tries to press-gang us."

They climbed back up the wooden ladder and slipped down the gangplank without notice. "Now go back to your hiding spot, where you won't bother my workers." The old Mesich was back, as unfriendly as ever, but Seba didn't care, because he had just been aboard his very first sailing ship!

Later that day, as the sun was setting, Papa finally disembarked from the ship. Seba was in his cozy hiding spot, contentedly eating figs he had plucked from the trees surrounding the shipyard as he watched the comings and goings of the crew and the shipbuilders.

Papa peeked over the bow of the unfinished ship's skeleton. "I'm sorry, Seba, you must be starving."

"No, Papa, I have these figs. And Mesich gave me some dried ginger from the ship."

Papa's eyes grew wide. "He did, did he?"

Seba wondered if dried ginger was in the same category as opium, which must be bad. But Mesich hadn't said not to mention ginger; he simply had taken the lid off a crate in the hold and reached his hand in to grab a fistful of ginger root, breaking a few pieces off and giving them to Seba, saying "One handful isn't going to make a difference. Put the rest in your pockets." Now Seba felt guilty, as if he and Mesich had done something wrong.

"Well, it was very nice of him to look after you," Papa said, and Seba relaxed at the sound of his father's reassuring words.

"Mesich showed me the silk fabrics and told me about the indigo and the dying process and the tulips and King George and the spices and—" He almost said, "And the opium," but caught himself short.

"And what, son?"

"And—the mastiha."

"Good for you. I knew you would enjoy this day. But now it's going to turn into night, because they want us to sleep at the shipyard and work extra hours to repair this mast. I'm afraid you are going to have to stay here with me. We won't have a delicious dinner like you are used to—just grilled fish and water from the spring. Do you think you can manage such deprivation with your old Papa?"

"Yes, Papa, it sounds wonderful!"

#

In the end, Seba spent several days and nights at the shipyard, and each day he learned more about shipbuilding, the Silk Road, trade with the west, the Ottoman Empire, Sultan Mustafa III, and the men who risked their lives to work on the seas.

"Papa, why do the men keep saying 'meltemi winds'?"

Papa smiled knowingly. "You remember the *Iliad* and the *Odyssey*, don't you?"

Seba nodded—Papouli's stories of Odysseus were some of his favorites, and had been written by Homer himself, born on this very island of Chios.

"The meltemi is a very unpredictable seasonal wind blowing from the north in the months of May through August. A ship might be in the middle of the North Aegean, making gloriously good time, when *whoosh*, the meltemia rise up at random from the sea, pushing it way off course. Why do you think it took Odysseus ten years to get home? It was the meltemi winds. They wreak havoc with the ships, Seba, and we have to build the ship to withstand these volatile winds as well as the storm gales rushing across the Ionian Sea."

Seba thought it sounded very scary, especially if the

winds descended on the ship's captain when he least expected it. "What do the sailors do when the meltemi winds blow?"

"They adjust, Seba. That's what all good sailors do. Poseidon is not to be toyed with, and anyone who tries is a fool many times over. I've heard stories of ships bound due west for Malta, blown all the way to Africa by the meltemi winds before they can get back on course. It is difficult—but exciting, too, don't you think?"

"Do you ever want to be on one of those ships, Papa? Sailing the ocean rather than building vessels here on Chios?"

'That's a question I've asked myself for many years. However, I believe it's not the sailing that is my passion— it's the design and creation of watercraft. Once the ship is completed, I don't want to take the helm, I want to start building another ship with a better, stronger, faster design. And so, this shipyard, with the sea breeze and the work I love, is just enough for me. Besides, how would I ever be able to leave you and your mother for such long periods of time? I couldn't bear it."

Seba understood. It was easy to see his father's happiness in measuring, constructing, taking apart and reconstructing, and testing his theories about the best methods for carrying cargo. Military ships were built for speed and maneuverability, but a cargo ship was built to float while carrying as much heavy lading as possible. Creating something to navigate the dance of wind and tide—that was Kostas's passion.

"See those dolphins out in the Strait of Chios? They know how to perfectly swim with the tide, rather than against it. No issue with the meltemi winds for them. Look! They are putting on a show for us, Seba."

Seba looked out across the Strait of Chios, and could see the rocky coastline of Anatolia eight miles away. The current was moving quickly north; Seba knew that it was deadly, but the dolphins were jumping and sporting as if it were a playground designed just for them. They spiraled around each other, then went under the surface of the water, only to shoot up in the air a great distance away. Seba marveled at their speed.

"Papa, they're playing! But I thought the Strait of Chios was dangerous. How do the dolphins do it?"

"It is dangerous, Seba, if you are afraid of it. The dolphins don't fear the water—they love it. The sea is their home, as natural to them as the air is to us. If we watch the dolphins, we can learn much from them. Once, right over there in that cove, I saw a fisherman throw his net over the side of his boat, but he lost the line and the tide was carrying his net away. I felt for the man—the net is his livelihood. He was crying and waving his arms, trying to row toward the net, but getting nowhere. He could think of nothing but the loss of his income."

Seba had not heard this story before. He looked out over the Strait of Chios and saw the waves crashing on the rocks of the opposite shore. It was beautiful but also foreboding.

"My hand to God, Seba, the next thing I saw was a pair of dolphins—just like those two out there—they caught the net in their teeth and brought it to him, just to the port side of his boat, like a dog fetching a bone! It was as if they knew his livelihood depended on his net. Or maybe they felt his pain. We believe compassion is something only we humans feel, but I disagree. In my experience, many of God's creatures feel compassion, especially dolphins. Never forget, Seba, the dolphins are our teachers, and I have seen them be in service to man. Whether you consider them a symbol of Poseidon or a symbol of Jesus, the fisher of men, it makes no difference. What's important is that dolphins are our friends. Always watch the dolphins, and you will be blessed."

6 THE *DAME*

It was mid-March, and winter was loosening its grip on the island. Seba had turned nine years old in December and had visited the shipyard with his father many times. The bursting forth of spring's growth was just around the corner and all of God's creation waited with anticipation for the season of rebirth. The latest English ship Papa had been working on was called the *Dame*, a 300-ton cargo ship — much bigger than the *Delight*, and with a much larger crew. It had been in the shipyard's cove for several weeks, and although Papa had only been home a few nights, it was all he could talk about. The English had heard how Kostas and the other shipbuilders had worked their magic on the *Delight*'s mast, making the ship faster while allowing it to carry more cargo, so there was a long line of ships wanting to be serviced at Mesich's shipyard. All the ships that arrived belonged to the Levant Company. As Mesich had told Seba, this group was no match for the Dutch East India Company, but they made their merchant members and their ships' crews very wealthy. They were generally a jolly bunch of men, to hear Mesich speak of them, and easy to work with because they often spoke Greek, French, and even Arabic in addition to their native English. To the extent that Kostas and the other Chians could speed up their ships, there was even more money to be made. The *Dame* had recently loaded up with cargo from Smyrna and was headed toward Gibraltar, when the meltemi winds pushed it off course, and made the voyage so difficult that the ship's captain decided to detour and replace the damaged mizzenmast with one of the celebrated Chian pine trees. Usually the ships in the cove carried no cargo, but this one had similar cargo to the *Delight*, including a bounty of wonderful spices: cinnamon, currants, ginger, frankincense, cloves, turmeric, nutmeg, saffron, and black pepper.

According to Mesich, the sultan was enamored of the English—especially their appetite for intricately designed Ottoman textiles and indigo cloth. Seba had stayed overnight in the shipyard with Papa for several days, and was in heaven. He loved spending time with his father and watching the dolphins dart in and out of the sparkling waves. On this particular day, Mesich was in an unusually good mood. Today the captain of the *Dame* would be paying him for the work that Kostas and his crew had done to repair the ship, and the ship would soon be ready to leave the cove. Mesich allowed Seba to follow him into the hold of the *Dame* to look around and to take a crate of spices or two in appreciation for a job well done. Seba learned that Mesich and the shipyard workers were often rewarded in this way—one of the benefits of working in the maritime trade.

The ship's crew was in a frenzy, trying to ready the ship for departure, and no one seemed to notice the two of them.

Mesich showed him some of the fabrics made in Smyrna, now on their way to King George's court. These were even more opulent than the ones from the *Delight*. There were plenty of indigo silks and velvets trimmed in silver, as well as a pattern of palm trees embroidered all in gold, outlined in deep red, on a field of pale green. The trees nearly leaped from the fabric as if they were living plants waving in an island breeze. These fabric coverings also bore the sultan's seal, an elaborate design that looked like snake curled into a pyramid, flanked on the left by what appeared to be a watchful eye, and topped with three vertical lines and two wavy horizontal lines. The seal was exactly the same as the one Seba had seen on the crates and fabrics aboard the *Delight*.

As Seba and Mesich beheld the unimaginable wealth surrounding them in the hold, they heard angry raised voices coming from above deck. Seba thought he heard his father's voice, urgently crying "No!" Seba ran to the ladder, and started to climb out of the hold. Mesich followed behind, and they both alighted on deck to see several Ottoman guards surrounding Papa in the captain's quarters. Ahmed, in all his silken glory, stood facing Papa, hands on his hips.

Mesich had gone pale, and his face was pinched. "Come on, math genius," he whispered fiercely. "We need to get out of here." He grabbed Seba's arm, but Seba was too fast. He pulled away, ducked past the ship's wheel, and ran under the window outside the captain's rooms.

"What's wrong?" he whispered to Mesich. "Why are they arguing?"

Mesich held his hand to his forehead, a pained expression on his face. "No, this can't be happening," he murmured as if to himself. Then he glared at Seba. "I need to get you off this ship right now. This is none of our business." He reached for Seba again, but missed for a second time as Seba slipped behind a huge pile of coiled lashings just outside the captain's window.

"What are they doing to my father? Shouldn't we help him?"

Mesich looked around at the crew, who had suddenly become very busy with the ship's lashings. As Mesich viewed the crew, a look of shocked realization crossed his face. "They *wouldn't*," he said under his breath. He turned toward the gang plank. "Seba, please. I told your father I would protect you. We need to leave this instant." Mesich's voice was shaky and tense.

"We need to protect my father. He needs us."

"What help could we be against Ahmed's guards? We can't help him. It's done."

Seba didn't understand. "What's done? Why are you leaving?"

Mesich's head flicked around as he looked again at the crew. "You're as stubborn as your father. I have my own family to think of. Come with me now, boy, or I can't be responsible for what happens to you."

He waited, but Seba stood firm. Mesich hesitated for a second, then turned and nearly ran down the plank toward the shipyard's office.

Seba was left on the deck, just under the window of the captain's quarters. He was well hidden from the crew, which allowed him to eavesdrop on the angry voices rising from inside the captain's rooms. Seba strained to hear what they were saying. He inched forward so his head was just below the windowsill.

He recognized Ahmed's oily voice, and his skin crawled. He was afraid to peer over the sill.

"Constantinople is a beautiful city. The harbor is enormous, the shipyard adjacent. The work is necessary, and there is no better city in the empire." Ahmed's voice sounded like the devil himself. He spoke in Greek, but the accent was thick and contemptuous. Seba shuddered, wishing just for a moment that he had listened to Mesich. He wanted to be as far away from this ship as possible right now, his father by his side.

"This is my home, and we do excellent work here." His father's voice sounded confident, but wary.

"Yes, Kostas, that is exactly why we are here. The sultan wants his best shipbuilders in the capital, not in some tiny shipyard on the east coast of an island miles away from the city center."

"Chios has been the center of trade since the ancient pharaohs of Egypt traded with Byzantium," Papa said. "We have a team of workers here who have established a rhythm and an excellent work product. These workers are the best in all of the empire. I can't leave them."

Seba moved his head slowly until he could just see over the windowsill. Papa was flanked by two Ottoman guards to the left, and Ahmed was standing across from him with his silk-gloved hands on his hips. Seba was looking across a great wooden desk that abutted the windowsill. On it were papers, a well of ink, a thin brush, and a black velvet pouch that was partially open, showing several large golden rings with wide round heads. Seba couldn't tell if the desk was for Ahmed or the English captain. Beyond the desk, Ahmed was even more terrifying in full view, gold rings glittering and black eyes looking like the depths of the darkest cave.

"Mesich has already identified the best three of your group, and they have agreed—quite willingly, I might add—to join us."

"Mesich knows about this?"

"Not precisely," Ahmed sniffed. "But he did fall all over himself to point out your most talented men, and to make his case for why their skills were unsurpassed. We agreed with his assessment, and took care of the rest."

"I appreciate the offer, Ahmed," said Papa, keeping his voice even. "but I must respectfully decline. My family is here. My wife's family has been part of the *mastichochoria* for three hundred years. Maybe if there were more acceptable terms—if you were not separating me from my only son—we could negotiate something."

Seba's covered his mouth so a terrified gasp would not escape.

Ahmed laughed derisively. "It's not an offer, Kostas. And you are not in a position to make demands. We're about to raise anchor. In a few days, we'll be in Constantinople, and you will be in a place where your work may be seen by the sultan himself. It is a great honor."

"If I am the best shipbuilder in the empire, as you say, then I must be of some value to you. I need to be here with my family, to teach my son to become a man, to share my legacy. My ancient Greek ancestors were the best shipbuilders in the world. I'm sure we can negotiate reasonable arrangements that satisfy everyone's needs."

Just then, the English ship's captain walked past Seba and into his quarters. The scene obviously surprised him.

"What's going on here?" he asked in perfect Greek.

Ahmed sneered. "The sultan is bestowing a great honor on one of his loyal workers, but this imbecile appears to be too stupid to recognize it."

The captain looked uncomfortable. "Well, maybe we could work something out. Is there anything I can do to help?" He bowed very graciously.

Ahmed's scornful voice made Seba's insides curdle. "We appreciate the sentiment, Captain, but the Ottoman Empire handles its own affairs—including this man's infantile behavior. It's precious, isn't it? He thinks this is a negotiation." Ahmed swung his silk-gloved hand in the air, as if batting away a pesky insect. Then he walked past the captain, purposefully brushing forcefully against the latter's shoulder.

Seba could see Ahmed lean down, drawing his face dangerously close to Papa's. His baleful voice was just a whisper. "You should be flattered the sultan wants you near him. People have died for less. The only negotiation my guards will entertain is negotiating your acceptance of your fate. And as you can see, they don't negotiate with words."

Ahmed stepped back and nodded to one of the guards, who lifted his sword, still in the sheath, and clobbered Kostas on the back of the head, causing him to drop to his knees.

The captain gasped; then, suddenly, all of the men lurched forward, losing their balance.

Seba, too, fell forward as the ship turned hard to port; he watched one of the rings roll out of the velvet pouch and across the desk. If it rolled onto the floor with a clatter, Seba would be discovered. Off balance because of the motion of the ship, he reached through the windowsill, grabbed the ring just before it slid off the desk, and stuffed it in his pocket. As he heard the crew shouting to each other, he realized they had lifted the anchor. Mesich had realized it when he saw the crew untying the lashings—the *Dame* was heading out of the cove!

"I apologize, Your Excellency," said the captain, "but I thought our business was finished here now that my ship has been repaired. As you know, the winds are preventing us from heading west, and I instructed my crew to make for Constantinople. Should I reverse the orders?"

Seba now stood just high enough to peer over the lashings, and saw that the *Dame* had already passed the jetty. As he turned to sneak another look through the window, he felt a pair of leather gloved hands grab him by the shirt-collar and lift him through the open window.

Seba kicked and screamed, trying to bite the guard, anything to make him let go. The guard slapped him hard across the mouth with his other hand, and Seba felt the salty taste of blood as his top lip split wide open.

"Don't you dare get blood on me, you little bastard!"

Seba looked up at his father, whose eyes were wild and fierce—a sight more terrifying than Ahmed. He stopped struggling and gaped at Papa. The man with the flaming eyes didn't even look like his father, but a chthonion demon recently arrived from the underworld. What could they have done to Papa to make him look like that?

Seba felt a jolt of electricity, as if struck. Papa glanced at Ahmed, then at Seba, and finally past both of them through the open window. He looked as if he were dreaming, and then as if a decision had been made.

Then, with a speed that shocked Seba, he ran across the thick carpet of the captain's quarters, grabbed Seba from the guard's outstretched hands, and shouted, "Didn't I tell you to stay on land?" The guard he looked at Ahmed, but the latter only smile wickedly. The guard shrugged and released Seba into Kostas's hands.

"Haven't you remembered anything I've told you?" Papa's voice was rough and angry. He carried Seba through the captain's open door like he would carry a melon under his arm, both of them lurching toward the port side of the ship. Seba could see the shipyard jetty, but the distance between the jetty and the ship was increasing at an alarming pace.

"Papa, I'm sorry! I'm sorry! I didn't mean anything! Don't hurt me! I'll be good—I promise!" Seba was too stunned to cry. The arms felt like Papa, but the eyes and the words coming from his mouth were all wrong. Seba wished he could wake up from this nightmare.

Papa whispered in Seba's ear, "I have to do this to save you. I love you, son. I might not be able to save myself, but I will not let the Ottoman vipers steal my son. Follow the dolphins." Then he yelled loud enough for everyone on deck to hear, "You are a disgrace and a dishonor to our family, and this will not be our legacy!"

Dumb with horror, Seba felt himself being tossed high into the air and off the side of the ship. Seba flew over the balustrade, fingers grasping for his father. The last thing he saw were Papa's wild eyes; Seba thought they were filling with tears, but he couldn't be sure. He hung in the air for what felt like an eternity, then smacked the water with a loud slap; he kicked his arms and legs just to keep his head above the waterline.

Raising his head, Seba looked around him for the ship. The *Dame*'s crew was letting out the huge white sails. The ship immediately picked up speed, its vast bulk receding into the distance, too far for him to reach.

The seawater felt like a wall of frost. The jolt of cold was so shocking, he thought he might freeze in place and sink to the bottom of the dark blue Aegean Sea. He was a good swimmer, but most of his experience involved being close to shore on hot summer days with half the village of Sessera enjoying the water with him. This was terrifyingly different, with the current pulling him away from shore, the jetty at such a distance as to seem unreachable, and the cold so intense that he thought his limbs might transform into solid ice. His survival instinct was the only thing keeping his arms and legs moving in the direction of the jetty. He couldn't even think about what just happened—only keep moving toward the shore. The captain would turn the ship around. He said he would. Then this would all be straightened out.

After a few minutes of struggling against the current, he realized he was not strong enough to make it. It was no use. He became so tired that the thought of lifting his arm for one more stroke was unbearable, and he started to slow down, sinking further below the surface where the water was even colder. As the wake from the ship pushed over his head, he got a mouthful of seawater and struggled to catch his breath, sputtering and splashing to gulp air and not water. As his head dipped below the water, he said goodbye to Mama, to Papouli, to the big sister he had never met.

I'm sorry, Papa, Seba thought, as darkness crowded in at the edges of his sight.

And then he felt a hand grab his hair, tugging him toward the surface. *Papa!* he thought. *I knew you would save me! I won't ruin your legacy, I promise!*

There was rush of air and streaming light, and a gruff voice shouting, "Get in here, you little troublemaker!" One large hand kept hold of his hair; another reached under his armpit to heave him into a little rowboat. Seba hung for a moment over the gunwale, coughing up seawater; then he dropped and curled up in a ball on the burden boards. He felt a thick, scratchy woolen blanket being thrown over him where he lay, limp and exhausted. Feebly pushing the blanket away from his face, Seba realized that the figure at the oars was not his father, but Mesich.

Seba could only lie in the boat, shivering, as Mesich

began rowing toward the shipyard. His mind could not process what was happening to him. *Papa,* he thought. *Why did you go? What have I done to make you so angry?* And then he thought nothing at all.

7 BACK AT HOME

When Seba woke up, he was lying on a straw cot in front of the hearth of his home, wrapped in two thick woolen blankets. The fire in the hearth was blazing, but he felt a shiver of cold. His top lip was swollen and painful. He looked up and saw Mama, Papouli, and Uncle Phillip, faces grim with worry as he opened his eyes.

"Bless us and thank the Lord Almighty, he's alive." Mama crossed herself.

Uncle Phillip leaned in and ruffled his hair. He and Papouli could have been brothers, they looked so similar. The only differences were that Uncle Phillip was a bit shorter, a bit thicker around the middle, and he walked with a slight limp. "Seba, you know I enjoy a bit of excitement now and then, but this is too much for your old uncle," he said. "It was your Papouli's constant whistling and humming that kept our spirits up. That, and our faith in the Lord."

Papouli stood up from the kitchen chair and walked

over, laying his warm and wrinkled hand on Seba's shoulder. "We're grateful you are safe, and it looks like Mesich here is a hero." He slapped Mesich's back with his other hand.

Uncle Phillip said, "Mesich has told us a little. It seems as if you nearly drowned. Can you tell us what happened?"

Seba remembered—and shut his eyes tight, shaking his head to push aside the memory.

Mama spoke, her voice scratchy and barely rising above a whisper. "Sebastian may need a little time, Phillip. Let him rest. We'll talk to him when he's feeling up to it. Sebastian, would you like some avgolemono? We've got some on the fire. It will warm you up."

Seba shook his head. The thought of his favorite soup now turned his stomach. He thought he might never eat it again; and just as quickly as the thought arose, the seawater mixed with bile also arose. He sat up, vomiting to the side of the little cot, partly missing the large earthenware jug Mama had obviously placed there for this purpose. The acrid smell of saltwater and stomach juices drifted up from the jug and Seba retched again.

Mama knelt by his cot and stroked his sable curls with one hand while she wiped his mouth with a cloth. "There, there, my baby. You're home and your Mama is here. Everything is going to be fine." Seba slumped into his Mama's arms to the sound of Papouli humming a lullaby.

Seba didn't know what time it was when he awoke again; there was no light streaming through the small kitchen window. The hearth fire was high, and the heat felt good. He thought it must be early evening, and he wondered why he was lying on a cot next to the hearth. He couldn't remember. Was he sick? How did he get there? Then he heard the sound of subdued voices coming from the kitchen table and remembered. His hand instinctively clutched at his stomach.

"Why would they have done this to us? And how could they try to hurt Sebastian? He's only nine years old. It's barbaric."

"Agnete, you know we can't explain or predict what those Ottoman vipers will do."

Seba turned his head toward the table. Mama, Mesich, Uncle Philip, and Papouli were sitting around the table with mugs of Turkish coffee in front of them, and Mesich had just disparaged his own countrymen.

"Aren't you a Muslim?" Mama asked in surprise.

Mesich drew a dark green bottle from his thick sash. Seba remembered seeing crates of those bottles in the hold of the *Dame*. Mesich said it was rum the English brought from the sugar mills of the Caribbean. He said the crew called it "firewater" and it could purge a man of all his sins by making him forget they ever happened. Seba thought it must be some kind of magic drink, even stronger than *tsipouro*.

Mesich uncorked the bottle and poured a long draught into his upturned mouth. "I'm sorry, Agnete, but I'm just as much a victim as you are. Not everyone who follows Allah agrees with the Ottomans. How naive could I be? I was unknowingly directing those predators to our best men. Oh, it's all my fault—you should have seen me, preening like a peacock, telling them how well Kostas, Samos, Ionnis, and Antonio worked together, and how there was no better team in the empire. I practically handed them to the sultan on a silver platter!" He raised the bottle of rum and thwacked it violently against his temple, splashing some on his balding head and leaving a pinkish spot that would grow into a goose egg.

Uncle Phillip put his hand on Mesich's arm, and removed the rum bottle from his hand. "Don't do this to yourself. None of us could have known this would happen. And you saved my nephew's life. I can't imagine what we would do without him."

"Phillip's right, Mesich," Papouli said. "If not for you, Seba would probably be at the bottom of the Aegean, and we'd be without a father *and* a son in this family. I don't think my daughter could bear it, and neither could I. We owe you a debt of gratitude."

Mesich spat into the fire. "Gratitude for offering the best men of Sessera up to the sultan like lambs to slaughter?"

"You said they are not being slaughtered—they've been requested by the sultan to work in Constantinople. It's not what we want, but it's an honor, isn't it?" Uncle Phillip was trying to sound confident.

"It sounds like slavery to me. They weren't even given a choice, and they weren't permitted to bring their families. What kind of honor is that?" Mesich leaned forward and dropped his head into his hands, wincing from the growing pink lump above his eye.

Seba wanted to ask questions, but he just kept remembering that his father said he dishonored the family. He didn't know how, though. Did Seba cause this to happen? If he had stayed in the shipyard office, would his father still be here? He felt as bad as Mesich looked.

"Do you know if the ship was stopping somewhere else before going to Constantinople? What if we went to Çeşme? We could ask Darius to take us in his fishing boat, and maybe find out more there." Papouli sounded optimistic.

Mesich grabbed the bottle of rum Uncle Phillip had placed on the table and slammed it down.

"Don't you understand? There is no negotiating, no

discussing, no reasoning with them! The Ottomans are far behind the Spanish, Italians, Dutch, and now the English when it comes to their navy and merchant fleet. The sultan is desperate to catch up, and will do anything to speed the process. There are rumblings that the sultan's currency is being devalued, and these damn Englishmen are everywhere, trying to make deals with every port they call on. They're bribing the local Ottoman tax overseers to look the other way when they want to deal directly with the locals. The empire is losing its tax base to those pasty white pigs and the only way it can catch up is to beef up its own fleet and get in on the trade. The sultan cares for nothing other than winning this competition of the seas."

Uncle Phillip looked pensive; it seemed to Seba that this was not the first time he had heard this story. He nodded in agreement, his forehead furrowed and his mouth a thin line of tension.

"That's why it is all my fault. Kostas gained a great reputation for his understanding of the English clipper ships' engineering. I told every sea captain who visited our shipyard that Kostas's knowledge and skills were unsurpassed. I should have known—the last time Ahmed was here, he mentioned that our little shipyard was not a proper place for one of the greatest engineering minds in the empire. I thought it was just a snide remark, but it wasn't!" He dropped his head into his hands, lurching forward in his chair. "What have I done?"

Papouli said, "This is not your fault. Every crew member and captain who visited the shipyard would have known Kostas's handiwork, as well as everyone who has seen his ships in every port in the empire. It could have happened anyway. Just as King Solomon said in the Proverbs: 'The crucible is for silver, and the furnace is for gold, and a man is tested by his praise.' I wish to God that Kostas was not tested in this way by the accolades he was given."

"We told Ahmed we would expand the shipyard here, but he never pursued it," Mesich said. "Now I know why."

Uncle Phillip said, "Seba is our priority now. We must ensure that he continues with his education. I personally vow, in front of Vaios, who once saved my life, that I will do all in my power to help Seba achieve the highest honor in Sessera, to carry on the Krizomatis legacy as a member of the *mastichochoria*, where his mother's family has worked among the skinos trees for twenty generations."

Mama blinked back the tears welling behind her lashes; Papouli stood up and hugged his best friend. "We are very grateful to you, Phillip. The loss of Kostas to the Ottomans is a disaster of cataclysmic proportions. It is our responsibility to support Seba. He may have lost his father today, but we will not let this stop my grandson from fulfilling his birthright."

The men separated, and Uncle Phillip looked over at the cot.

"Speaking of which, I think your grandson might be ready to talk to us."

Seba sat up but said nothing. He still wondered if his father wanted to see him. He felt confused. He wanted to run to the shipyard right now and board a ship for Constantinople, but his father had thrown him overboard. He was not going to tell anyone that, lest they think his father didn't love him. He wanted to see his father, but now he wasn't so sure his father wanted to see him. His father had whispered something to him before he tossed him overboard and his eyes had welled with tears for an instant, but now Seba could only remember the loud words shouted for all on the ship to hear, saying that Seba was a dishonor to the family.

"It's too soon, Phillip. And he needs to eat. Sebastian, would you like some mastiha bread? Phillip was kind enough to share some of the council's mastic tears with me. It will settle your stomach."

"Then you can tell us what happened and how the English captain was involved." Uncle Phillip was not going to let it go; Seba knew he would have to tell them something about the incident at some point. He wasn't sure what he would say.

Papouli said, "Mesich, are you going back to work at the shipyard?"

"Yes, we have thirty other men who still have jobs and a great backlog of work to accomplish. I hope Kostas and the others have taught them well, because they will have to find a new leader."

"Can I work at the shipyard?" Seba hadn't planned to say that – it just slipped out.

His mother dropped the knife she was using to cut the mastiha bread; it fell to the floor with a loud clang. "Absolutely not!" It was the same shrieking sound Seba remembered from the day of his encounter with the snake. He looked at her mahogany colored eyes, which seemed to be on fire. She made a fist and banged it on the cutting board, then crossed herself and looked to the heavens, as if asking the Virgin Mary to intervene.

Papouli's bushy eyebrows nearly hit the ceiling, and he said, "Seba, why don't you eat something? You've had a shock and you need a bit of normalcy. Let Mesich handle the shipyard for now. Phillip, why don't you tell us how the skinos trees are faring this season? I think Seba is ready to wield the *kentitiri*, the sacred embroidery stiletto, now that he is nine years old. He's practically a man."

Seba knew it was a bribe. Uncle Phillip (not really an uncle, but Papouli's best friend) was the leader of the village. He made the rules, and he had never let any child in Sessera embroider the skinos trees until they were ten years old. That was the age of the passing of the knife ceremony. Seba would not be eligible for the ceremony for another year. He wondered if Uncle Phillip was going to let Papouli down gently or loudly scold him for suggesting they break the rules.

But Uncle Phillip's response shocked him. "Vaios, I couldn't agree more. As leader of Sessera, and judge appointee of Sultan Mustafa III, I would be honored to train Seba in the ways of the embroidery. From what I've seen and what your grandfather tells me, young man, you already have the wisdom of ten years. I think we can make an exception and celebrate the passing of the knife ceremony with you this season. You will be my special apprentice, and it will be our secret—that is, if your grandfather can manage to keep a secret."

He winked. Seba was grateful for the kindness. Having his Uncle Phillip, the most important man in Sessera, offer to step in and treat him like a son was a great honor. But Seba knew that he was doing it because he felt sorry for him, to distract him a sliver of hope after his loss. It felt more like pity than honor.

Mama wiped her eyes with the corner of her headscarf. Seba knew she had always wanted him to join the mastic council and work for Uncle Phillip. To her, that was the highest honor that any Greek man on Chios could receive. But the look on her face told Seba that if losing her beloved husband was the price to pay to gain that honor, it was too much.

Seba frowned and Uncle Phillip sat down next to him,

patting him on the knee. "And don't think I'm doing this just because you lost your father, Seba. It is a tragedy that our village will suffer for a long time, but it has nothing to do with my decision. I've been watching you—the way you observe and consider before you speak. That is a rare quality, and one that we will need on the mastic council in the coming years. The world is changing. With you as my special apprentice, Sessera will maintain its place of prominence on Chios."

Seba offered a shallow smile. It was all he could muster, even with the most important adults in his life looking at him expectantly. He took the bread Mama held out to him, smelling the piney smooth aroma of the mastiha mixed with the yeasty warm bread. His stomach rumbled, and he realized he hadn't eaten in a very long time. At least the smell of mastiha didn't make him sick, which was good, since it seemed from now on he would be spending much more time among the skinos trees.

8 THE HARVEST

Five years later

The Tears of Chios wept. It was as if the mastic trees had squeezed their eyes shut so tightly that thousands of tiny translucent teardrops appeared. The white resin of the mastiha hung from the gnarled and twisting limbs like tiny elongated jewels. They had hardened in the cool predawn breeze, but if left out in the July sun too long they would become soft and sticky. The villagers had to work quickly to harvest the tears and get them into the shade before the sun illuminated the whole valley. Seba, now fourteen, did the backbreaking work of carrying the tears from the mastic grove back to the village to be processed. His woven basket was bulging with the weight of the pebble-like tears, the long rope handles rubbing his sweaty shoulders raw. The sun peeked over the tops of the surrounding mountains, but the growing heat was already brutal. Seba couldn't tell if the high-pitched buzz in his ears was the insects sweeping over the grove or the sizzling of his skin. He dared not complain. The entire village was on the terraced groves today, the harvest day, everyone working feverishly to gather the tears before they softened in the sun. They had to be cut from the tree limbs, gathered off the ground, and transported to the village before they were ruined. The economy of Sessera—even their very lives—depended on everyone's speed.

Seba, Mama, and Papouli had been working with Uncle Phillip and the other villagers since before sunrise to harvest the precious tears, now his family's only source of income. He inadvertently cringed, remembering the sight of his father's flaming eyes as he threw Seba over the caprail of the *Dame*, nearly drowning him. *You are a disgrace and a dishonor to our family.* How many times had Seba replayed the scene in his head over the last five years? Every time he heard those words in his head, his body flushed with shame. He slapped the side of his temple. If anyone had been watching, they would think he was swatting at a fly. In a way, he was; but this fly was inside his mind, and it never stopped buzzing.

The mastiha copse smelled strongly of pine, cedar, mint, and herbs, and Seba's head was spinning. He had an uncanny feeling that he shouldn't be in the dusty heat of the skinos groves, but instead out on the blue waves of the Aegean, looking for his father. But there were no sailing ships for Seba ever since That Day, which is what Seba began calling the day of his father's kidnapping. That Day, the only ship that mattered to him had sailed out of the shipyard's cove, taking his dreams—and his father—with it.

Dizzy and off-balance, he found a spot of shade at the end of the terraced grove, dropped the basket, and slumped to the ground. Looking up through the tangle of tree limbs, he spotted a broken fragment of a resin-filled tear still clinging to the tree. "Uncle Phillip must have missed this one," he thought, as he reached up and scraped the minuscule hardened fragment from the tree with his dirty fingernail.

He raised it to his mouth, breathing in the earthy, minty smell.

"Sebastian, *no!*" His mother appeared out of nowhere and violently slapped the tear from his hand. It fell to the dirt.

"Are you trying to ruin what's left of our family? You know these are more valuable than gold! After everything Uncle Phillip has done for you, how could you? I've told you a thousand times they cannot be wasted!" His mother's dark eyes were blazing, and she looked like Medusa, about to turn Seba to stone. Still dizzy, Seba imagined a tangle of snakes slithering under Mama's headscarf and he decided not to look her in the eye.

"Why is it wasted if I'm eating it?" Seba, hot and exhausted, looked at the ground. His empty hand still stung.

"How dare you speak to your mother that way?! This is what allows our family to survive now without—"

She was going to say "your father," but stopped herself. Her eyes were still aflame. "You know these tears are our lifeblood. How can you be so selfish?"

Seba stood to his full height, which had recently surpassed his mother's. His eyes, the gray-green color of a stormy winter sea, shone with a fire of their own. "One tiny tear is not going to make a difference."

"Sebastian, you're wrong! This is all we have—if we squander it, we'll have nothing! Uncle Phillip would have to banish us from the village if the Ottomans catch you stealing. What if they cut off your hand? I couldn't bear it! You know what the Ottomans are like. We'd be homeless, with no access to food and no future. I will not let you ruin our family's legacy. We have worked too hard, and I won't let you throw it away."

She was straining not to raise her voice; her face was blood-red and the veins in her neck nearly erupted from her skin. Her long black skirt didn't move, but Seba could feel the anger coming off her in waves. She brought her face within inches of Seba's, and grabbed the hair at the back of his neck, twisting it as if she wanted to rip it off, skin and all. "We are proud descendants of the mastic growers of Chios, and I will not let you carelessly discard your family's heritage. What if Uncle Phillip saw you? We would be humiliated! You have been chosen. You are Phillip's heir apparent. Do you want to ruin your life? You have no idea what life is like outside the safety of the village walls. You would be alone, fending for yourself, and maybe me and Papouli with you! Is that what you want?"

Seba squinted from the pain of wispy brown hairs being pulled out in clumps from his neck, but he made no sound. He would not give his mother the satisfaction. "Papouli eats them while we're working—he says they are ambrosia and we are the gods. He says we are the true caretakers of this mastic island, not just slaves working for whoever happens to be ruling us this century."

His mother whipped her head around, as if an Ottoman overseer would appear on invocation. She exhaled loudly and her shoulders rolled forward. She released the hair at the nape of Seba's neck. "Your grandfather is an old dreamer. He doesn't consider your future."

"What future? What's wrong with not wanting to be a slave? We break our backs to grow the mastic. Why can't we enjoy one tiny piece? It's not fair! What if Papouli is right? Aren't we meant to be happy?"

Seba immediately realized he had overstepped a precarious boundary. He could feel her five feet of fury about to erupt like a volcano.

His mother reached up and slapped the side of Seba's head with her right hand, somehow managing to make the sign of the cross with her left. "You'll think nothing when I'm through with you! Holy Mother of God, give me strength!" Then she picked the tear from the dirt and waved it wildly in Seba's face. "You go tell your grandfather I won't tolerate his blasphemy any longer. There is one God, and He has bestowed on us this mastiha! It is our birthright and *I will not allow you to waste it!*" She turned abruptly and ran back to Uncle Phillip, who was standing at the far end of the skinos grove, surveying the harvest. Running as if chased by the devil, she cried, "Phillip, look! Sebastian found a little tear that someone missed—another for the harvest! I tell you, he has the eyes of a hawk, my son!"

Seba wondered if he would ever understand his mother, especially now that his father was gone. At first, she had been like a mother hen, hovering over Seba like he was a fragile injured chick. But as the years passed, it was clear she expected Seba to work for Uncle Phillip and possibly become leader of the mastic council. She acted as if the sea didn't exist, and as if Papa were simply a ghost of their collective imagination.

Just a few weeks earlier, the entire village had been in the mastic groves for the embroidery of the trees. It was a special occasion, leading up to the summer harvest. Coaxing mastiha from the trees was a never-ending, painstaking process that the villagers and their ancestors had undertaken for more than a thousand years. Seba had once loved learning about the mastic production. Uncle Phillip was a wealth of knowledge, and Seba had always looked up to him. Seba wondered how Uncle Phillip would have fared with the Ottomans on that English ship so many years ago. Could he have saved Papa? Uncle Phillip worked with the Ottoman tax collector and local politicians to manage the production, supply, protection, and sale of mastiha for the sultan. Seba knew that to the extent the Ottomans would respect any Greek man, they had a high regard for Uncle Phillip—at least according to Papouli and the men of Sessera, who extolled Uncle Phillip's finesse and wiles late into the evenings in the village square. Mesich had said that Uncle Phillip had no power, but what did he know? He admitted that it was his fault Papa had been taken. Seba had not spoken to Mesich since the day he nearly knocked himself out with a bottle of rum. He would be happy if he never saw Mesich again as long as he lived.

Uncle Phillip, true to his word that day in the kitchen, had made it a point to give Seba every advantage when it came to understanding the ways of the mastic village. He was never too busy to show Seba how to care for the trees, or even show him the accounts given to the Ottoman tax collectors at harvest time. Seba got extra attention, but it wasn't just Seba he taught—he often spoke like a teacher to all the children of the village, explaining the ways of the *mastichochoria* that had been passed down for hundreds of generations.

"Did you know the resin of these skinos trees has been harvested on this island since before the time of Homer?" Uncle Phillip was somewhat of a celebrity in Sessera, so when he was teaching, the children listened. Even Thaddeus and Nikos stopped bickering.

"The mastic teardrops are a form of currency even more

valuable than gold here. They have been prescribed for a thousand different ailments, maybe more, from digestive pains to open wounds."

Seba knew women in the village who baked mastiha into their breads and pastries for their families with the minuscule allotment of tears the sultan permitted each family to retain; but after Papa was taken, Mama said the mastiha was too valuable to waste on everyday food. She saved it and used it only on rare occasions.

"The embroidery is one of the most beautiful and sacred dances between us and the trees. It has been so since the time of Hippocrates."

For years Seba had watched Uncle Phillip and the other men use a special knife to make little cuts all over the trees' limbs, usually just after midsummer, when the sun was hot and the land was dry.

"We must wait until the trees are at least five years old before we can begin coaxing out the tears." Uncle Phillip, ever the teacher and showman, held up the small sharp knife with a grooved point.

"This kentitiri was specially designed for the embroidery. We are like surgeons, barely breaking the surface of the bark, making quick, sharp cuts, only as long as my thumbnail. You see, these trees and the villagers have an understanding. We make only the smallest prick necessary to draw out each tear, and in return, these beautiful trees provide their precious nectar. As it weeps from the trees, the summer winds help the resin form a protective shell that lets the tears retain their characteristic shapes, hiding the treasure of the mastiha inside." Like the other embroiderers, Uncle Phillip's hands expertly flew across the tree bark while he spoke. It was a marvel how the men made delicate patterns on the tree limbs with the special knives.

It was inevitable each year that one child or another would ask, "Does it hurt the trees, Uncle Phillip?"

"Excellent question, my young student. Absolutely not! When we embroider the trees, we are decorating them and making them beautiful. After the embroidery, the tears emerge like diamonds. These trees were made for this purpose, and they know we appreciate them—down to every last droplet that emerges like magic. It has been this way for many thousands of years."

Seba had been told countless times that Sessera was fortunate to have this legacy.

"But remember, children, we don't get greedy, do we? No. If we make too many cuts or make them too close together, we overburden the tree, and it stops producing."

Usually by now the younger children would look concerned. "Don't worry, little ones. Over a thousand years of practice has taught us exactly how much embroidery to place on the trees to get the most from them." As he flicked his knife over the trunk of the tree, Papouli came up behind them and clapped Uncle Phillip on the back.

"A whole new crop of embroiderers, eh, Phillip? You don't need my help, do you?"

The two old friends smiled broadly at each other. Seba had noticed that no one else ever dared interrupt Uncle Phillip when he was speaking: only Papouli. Uncle Phillip never seemed to mind. "My young students," he said. "Have I ever told you how this man saved my life when I was a boy?"

Seba was shocked. Papouli was a great storyteller within the village, but he had never mentioned this tale. In fact, he looked embarrassed. "Oh, not that tired old yarn again! They don't want to hear that! Pick up your knife, let's get on with the embroidery."

"No, Vaios, I think they should hear it. Children, did you know I owe Vaios my life? Do you want to hear the story?"

"Yes, please, please!"

Papouli stomped his foot. "I will not tell it. He who boasts much is punished in equal measure. I prefer the humility of Socrates." Papouli put his hands together in front of his heart and bowed.

Uncle Phillip laughed and said, "Don't quote the ancient Greeks to me—you will lose that battle, my friend. For now, I'll take the side of Aristotle and say that humility represents a deficiency in the virtue of sincerity."

"Wasn't it Aristotle who said, 'It is the mark of an educated mind to be able to entertain a thought without accepting it'? If so, I entertain your humble thought without accepting it." Papouli bowed even lower this time.

Uncle Phillip guffawed and slapped his leg. "Aristotle also said, 'The energy of the mind is the essence of life.' That is why, young students, you should study your lessons and try to keep up with Vaios and me. And don't let him distract you. I said I was going to tell a story, and he's not going to stop me!"

Papouli smiled and said, "Fine, but I warn you that if every man in the village square buys me drinks tonight instead of you, we'll all know who to blame."

Uncle Phillip said, "Grand idea! And I'll buy you a drink myself."

He bent down and looked very serious. "Children, I would not be here to harvest these tears had Vaios not saved my life many years ago, when I was only a boy of ten years. It was the damned *klefts*, raiders from the north. You know them—bastard bandits who roam the countryside and steal from Muslims and Christians alike. Those devils attacked

Sessera by night, and by the time we turned them away, it was daylight. The villagers of neighboring Kokoria were heading to their mastic groves, and we knew they would be next. We had tried to signal their watchtower, but didn't receive a response. I climbed down the outer wall of our village, thinking I could warn the Kokorians before the raiders got there. I knew the path through the ravines would get me to the Kokorians before the klefts' horses could arrive.

"What would I do when I got there and the Ottomans soon followed? Well, I hadn't thought that far. Stupid? Yes, of course, but as the great historian Thucydides said, 'Ignorance is bold, knowledge is reserved.'

"I kept hidden in the brush, making my way along the ravine. I could hear the raiders on the path high above the gorge. If I could get to the other side before them, I could warn our neighbors as they reached the fields. Well, I guess those horses were faster than I thought, because the raiders caught up to me. The next thing I knew, rocks were flying down the ravine straight at me, and the whole hill shifted. Those bastards had started a rockslide! I couldn't outrun it. I tumbled down the mountain, rocks and boulders raining on me as I tried in vain to gain my footing. I felt the bones in both arms snap, as well as several ribs. When everything stopped moving, I was buried underneath the boulders, cut and bleeding at the bottom of the ravine. My arms were useless, and I tried kicking the rocks away, but my hip was also useless and I was as good as dead."

Papouli looked grim and said nothing.

"The raiders laughed as they rode above me. I said my prayers because I felt crucified, dead, and buried. I'm sure I was delirious with pain by then. Night began to fall and imagined myself in the tomb with the Savior, the stone blocking the exit. Then I heard someone whistling the *tripatos* and said out loud, 'Jesus, when did you learn the Greek folk tunes?'"

Papouli whistled a few lines from the *tripatos*, and everyone clapped and laughed.

Seba laughed, too, remembering all the times Mama scolded Papouli for humming, tapping, or whistling around the house. Seba could picture him as a young man, whistling on the road to Kokoria's mastic groves.

"I then realized my own resurrection might be at hand, and I started yelling—probably frightening Vaios to near death, but I had nothing to lose at this point. When I yelled that the raiders had done this to me, Vaios steered his donkey down the ravine and began clawing at the rocks until my face just peeked out into the twilight. He helped me onto his donkey, and those two miles back to Sessera were both the worst agony I've ever felt, and the happiest I've ever been."

Finally Papouli spoke up. "It was pure dumb luck that our paths crossed. The monks at Nea Moni were donating a donkey to each of the villages, and I had the lucky job of collecting Sessera's new donkey. It was a special honor. Brother Stephen, who worked in the monastery's kitchen, plied me with smoked fish, mastic bread, and peaches from Nea Moni's orchard. I stayed far too long and had to spend the night in the monastery. I knew my father was going to beat me for being gone all night, so I got up several hours before dawn. I passed by at the right time."

"Didn't you worry you would be robbed in the dark?" Thaddeus asked. They had heard stories of the robbers on the roads between the villages and the port at Chora, which is why Mama said they needed to keep the village locked up tight at night.

"Well, to tell you the truth, Thaddeus, I didn't even consider it."

Nikos asked, "What about the raiders? Did you see them?"

Papouli shook his head. "No, I didn't see or hear them. I guess we both were stupid that day, eh, Phillip?"

"Well, my friend, then stupidity is the reason why we are great friends!" He clapped his hands together and stood up.

"All right, children, story time is over! I want you to walk these terraced groves and watch the miracle of the tears emerging from the tree limbs. The day of embroidery is a sight to behold, and we on this island are the only ones fortunate enough to see it! Drink it in, my young students—this is your heritage and your legacy!"

The children scattered, watching the embroidery. If Seba sat still long enough, he could actually see the mastic trees began to weep, the clear resin sluggishly appearing in the cuts. It took several weeks for the resin to slowly appear and harden into clear, perfect tears, hanging from the mastic limbs like jewelry sparkling in the sun. It was as if the stars had dropped from the sky and were now caught among the branches, shining in the bright daylight.

They made Seba think of the sun sparkling on the sea, like diamonds illuminated by the rays of the sun. Was his father looking at jewels on the sea in Constantinople? Even though he didn't know if his father wanted to see him, Seba wanted to find him—to apologize, and to ask penance for ruining the life of the best man he had ever known. Maybe if he hadn't been on the ship That Day, his father would still be here, and they would be working happily in the shipyard together.

He turned and looked at the skinos trees. The glistening jewels of mastiha dripping from the trees were once an enchanting sight to him. But today, Seba only saw grief and sorrow oozing from trees that had been maimed.

9 CHARITY

The next day, Seba plodded through his daily chores in a daze, watching the brown dust rise up from the path to the skinos grove, covering his boots with umber earth. The recollection of how his mother had slapped the tiny fragment of mastiha from his hand caused every cell in his body to erupt in anger, heating him to his core. It felt like waves of red flames were crackling outward from under his skin. His hand still stung where his mother struck him. From the opposite end of the grove, Uncle Phillip was gesturing to him. Every time he took a step in Seba's direction, however, he was accosted by one villager or another who urgently needed his advice. Uncle Phillip was always in demand, with everyone in the village relying on his guidance to ensure a fruitful harvest. Before he was interrupted for the hundredth time, he managed to say, "Seba, I need to speak to you about some very important business I need you to do for me—for the council. If I ever get a free moment, I will come and find you."

Seba had no idea what "important business" Uncle Phillip needed to discuss with him. He hoped he was not going to be castigated for disrespecting his mother in the skinos grove the day before. Seba felt a knot growing in his stomach.

Seba and Papouli walked back to the village together after a long day of work. The latter, seeing the look of utter dejection on his grandson's face, said, "Why don't we buy some fish from Darius for the evening meal? I'll even let you choose the biggest one."

Seba agreed. At least Mama still let them eat fish, even though they came from the sea. Ever since That Day, Mama pretended that the sea did not exist. Seba knew that she was hurting, but he didn't agree that the solution was to erase all memories of Papa from their lives. Seba and Papouli walked together to the village square, where Darius the fishmonger had a wooden crate filled with the day's catch for sale to the villagers returning from the fields. He didn't have many teeth, but he had a wide smile and an easy manner. As Papouli was putting the fish in his carrying basket, Thaddeus and Nikos appeared in the square, arguing as usual, and oblivious to anyone else in the village, as usual. Truthfully, they had never stopped fighting since the day they had saved Seba from the Ottoman viper.

They were quite a distance away, but Seba could make out bits of their conversation, which made his insides boil.

Thaddeus pounded his fist into the open palm of his other hand. "I think he fought them, refused to make their ships! That's what a strong Greek man would do. Maybe he escaped, and he's making his way back to Chios, like Odysseus after the Trojan War!"

Nikos sneered. "Thaddeus, he's not a moron like you, he would never do that. They're probably paying him well to build their ships."

"Then where is all the money, Nikos? No one's heard from him for years. A group of men asked Phillip for permission to go find him, and he refused, saying it was too dangerous and he didn't want to antagonize the sultan. Kostas is probably just a slave like the rest of us. If they were paying him, he would send the money back home, wouldn't he?"

"How should I know? Do I look like the authority on Ottoman shipbuilding? They have all the power, and they take what they want. They wanted Kostas, and they got him. There was nothing any of us could do about it. That's how it works. Even a fool like you should be able to understand that."

Thaddeus's fingers were still curled into a fist; he was barely holding back his wrath—but it was Seba's anger that broke first. Seba ran across the square in a fury, stopping between the two of them, his whole body shaking with rage.

"Nikos, my father is not a traitor! You don't even know him. He was the smartest, kindest, most honorable man in Sessera. You wouldn't know anything about honor. All you do is talk behind people's backs and cause trouble. Don't *ever* mention my father again."

Nikos said nothing, his fingers pressed tightly together in a ball. He had never seen Seba lose his temper, and he wore an expression that fell somewhere between wariness and curiosity, like a dark cat ready to pounce.

Seba whirled on Thaddeus. "For the past five years, people in this village have gossiped about the most important person in my life. Do you know what it's like to be forever reminded of my worst nightmare? The constant murmurs behind my back, people falling silent when I walk by. I can never get away from it. You and I have always been friends—I didn't think you would do this to me. Every mention of my father feels like a dagger in my back, but I never thought you'd be the one twisting it."

Nikos took the opportunity to slink away. Thaddeus's face flushed pink, and then a deep shade of red. His fists uncurled and his shoulders fell. "I'm sorry, Seba. I never meant—"

Seba saw Thaddeus's pained expression and his anger dissipated. He held up his hand. "I know, Thaddeus. I'm sure people talk about your father as well, and I know you didn't mean anything by it, but I hate the thought of people disrespecting my father. And today it feels even worse than before."

"Worse than the day they took you father from you? What could be worse than that?" Thaddeus's face was still red, but now his eyebrows were arched inward, as if he were ready to pummel whoever was causing more pain to his friend.

Seba lowered his voice. "I argued with my mother yesterday. She keeps pushing me to be my Uncle Phillip's special pet—as if I don't have any thoughts or ambitions of my own. And now Uncle Phillip says he has some business he needs me to do for the council. You know all I ever wanted to do was work with my father in the shipyard. Every year that passes takes me away from my dream. It feels like my mother and Uncle Phillip are closing in on me, like I'm an animal caught in a snare. Am I a traitor? Should I have gone to look for my father years ago? Now it's too late. I feel like everything I do is a betrayal of someone I love."

"Seba, I'm really sorry." He put his hand on his friend's shoulder and said, "I know what would make us both feel better. Do you want me to beat up Nikos?"

Seba couldn't help but laugh out loud. Seeing Thaddeus beat up Nikos just might make him feel a little better.

Thaddeus made a fist and pounded it into the open palm of his other hand, just as he had done minutes before. "I can't stand that snake in the grass. He never lets me forget my family is poor and his family is on the council."

"My Papa used to say it's best to ignore boys like Nikos. The only reason they speak is to get a reaction, so if you deny them the thrill they'll walk away."

"I've tried, Seba, but he follows me around reminding me—and everyone in this whole village—that he's better than me. I just wish for once I could prove him wrong."

"I'm sure you'll get your chance. Papouli says pride comes before a fall, and Nikos is the most prideful person in Sessera."

Thaddeus nodded in agreement. "I know exactly what you mean about feeling like a trapped animal. Every day here is the same. Open the gates, work the fields, close the gates, tend to the village. We weren't meant to be imprisoned within these walls for the rest of our lives." He stood tall and thrust out his chest, mimicking the Ottoman soldiers who guarded Sessera's gates. "'These are my swords, so hand over your mastiha; I'm the sultan, so you must do what I say.' I can't stand it!"

"It's so confusing. Papouli says we're lucky to live in Sessera. Otherwise you or I might be sent as tributes to the Ottoman army. They have it much worse on the north side of the island, where the mastiha doesn't grow."

"Ugh! I just wish we could grow our own food without interference. Why do the people on the council get more than we do? Shouldn't we all share in the fruits of our labor? And the mastiha—our birthright? Ha! We barely get to keep any of it. A few measly little tears with every harvest, after we break our backs for the Ottomans all year long. That's an insult, when we're the ones who do all the work. They couldn't produce it without us."

Seba agreed with Thaddeus on one level, but it felt dangerous to say such things aloud. No one had ever spoken like this in the village. "Aren't the Ottomans everywhere, even across the Strait of Chios? The English captain looked like he was scared of Ahmed the day they took my father. Mesich said even the westerners, with all their navies and merchant fleets, can't compete with the power of the Ottoman Empire. All the silks, spices, gold, gems, and valuable resources are managed by the sultan in Constantinople. The westerners have to accept the rule of the Ottomans, too, and they won't challenge the sultan. Mesich says they'd be stupid to try. I guess we would be, too."

Thaddeus shook his head, irritated at the direction of this conversation. "I'm sorry, Seba. I would like to stay and talk to you, but my father needs Mrs. Lampros's salve for his back."

Seba was relieved. He didn't like the direction of the conversation either; it felt like another betrayal. "Yes, Mrs. Lampros is wonderful—we buy her honey and bread for special occasions."

"Thank God for her and her medicines. She's amazing. I wish we didn't have to rely on her charity, and that of everyone else in the village—but with twelve children, we never seem to have enough. My father is getting these disgusting black sores on his spine and the backs of his legs, probably because he never moves them. I feel so bad for him. I shouldn't keep him waiting."

After saying goodbye to Thaddeus, Seba walked over to Darius and Papouli, who had been deep in conversation about a recent fishing accident in the Strait of Chios. One of Darius's fellow fishermen had fallen overboard, and his fishing boat was dashed against the rocky coastline. The current was so strong that the poor man nearly drowned. Darius, who had been fishing nearby, rowed furiously against the tide and scooped him out of the sea before the current dragged him away. Unfortunately, the man had lost his boat and his livelihood.

Seba knew how the fisherman felt. He thought of his father, toiling away for the Ottomans in a city far away. Papa's livelihood was taken from him, as well as his family. It wasn't fair.

Seba's thoughts were interrupted by the warm voice of Brother Tim. "Blessings to you in the name of our Lord Christ. What a fine evening it is! And what do you have, Vaios? Is that *barbouni*? A delicious fish, especially grilled over a fire. My mouth is starting to water just at the thought of that crispy skin and flaky white meat."

Papouli opened the basket to show him the fish. "Then bless us, Brother Tim. Would you like to join us for supper?"

Seba's favorite teacher was not known to refuse a hot meal. "What a kind offer. Much better than me dining alone in my little room behind the church. Yes, I accept. But first I have a bit of business to attend to for the church."

"Do you need any assistance, Brother Tim? Seba would love to help you. Afterward, he can escort you back to our home for supper." Papouli must have seen the argument between Seba and Thaddeus and thought that Seba could use the wisdom of a man of God. Papouli was very observant like that sometimes.

And in truth, Seba would be glad of the monk's company. Since That Day, Brother Tim's presence had been one of Seba's few comforts. He often quoted the Greek poet

Menander's words: "Time is the healer of all necessary evils." Seba wasn't sure the kidnapping of his father by the Ottoman Empire was a necessary evil, but he did know time had not yet healed it.

Brother Tim also said, "God makes all things work together for our good," which was his personal paraphrase of Romans 8:28. Seba thought that lots of things in the world were not working out for his good, but Brother Tim meant well, so Seba kept quiet and tried to be grateful for what he had, as he suggested.

Brother Tim nodded his thanks to Papouli and said *"Whoever is kind to the poor lends to the Lord, and He will reward them for what they have done.* Proverbs 19:17. Seba, if you will help me with the Creator's charity work this evening, I would be grateful."

Seba nodded and followed Brother Tim as he conducted the business of the church—visiting the elderly who could no longer leave their homes, and bringing food to the fisherman who had lost everything. As they walked through the narrow alleys of Sessera, Brother Tim looked earnestly at Seba.

"How is your mother?"

"*Kala.* She says her prayers to the Virgin Mary day and night."

A smile escaped just above Brother Tim's bushy beard. "Yes, she is an example to others of a certain rare devotion."

Seba remembered why he liked Brother Tim. Like Mama, Brother Tim was a steadfast Christian, but his practice of the faith was much more serene than hers. He did not judge anyone, ever. He told the truth in a way most people did not—with kindness, humor, and a sense of joy.

After leaving the fisherman with a loaf of bread and several rounds of farmer's cheese, Brother Tim said, "We have one more stop, and then on to the mouthwatering barbouni."

Seba could tell from the direction of Brother Tim's steps that they were heading toward Thaddeus's house. Seba recalled the conversation with Thaddeus, and how he hated accepting charity.

"Um, maybe I should just wait here while you finish up."

"Is there a problem, Seba?"

"It's bad enough that poor Thaddeus's family needs donations to survive, especially after all the work he does. If he finds out I participated in giving him charity, he will feel even worse."

"Seba, you're not making it worse for him. It's his own insecurity. He's a child of God, just like you and me. If he views his worth through the eyes of men, the best thing we can do is show him he is valued and cherished as our brother in Christ. He must see himself through the eyes of the Creator."

Seba thought it might be a good theory, but probably not realistic. He nodded and said nothing.

Brother Tim's mouth twitched with amusement. "I see you may need more convincing, just like our friend Thaddeus." He pointed to the east. "Saint Paul visited the ancient city of Ephesus many times. It's there—just across the water, southeast from our beloved Chios. The early Christian church in Ephesus struggled against Roman rule, much like we Chians struggle with the Ottomans."

Seba was amazed. He had no idea that Brother Tim knew about the struggles with the Ottomans. He thought the priests spent their time praying, reading the Bible, and teaching children in the schools. Despite Brother Tim's vast knowledge, Seba had never heard him speak of politics. This was very interesting.

"Saint Paul wrote letters to the church in Ephesus, to encourage them and give them hope. In Ephesians 2:10, he said: *For we are his workmanship, created in Christ Jesus for good works, which God prepared beforehand, that we should walk in them.*"

Brother Tim saw Seba's confusion and continued, "You see, Seba, Saint Paul knew we were God's perfect creations—but he also knew that we often forget our perfection. Sometimes we need a reminder that we are treasured by God. Maybe your friend Thaddeus has forgotten he is God's creation, and sometimes God's creations help each other."

Seba thought it sounded reasonable, but he was pretty sure Thaddeus would not see it that way. Brother Tim could tell Seba was still uncomfortable. "Did you know that I, Brother Timotheos, was named for the first Christian bishop of Ephesus? By all accounts, he was a very wise man. I don't claim to have his wisdom, but I know enough not to cause the ruination of a friendship." He reached into his vestment and gave Seba a few coins from his pouch. "Why don't you go buy some bread and honey for us to share with your family this evening? Saint John the Baptist would have also added locusts, but I think we can skip them just this once."

Seba laughed. You'd think Brother Tim would be rotund for as much as he talked about food, but in reality he was average size, with little spectacles that slid down his sweaty nose. He had a habit of constantly pushing them up with the back side of his wrist, which he did right now.

Seba left Brother Tim and walked to Mrs. Lampros's house and tried to buy honey from her, but she would not hear of accepting payment from the grandson of Vaios Georgelous.

"You tell that grandfather of yours a piece of my hearth

fire-hanger has broken off, which means I cannot make any soups over the fire until it's fixed. I understand he is skilled at the forge, and I could use his expertise. Would you send him over some time, please?"

Seba smiled and nodded. Papouli was a good welder—all of the firedogs, spits, and metalwork in Seba's home were the most beautiful and the strongest in all of Sessera. Papouli had worked as a blacksmith when he was younger, but now at his advanced age, he worked the skinos trees with his daughter and grandson. Nevertheless, he had not lost any of his welding skills and he was still like Hephaestus with iron and fire.

"Yes, Mrs. Lampros. I'll send him over."

"You look different today, Seba. Has something changed?"

How could she possibly know? Yes, he lost his temper with his mother, yelled at his best friend, and was being hounded by Uncle Phillip to do some special work for the council that made him feel like he would never see his father again. He felt like his whole world was turning upside down; but he wasn't going to admit it to Mrs. Lampros. "Not that I can think of," he said.

She smiled at him, and he could tell she saw right through him. "Well, my young man, I am always here for you. That's how it has been in this village and ones like it for thousands of years. We are a family, carrying on the honor and the legacy of the original mastic growers of ancient Greece. We take care of each other and share each other's burdens. That's what families do. And I, for one, am honored to be part of it."

She wrapped up the earthen jar of honey in a cotton towel and handed it to Seba, then gave him a hug. Seba understood why Papouli liked her so much. She was a great cook like Mama, but sweeter and warmer, like the honey she had just given him.

Seba left Mrs. Lampros's house and stopped by the kafenion to buy two loaves of braided olive bread from Sotirios, the owner. As he waited for Brother Tim, Seba realized he was smiling. He was looking forward to this dinner.

As the sun began to set, Brother Tim returned from Thaddeus's house and they walked together to supper. The priest had a way of complimenting his mother without agreeing with her statements, and Seba knew this dinner would be pleasant—maybe the first pleasant meal his family had shared in a very long time. Seba thought of That Day, and clenched his fists together, willing the memory to disappear.

As if he could feel Seba's painful memory, Brother Tim stopped and looked at him intently. "You know, don't you, Seba, when our loved ones are not near, we are still connected to them through the Holy Spirit?"

Seba did not know this. He frowned, bewildered.

"When Jesus's work in physical form on this earth was complete, He ascended into heaven. But He did not leave us alone, Seba. He introduced us to the Holy Spirit, a part of Him and a part of us that connects us all. Do you understand?"

"Not really."

"Have you ever felt connected to anyone—your father, say—when he was not near you?"

"Well, there are times when I'm in my bed on the roof, looking at the stars, and I think of Papa looking up at the very same stars in Constantinople. Is that what you mean?"

"Yes, that is part of it. The Holy Spirit facilitates the connection, and offers us so much more. Tell me, Seba, how do you feel about your place in this mastic village? Does it feel like the Holy Spirit is with you when you are coaxing those tears from the trees?"

"I don't know. I didn't mind working in the groves when Papa was here."

"Is it because you always thought you had a choice—maybe to go somewhere else or do something else?"

"Maybe."

"Will you do something for me, Seba?"

Seba nodded.

"Tonight, after our meal, go back up to the roof, alone. Sit quietly. Don't think of anything. Just invite the Holy Spirit to visit you. Then listen. Don't force it—just be still and listen. What does the Holy Spirit tell you about your place in the world? I'm very curious to know what the Holy Spirit tells you."

Seba didn't say anything, but he had the strangest feeling the Holy Spirit had already told Brother Timotheos the location of Seba's place in the world. He promised himself he would go to the roof and find out for himself. For some reason, this made him feel just a little bit better.

When they reached Seba's house, they were able to bypass the animal pens; there was a series of steep stone steps leading directly into the family's dwelling. Mama said those stairs were only for guests, so Seba rarely used them. He felt special bringing Brother Tim to the "guests only" entrance.

When they walked through the door, Mama began making the sign of the cross before Brother Tim could open his mouth to greet her. "Mother of God, what a blessing it is to have you in our home, Brother Timotheos! The Lord has smiled on us to bring you to our table today. We thank the one true God for his generosity and the miracle of his blessings."

"Thank you, Agnete. You are truly a blessed servant of God."

"*As for me and my house, we will serve the Lord,*" she quoted.

"*You are hospitable, a lover of what is good, sober-minded, just, holy, self-controlled,*" Brother Tim quoted back.

Mama put her hands together in front of her heart. "*Humility is the fear of the Lord; its wages are riches and honor and life.*"

Brother Tim bowed. "*For thus says the One who is high and lifted up, who inhabits eternity, whose name is Holy: 'I dwell in the high and holy place, and also with him who is of a contrite and lowly spirit, to revive the spirit of the lowly, and to revive the heart of the contrite.'*"

Mama and Brother Tim could have exchanged Bible verses all night long, and then Seba would have gone to bed hungry, but Papouli surprised them all by saying, "*I have heard the grumbling of the Israelites. Tell them, 'At twilight you will eat meat, and in the morning you will be filled with bread. Then you will know that I am the Lord your God!'*"

Brother Tim laughed heartily. Mama looked slightly irritated that her demonstration of Bible knowledge was cut short, but she quickly rallied and put a platter of grilled fish on the table. Not one to let Papouli have the last word, however, she said quietly, but loud enough for everyone to hear, "*Man shall not live on bread alone, but on every word that comes from the mouth of God.*"

It was all Brother Tim could do to stifle a guffaw by coughing violently into his sleeve.

10 SESSERA

Several months later, a warm September breeze scented with olives and ripening grapes flowed through the home's small windows. The fattening sun was low on the western horizon, glowing the color of a fresh squeezed blood orange. This had once been one of Seba's favorite times of the year, just before the second embroidery of the skinos trees. Now, it just seemed like the end of a season of living outdoors, and a chilly precursor to the winter season when the villagers were cooped up like animals to protect themselves from the cold.

Seba was sitting in the kitchen, staring into the evening fire, lost in thought, when Mama stepped between him and the hearth. "Sebastian, I need you to run an errand for me. Mrs. Lampros's offered me some sour oranges from her garden. I meant to ask your grandfather to pick them up, but you know he always runs out of here as soon as the evening meal is over so he can get to his storytelling."

After long days toiling in the mastic groves, tending the

olive trees, and foraging for *chora*, the men in the village would meet at the kafenions around the village's central square, drinking thick, rich Turkish coffee, debating whether life was better under the Ottomans than the Genoese, talking politics, and making predictions about the mastic harvest. Papouli was always the center of attention, telling stories that usually caused a roar of raucous laughter from the men drinking from their small ceramic cups.

Mama generally disapproved of the men "wasting time" in the village square. But lately, she had started practically pushing Seba out the door to keep him from sitting in the chair in the kitchen, staring into the fire in the hearth like a ghost.

"Sebastian, did you hear me?"

Looking up, Seba saw she didn't look angry. No, she looked worried.

"Yes, Mama. I'll get the oranges from Mrs. Lampros."

"No, Sebastian, I want Papouli to do it—I think Mrs. Lampros likes him. I can't believe it's been almost ten years since Mr. Lampros died. I thought she would have remarried by now. I've seen the way she looks at your grandfather. That poor man has been a widower since long before your sister, rest her soul, left this earth."

"Yes, Mama. I'll tell him to get the oranges."

"That's my good boy. While you're in the square, why don't you stay for a while? The company will be good for you."

"Yes, Mama."

Seba didn't want to go, but he also didn't want his mother circling him all evening, trying to get him to talk— or worse yet, planning his future as Uncle Phillip's special assistant. He didn't want to talk to anyone. Mama liked to fix things; often, she succeeded at it through sheer willpower, but Seba was something she could not fix.

He went to the village and gave the message to Papouli, who was talking to Sotirios, the kafenion owner. Upon hearing the news, Papouli's bushy eyebrows bounced up and down in amusement. "Ah, my daughter, always looking out for my heart, eh, Seba?" Papouli didn't really want an answer, and Seba didn't know how to respond anyway. "What do you think about Mrs. Lampros, grandson?"

"She makes the best *loukoumades*. I think it's because she uses fresh honey from her own bees."

"Right you are, Seba. And I won't tell your mother you prefer Mrs. Lampros's loukoumades to hers." He winked conspiratorially. "Barbara Lampros is a fascinating woman. She knows a little bit about almost everything."

"Mama says you should marry her."

"Oh, she does, does she?" Papouli rolled his eyes at Sotirios, who discreetly excused himself. As owner of Sessera's most popular kafenion, Sotirios was well versed in the art of diplomacy. He knew better than to get involved in Vaios Georgelous's relationship with his daughter Agnete.

Papouli held up his hands, palms facing out, as if to push away the idea. "Well, I won't be rushed by my daughter. In the words of Plato, 'To love rightly is to love what is orderly and beautiful in an educated and disciplined way.' Mrs. Lampros is one of the most orderly and beautiful women I know."

Papouli held his hands crossed over his heart and recited dreamily:

The stars around the beautiful moon
Hiding their glittering forms
Whenever she shines full on earth...
Silver...

Seba knew that Papouli must be in love if he was quoting the poetess, Sappho. Brother Tim had taught them that Sappho was one of the most prolific lyricists in ancient Greece, writing poetry that was intended to be accompanied by music. Her favorite subject was romantic love.

Papouli continued, "I will court that rare and beautiful flower as I see fit, and not on your mother's timetable. Now, enough of this love talk, Seba—if I don't get to my table over there, Phillip will steal my audience and get all the attention!"

Papouli walked over to the men sitting at a large table, open to the darkening sky, and was welcomed heartily. He was always prepared to share a lively story and immediately launched into a hilarious tale that involved dozens of stolen pears, a wasp's nest, and a near-whipping by his father. In minutes, the village square was alive with the sound of laughter.

Seba stood there for a few moments, taking in the scene. Papouli was holding court and entertaining the men in the village who were seated at small wooden tables which bore steaming mugs of Turkish coffee and cold cups of tsipouro. Mrs. Lampros was sliding her heaven-scented freshly baked peach pies onto her windowsill. Seba noticed that as she leaned forward through the window, she saw Papouli and blushed. Everyone seemed so happy—happy to be together, happy to be alive, and happy to be safe inside the walls of Sessera.

"It's a beautiful place, isn't it?"

Seba wheeled around to find Uncle Phillip standing beside him with one hand in his pocket and the other holding an argentine-colored tobacco pipe. A long wooden stem fit into the bowl of the pipe, and a mouthpiece of amber was between his lips. A smoky sweet smell of tobacco wafted from the top of the pipe's bowl and swirled around Uncle Phillip's graying beard. He looked handsome and regal, comfortable in his surroundings.

Seba breathed in the pipe smoke and swallowed. "Yes."

"I've been thinking, Seba. Do you remember the day when I promised your mother and your grandfather I would take care of you?"

Seba nodded, the feeling of nausea that he had felt that evening coming back to him, as if he were nine years old again.

"I've taught you much about the ways of the *mastichochoria*, but I believe you are ready for more."

Seba looked up at Uncle Phillip through the haze of smoke. He could no longer hear the laughter of the men in the square, and his stomach lurched as he waited for Uncle Phillip to continue.

"The life of a council member is challenging, but with it comes great honor. There are few with the skills or temperament for this difficult position. Keeping the villagers safe, negotiating with the Ottoman Empire, studying the skinos trees to make them produce, managing the guards, setting prices, maintaining the peace with twenty other mastic villages, buying and selling with merchants around the world. Some might even call the task Heraclean."

Seba continued to peer through the smoke and the pace of his heartbeat increased.

"This position requires superior skills of the mind, fortitude, prowess, good judgment, adaptability, prudence, and a fair bit of political savvy." Uncle Phillip sucked air through the pipe and exhaled slowly. "I am not complaining, Seba. Please understand. I know everyone in this village looks up to me and always expects me to make things right. It is a lonely job, though. And I need someone I can trust to assist me."

"What about Nikos's father? I thought he was the most important man in the village—after you, of course."

"Yes, he is a good man. But he is too important to be of assistance to me. I need someone with discretion, who can watch and learn without divulging my secrets. No, no, Eugenio Lykaios is not the man for the job. He lacks discretion—and his son has not shown promise in that area, either."

Seba wondered why Uncle Phillip was confiding in him. There were other men from Sessera who sat on the mastiha council, and there were many more from the twenty other villages who had experience working with the skinos trees. They already knew how to bring the valuable tears to trade in the world, and they had experience navigating the politics of the council.

"I need an apprentice, Seba. Someone who will be by my side at all times, and train to become the next leader of the council." He took a deep puff on the pipe and slowly blew the smoke into the air. "You are the person I need."

"Me? I don't think I'm qualified."

"Of course you are, Seba. Like no one else in this village, you know how to hold your tongue and observe everyone around you. There is a degree of humility required to do this job. Anyone who gets too big for his pantaloons is bound to make mistakes. You will never do that, and I know you would never betray me."

Seba had his doubts; surely Uncle Phillip was making the biggest mistake of his life. But then Seba imagined his mother's face if she found out he had refused this momentous offer from the most important man in Sessera.

"I need your answer, Seba. Will you work for me and with me, as my special apprentice? I'm sure you are the only person who can do this job for me. Your village needs you. I need you."

Instead of picturing the villagers and the skinos groves, however, the vision that appeared in Seba's head was his father, on That Day, at the mercy of the Ottoman Empire. Something about this conversation with Uncle Phillip felt wrong.

Seba pushed the thought way down inside. "All right," he said. "I will be your apprentice."

Uncle Phillip took his hand out of his pocket and handed Seba a small brown velvet bag. "I was hoping you would say that, Seba. Here is a small token of my appreciation, and a symbol of my commitment to you." The bag was fragrant with mastiha. "Do with these what you want, and when you want. If anyone sees you with the bag, you tell them that you work for the mastic council and to see me if they have a problem. In exchange, all I ask is that when I need you to do something for me, you do it—without question. Agreed?"

Seba took the bag from Uncle Phillip's hand and opened the drawstring. Seba was shocked—the bag was brimming with the sparkling white jewels of mastiha—just like the one Mama had slapped from his hand, but bigger. Seba had never known any villager to ever have so many tears in their possession. If a worker was caught with mastiha in excess of their meager allotment, they were brought before the Ottoman guards and interrogated to determine whether they were stolen. Seba knew Uncle Phillip was important, but the fact that he was permitted to carry a pouch full of mastiha like this showed his stature with the Ottomans was even more significant than anyone knew. And now he was offering the same opportunity to Seba. He looked up at Uncle Phillip, who was holding out his free hand.

Head spinning with the prestige and possibilities, Seba grasped Uncle Phillip's hand and they shook.

"That's my good boy. You put this bag where your grandfather won't find it. If your mother asks, it is a gift from me to you for the work that we are doing together on the council, and is yours to do with what you see fit."

With that, Uncle Phillip walked away, calling out to Papouli, "Vaios, why don't you tell them about the time we swam Mavra Voila with those girls from Olympi?"

Stunned, Seba absently walked through the doors of Sotirios's kafenion and waved to Sotirios, who was busy boiling coffee in copper brikis over the fire. Sotirios had always been kind to Seba, and he knew Seba liked to access the village's rooftops through the ladder at the back of his cafe. It was their little secret, and Seba was grateful for Sotirios's discretion, because Seba needed some time alone to process what had just happened.

Sotirios looked up from the brikis, his back bent from hunching over the fire, stirring coffee day and night. "I wish my knees weren't so stiff, Seba, or I'd join you on the roof. I used to go up there all the time when I was boy. The fresh air, the view of the sea, the mountains that protect us, and the beautiful colors of the sky—there's nothing like the freedom to enjoy the treasures of God's earth."

"I can help you climb up if you want to join me."

Sotirios waved him off, nodding his thanks. "Another one of God's treasures is the glorious smell of this boiling coffee. Don't worry about me. You go enjoy yourself up there. If you see that cat, Artemis, tell her I appreciate her hunting. She keeps the mice out of my coffee shop." He returned his attention to the fire and the bubbling coffee.

Seba sat on Sotirios's roof, looking up at the twilight. Venus was in the eastern sky, so bright that it shined even before night had truly fallen. He thought about what Uncle Phillip had just offered him. Every boy in the village, especially Nikos, and maybe even Thaddeus, would kill for that opportunity. However, Seba couldn't shake the uneasy feeling that this decision was pulling him further away from his father. *Papa, I wish you were here. You would tell me whether this is the right decision. I just don't know.*

He made his way across the rooftops of the connected houses in the village until he reached his own home. He flopped onto his straw mattress, feeling wretched. He had a pouch full of mastiha and he didn't even feel like chewing any of the mastic tears. *I guess it doesn't matter now, Papa, because it's done—I've already said yes to Uncle Phillip.* Crossing his ankles and putting his hands behind his head, Seba could hear Papouli's voice wafting up from the village square.

To hear Papouli talk, one might believe he had lived in the village for centuries. "Sessera is the best of the mastic villages, my friends! You think they get more from the trees in Vousta? Olympi? And Pyrgi—that precious 'painted village'? Ha!" Papouli spat, or at least that's what it sounded like from the rooftop. "They cannot hold a candle to Sessera. We are the best mastic village on the island. That's why our walls are the highest, nestled in the best valley on the island. No one can find us here—we cannot be seen from the sea. No raiders will ever come to Sessera! Our mastic is safe!

"And just let them try! It will be like the Labyrinth of Daedalus! Ha! They will run in circles and dead ends, and wish they had never tried to defeat the men of Sessera! They would never make it out alive, right, my friends?!"

"Opa! Opa! Sessera! "

Seba could hear the pride in his grandfather's voice. Sessera and all of the twenty-one mastic villages truly represented a masterful feat of engineering by the former Genoese rulers of Chios who had established them more than four centuries ago.

"Our mastiha travels all over the world — to Egypt, Italy, Asia, Spain, England, and even to the farthest reaches of the vast oceans. It may be reaching people all over the earth! All from Chios! And the best from Sessera!"

Seba guessed that if Papouli had not been a mastic farmer in the village, he probably would have been a great leader of soldiers. He sure knew how to rouse their passion and pride, and get them to agree with anything he said or did. Of course, he always had the assistance of the thick dark coffee and tsipouro they drank every night.

The men would talk and laugh long into the evening, sometimes only sleeping a few hours before dawn, ready again to join their fellow Sesserans in the skinos groves. Many times, the evening stories would evolve into the men singing their favorite songs, passed down for generations, even before the walled villages of the *mastichochoria* had been built.

εκεί κάτω από την εκκλησία
δίπλα στην εκκλησία του Αγίου Σιδέρου
η εκκλησία, αγία παρθένε
η εκκλησία της αγίας Κωνσταντίνου
είναι μαζεμένοι
σε άπειρους αριθμούς
από τον κόσμο, αγία παρθένε
από τον κόσμο, ό,τι καλύτερο!

He could hear Matilde the donkey braying and the family's hens clucking from the ground floor below. Venus was still bright and low on the horizon. The Romans called her Venus, but Seba preferred the Greek name, Aphrodite. Papouli must have been thinking of Aphrodite as well, because Seba could hear him telling the story of her creation, his voice floating up past the stone walls of the village. Aphrodite was born of foam from the sea, foam that rose up from the water after Kronos castrated his father, Ouranos. The old Titan's genitals fell into the Aegean, and a great froth rose up from the water, creating the goddess of love and beauty.

It was a curious story; to think that something beautiful could come forth from violence and disaster. He wished he could believe it was true.

In time, Seba fell asleep. In his dreams, he and his father were born of the foam of the sea, the two of them traveling the Aegean on a pair of sleek white dolphins, laughing together as they bounced over the effervescent waves. He slept, his hands curled as if holding the dolphins' reins, lips pressed together in the languid arc of a smile. He could almost feel the salt spray on his face.

11 TRAPPED

Several days later, Seba had chewed a few of the mastic tears from the brown pouch Uncle Phillip had given him, and he was feeling a bit better. Maybe being Uncle Phillip's apprentice wouldn't be that bad, after all. Seba whistled the *tripatos* while he milked the goats, whom his mother had named Myra and Sheba. They were sisters, and were not unlike Xenia and Demetria—Myra was a mouthy busybody, while Sheba was easygoing, a pleasure to be around. Seba's whistle was not quite as good as Papouli's, but similar enough that he thought one day he might fulfill his grandfather's musical legacy. He returned to the kitchen with a brimming pail of milk, and what he saw caused the pail to nearly slip through his fingers, as that old knot in his stomach squeezed him hard.

Xenia was sitting at the kitchen table with his mother.

When her eyes met Seba's, she jumped out of her seat and lunged toward him, her brown curls escaping from her tight braids. "Silly, don't drop the milk after you just spent the morning filling the pail! Let me help you." She reached for the pail, but Seba stepped back and gripped the handle tightly. Xenia's arms swept through the air like she was trying to catch a butterfly and missed.

"What are you doing here?"

His mother shot him a look of daggers, her forehead heavily furrowed and eyes piercing through Seba as if to impale him with an invisible force. "Sebastian, where are your manners? How dare you speak to our guest like that? Apologize immediately! And please, dear Lord, forgive Sebastian for his impertinence. I did not raise him to treat his neighbors this way. Sebastian, have you forgotten to love Xenia as yourself?" Then looking conspiratorially at Xenia, she said, "Don't mind him my dear, he's not awake yet. Sometimes in the early light of day, he doesn't remember how to express himself the way Christ taught us."

Seba was nonplussed, looking from his mother to Xenia. Of course, Xenia, who never missed an opportunity to speak, was completely undisturbed by Seba's reaction. She sashayed gracefully back into the chair opposite Seba's mother and leaned in.

"Oh, Mrs. Krizomatis, Seba just isn't much of a lark, is he? That's all right, I'm a lark and an owl rolled into one, so I have enough energy for both of us."

Mama smiled approvingly.

Xenia continued, "Seba, I was just telling your mother that Thaddeus and Nikos have been fighting again. Do you know what it's about? I even saw you arguing with them some time ago in the village square."

Seba was surprised; he didn't even realize Xenia had been in the square the day that he had lost his temper with Nikos and Thaddeus; but she obviously made it her

business to know everything that happened in Sessera—
especially if Seba was involved. But he only shrugged: "No
idea," he said.

"Seba, I know their feud is getting worse. Don't lie to
your future wife." She looked over at Mama to see her
reaction. Seba couldn't tell if that statement was for him or
for his mother, but he didn't like it. Mama smiled sweetly at
Xenia and nodded her head in agreement. Seba thought that
this day couldn't have started any worse. He wanted to
climb back up to the roof, burrow into his mattress, and not
emerge for days.

"Xenia, I'm only fourteen years old, and you are not my
future wife."

His mother held her finger in the air and clucked her
tongue. "Sebastian, you do not know what the future holds.
Xenia and I were just talking about the sacrament of
marriage. Two beautiful young people, full of integrity and
intelligence, growing together in love as they work toward
a common goal—that's what makes a marriage blessed in
the sight of God. It's time for you to start planning for your
future. We have been a mastic family for generations and
Xenia's family is well-respected in this village. It is a perfect
match, just like Kostas and me."

At the mention of his father, Seba wished he was here
right now, stirring a pot of homemade avgolemono. Seba
would give anything to see him walk through the door at
this moment. He would never force Seba to marry the
village busybody.

He needed reinforcements. "Where's Papouli?" he
asked.

"Your grandfather and Uncle Phillip have a meeting
with the mastic council members later. They're at Uncle
Phillip's house, looking over the production figures. The

Ottoman tax collectors will be here to inspect the harvest any day now. I expect your grandfather will be finished by this evening."

Xenia steered the conversation back to her favorite topic. "Oh, Seba, you know no one picks their own husbands and wives in this village. Your mother and I were just discussing this. She has spoken to your Uncle Phillip, and you know he is the most respected leader in the village. He agrees that we are right for each other."

Seba looked at his mother. "You said something to Uncle Phillip, and didn't even tell me?"

"Sebastian, these matters are for the adults to manage in the best interests of all of our families. Uncle Phillip knows both families well, and believes this to be an excellent arrangement."

"That's news to me."

"Sebastian, I've had quite enough of your rude behavior. We'll have plenty of time to discuss it before any specific plans are made. Xenia, thank you so much for visiting this morning. I'm going to clean up these dishes. Why don't you two take this goat's milk over to Father Jacobos before we go out to the mastic groves this morning?"

Seizing on the opportunity to be alone with Seba, Xenia grabbed the pail that Seba was still holding, making sure that their hands touched, and said to Seba's mother, "Thank you so much, Mrs. Krizomatis. We'll take this over to the chapel right away."

Seba was on the verge of protesting, but his mother shot him a look – it was like a dart full of poison aimed right between his eyes.

"Yes, Mama."

"There's a good boy, Sebastian. You two give my best to Father Jacobos and Brother Timotheos. I'll see you later in the mastic groves."

Seba and Xenia walked to the chapel; the irony was not lost on Seba. Xenia couldn't contain her smile. Her pale overskirt, embroidered with green vines and delicate yellow diamonds, swished back and forth, dancing with the deep orange sash that flapped up and down with each step. Her gait was so full of energy that her headscarf fell to her shoulders, revealing the thick braids that reached all the way to her sash. Seba wondered if she was really human, or simply a lightning bolt in physical form, complete with an overactive voice box.

How long had they been planning this, Xenia and his mother? Seba gritted his teeth. *Let them plan all day and all night if they want,* he thought. *I am not going to participate.* Xenia was the last person he would want as a wife—already the town busybody at the young age of fifteen. Seba didn't even want to imagine what she would be like in a few years—especially if his mother was helping her along.

Xenia chattered away as they walked. "Seba, I'm serious about Nikos and Thaddeus. It upsets me that they can't get along. I don't understand why Nikos even cares anything about what Thaddeus does. Nikos's family has all the power in this village—I mean, other than your Uncle Phillip, of course—so why must he antagonize the oldest son in a family of twelve children? Maybe it's because Thaddeus is so tall and handsome. Nikos probably can't stand it! Too bad Thaddeus's family doesn't have any money or prospects. I mean, after you, I'd marry him in a heartbeat. He looks just like Heracles to me. Don't you agree? Seba, did you hear what I said?"

Good Lord, does she even breathe? Seba heard Xenia say his name, but he hadn't been listening, so he answered with a shrug.

"Oh, Seba, we will have such a wonderful life together," she went on, undaunted. "And our children will just be beautiful. Well, I mean, as long as they look more like me than you." She jabbed him in the ribs with her free hand. "You know I'm only kidding, right? Oh, won't it be wonderful? Me in my green and gold wedding dress, covered in lace, walking down these adorable village streets with all of our friends and family around, congratulating us on our special day! It will be so beautiful, I can't wait!"

With the way she went on despite his complete lack of enthusiasm, Seba felt as if she hardly noticed him—not the real, flesh-and-blood Seba, anyway. He felt like a proxy for her idea of a husband. He might as well be a carved figure, like the statue come to life in the story of Pygmalion. To make matters worse, every elderly woman in all of Sessera chose this exact time of day to sweep her steps and put a dish of milk out for the village cats. They all smiled at Xenia and Seba, walking together to the chapel, Xenia chattering away and Seba seething in silence beside her.

"Don't you just love our little chapel here in Sessera, with the bells chiming throughout the day? Maybe our little boys will be the ones to pull the cords to the chapel bells one day! Wouldn't that be so adorable? I mean, we should have girls, too, because they would have my gorgeous olive skin and curly brown hair, so every little boy in the village would want to marry them. Life just could not get any better, Seba! I mean, Nikos is kind of a pain sometimes, but even he is from a good family, and everyone can improve themselves in one way or another, right?" Seba, only half-listening, thought: *Where did that come from?* "I'm sure that Nikos will come around. You know, sometimes boys just take longer to mature than girls. Nikos will probably be a wonderful man, and a good husband for one of the village girls. He's not as handsome as Thaddeus, of course, but he's got his own kind of charm. Just like you do, Seba, with your brooding silence. I think it's very mysterious. And a perfect match for me."

Seba wondered why he was being subjected to this torture. Would he ever be able to make any decisions for himself? He felt like he was suffocating, just like Uncle Phillip in that landslide. He wondered if there was anyone like Papouli who would come along and dig him out.

His thoughts were interrupted by Xenia's shout, "Oh, Mrs. Lampros! Weren't you asking the other day what my mother puts in her feta cheese to make it so tasty?"

The sight of Mrs. Lampros, walking sprightly along the path to the chapel, broke him out of his claustrophobic thoughts. Her clothes were immaculate, as always, which Seba could never understand. She was constantly baking something delicious: How was her skirt not streaked with flour, or her hands sticky with honey or stained with oil or herbs? Papouli said that Mrs. Lampros was touched by both Hestia and Aphrodite, displaying their best qualities: Hestia's calm, gentle hospitality as goddess of hearth and home, and Aphrodite's beauty and grace.

Mrs. Lampros waved cheerfully to the two of them. Did she know about Xenia and his mother plotting against him? Was she part of their conspiracy? No, he decided: Mrs. Lampros would never trade in that kind of gossip. He would make a point of asking Thaddeus if he had heard about their ridiculous plan to marry him off to his polar opposite.

"Seba, I have to go tell her that I would never divulge a family secret like that—you know that each family's feta recipe is sacred. You'll be a sweetheart and take this milk up to Father Jacobos for me, won't you? Of course you will! See you later!" She blew him a kiss, pulled her white linen headscarf back over her braids, and sashayed off to Mrs. Lampros.

And with that, she was gone, like a violent cloud of dust that spins into existence in a windstorm, and then disappears just as quickly.

12 A CHALLENGE

The weather in Sessera was beginning to change. The bright sunshine that warmed the ground from April through October was partially obscured by the approaching winter clouds. The high domed sky, once clear and bright blue, was now gray and hazy, its ceiling closing in like a thick cocoon. Beginning in November, it rained frequently—a cold, misty rain that seeped through Seba's woolen trousers and long jacket, driven in by the relentless press of air pushing from the coast. The brumal winds funneled through the mountains and shrouded the valleys of the mastic villages like a soggy gray blanket.

The worst part for Seba was that the low clouds occluded his rooftop view of the sea. Brother Tim said that the earth needed balance—warm, bright sun in the summer and cool, misty rain, or even snow, in the winter. Seba understood the need for balance, but it didn't stop him from yearning for his view of the sea. Reluctantly, he brought his straw mattress down from the roof and settled his bed in front of the large hearth for the winter.

It was frosty outside, and it had been a difficult day in the groves. They had scoured the ground for any stray tears that had fallen from the skinos trees and were buried under leaves, white lime, or dirt. Seba's back was sore from bending under the low branches all day; his muscles grumbled at him angrily. After washing up and feeding the animals, he climbed up the ladder from the ground floor and threw himself onto the end of his bed that was closest to the crackling fire. Huddled on his straw mattress, he held his palms up to the flames that rose from the glowing logs.

His mother was facing away from him, stirring a large pot of lentil stew. The earthy smell of the lentils, mixed with onions, carrots, parsley, oregano, and red wine vinegar made Seba's mouth water. Mama often topped this simple stew with a combination of yogurt and feta, married with a squeeze of lemon juice.

"Sebastian, please watch out for sparks from the hearth. The last thing we need this winter is a fire. If you're not careful, your bed could disappear in flames in a matter of minutes. Then you'd be sleeping on the cold stone floor."

Seba stared at the back of her head—she hadn't even turned around! How did she know where his mattress was? Papouli said that she had eyes in the back of her head, but even that was covered with a bright red scarf. Seba remembered a few days earlier, when his mother had nearly impaled him with a venomous look. Maybe there was something to Papouli's jokes about Mama's "evil eye." Seba had heard other people talk of *matiamenous*—the curse of the evil eye—and many of the villagers believed in it, even if they wouldn't admit it. Brother Tim laughingly told Seba one day that the *mati* had been around since the time of Plato and the Christians hadn't been able to eradicate it yet.

Mama said no self-respecting Christian would believe in the evil eye. *But, still . . .* Seba pushed his mattress further from the hearth, and made sure that there were no stray pieces of straw poking out from his cotton bedcover. Papouli had a similar mattress, but he had made a simple bedframe to keep his mattress off the floor, and there was large expanse of cotton fabric hanging from a rope across the ceiling that could be pulled in front of his bed to make a little room for him. Papa and Mama had their own small bedroom at the front of the living space, with a double bed that was also on a low wooden bedframe. Mama complained that she no longer needed a double bed, and had tried to convince Papouli and Seba to sleep together in the double bed while she took Papouli's single mattress. Even though Seba was only nine years old when his father was taken, he balked and put up such a fight that he was allowed to keep his movable bed. For the last five years he had dragged his bed to the roof in spring and only brought it inside when the rainy weather made it too uncomfortable to sleep outside. Mama threatened to sell or give the double bed to someone who could use it, but she never did.

"Sebastian, will you please put the soup bowls on the table, with some olives and what's left of this morning's bread? I believe that your grandfather was invited to dinner by Mrs. Lampros, so it will be just the two of us." She was still stirring the stew with a large olive wood spoon and still hadn't turned around. "That is, unless you'd like to invite Xenia to eat with us."

Seba's breath came out in a heavy sigh, and he thought about the many reasons he didn't want to eat dinner with Xenia, now or in the future. However, the deep breath seemed to calm him. He was learning not to react to Mama's provocations. Instead of sparking Mama's five feet of fury, he simply said, "Not tonight, Mama."

His mother stopped stirring and looked over at him. It was clear that she took this response as acquiescence that Seba would invite Xenia for dinner some evening. She gave a little smile, then went back to stirring the lentil stew, crushing a few leaves of oregano into the pot.

Seba put two earthenware bowls on the table, and scooped a few cured olives from the large stone jar onto a plate. He poured two cups of goat's milk, and reached for the bread. He started to break a piece of the crust from the bread to filch a little bite before dinner.

"Don't eat that until we've blessed the meal," his mother said—again without turning around. Seba had his confirmation; it was definitely the mati.

Mama said the blessing, and soon Seba's stomach was full of the warm, earthy lentil stew spiced with the fresh bite of parsley mixed with lemon, feta, and yogurt. Seba wiped the inside of his soup bowl with the crusty bread, and ate all of it until he thought his stomach would burst out from his trousers. This was the kind of meal that made him forget that his back was sore from crawling under the skinos trees and digging in the dirt all day. He said a silent prayer of thanksgiving for his mother's skill in the kitchen; he didn't care if she gave the evil eye, her cooking was that good. The only woman in the village who could match Mama's magic with food was Mrs. Lampros.

He helped his mother clean up the dishes and placed a few more logs on the fire. Without the freedom of the roof, Seba felt penned inside. He couldn't fathom staying in the house until sleeping time. He was afraid that his mother would start talking about marriage again. "I'm going to have a coffee with Papouli in the village square," he said.

Mama smiled at him approvingly. "My little Sebastian is

growing into a man."

If that's all it takes to keep her from pestering me, Seba thought to himself, *I'll drink coffee in the village square every night of my life.*

The men were jammed into Sotirios's kafenion, as they often were during the winter months. Even Thaddeus was there, drinking a steaming hot mug of Turkish coffee, having earned a few extra coins for doing errands for Uncle Phillip. Nikos sauntered into the kafenion as if he owned it and walked straight over to Thaddeus, who was sitting with a few of the older boys in the village. Very loudly, he said, "Thaddeus, yesterday I was talking to Demetria and she compared you to Heracles."

Thaddeus almost dropped his mug. He flushed so much that the red in his face flowed all the way down to his hands, which looked like two steamed langoustines.

"So what?"

"Well, I was thinking."

Thaddeus scoffed. "Don't hurt yourself."

Seba held his breath. Whenever conversations between Thaddeus and Nikos started like this, they usually ended in a brawl.

Ignoring the barb, Nikos continued, "The families on the east side of the village have a huge pile of firewood that has been collected for the winter, but it needs to be stacked on the ground floors of all the east side homes to keep it safe and dry before the soaking rains come. The delay in the harvest this year has us behind schedule, and the Ottomans are telling us to expedite the cleaning and sorting of the mastiha, so the villagers don't have time to get the firewood stacked. I told Demetria that Heracles probably could stack all of that firewood in one day."

Thaddeus bristled. Seba could tell that he didn't like the

thought of Demetria talking to Nikos, even if it was about him. "What does that have to do with me?"

"Well, she said that was probably too ambitious, even for Heracles, but when I said that I thought our very own Thaddeus could do it, her whole face came alive."

"Oh, did it?" Thaddeus voice was indifferent, but in the dim evening light, Seba saw Thaddeus's knuckles turning white; he held his coffee cup in a death grip.

"So I thought maybe you could test my theory for Demetria in exchange for a little extra cash for the winter."

"And what theory is that?"

"I told Demetria that you were the embodiment of Heracles, right here in Sessera, and you could probably stack all of the firewood for the families on the east side of the village." He paused and said, "In one day."

Several men sitting at the tables, including Papouli, protested.

"That's absurd!"

"He'd kill himself trying."

"The east village families can stack their own wood, Sessera is not that far behind on the mastiha production."

"I live on the east side, and I can stack my own firewood, thank you."

But there were others who also saw Thaddeus's coffee mug shaking, and egged him on.

"Thaddeus is our very own Heracles. He can do it!"

"That's nothing for him."

"What's at stake? He certainly isn't going to test your theory for free!"

"Yes, how much are you going to pay him?"

"There needs to be a bet."

"Yes, a bet!"

"But don't tell my daughter," laughed Papouli. "You

know how she hates gambling."

Seba was surprised by how many people laughed along with him. Many of the men nodded their heads in agreement, as did the boys who had been caught by Agnete throwing dice or gambling with sheep bones in Sessera's narrow alleys. Seba hadn't realized until now that his mother was the gambling police of Sessera.

Nikos was basking in the attention. "Of course, Thaddeus would be well compensated. I was thinking that if he can finish in one day, we would offer him six month's wages."

Everyone gasped. That was an enormous sum of money, even for Nikos's wealthy family. It showed Seba how slim Nikos judged the chances that Thaddeus would succeed.

"What if he can't do it in one day?"

"Nothing. Just a few families in the east village who will have to stack the rest of their firewood, and Thaddeus might be a bit tired with nothing to show for it."

Seba knew that wasn't all. Nikos would never let Thaddeus live it down if he failed at a task set by his archrival. If Thaddeus failed, no one would ever call him "Heracles" again—which is probably why Nikos orchestrated this elaborate proposition.

Seba repeated in his head, *Don't do it, don't do it, don't do it.* He prayed that Thaddeus could hear him or feel the warning, which radiated out from his body like heat from a fire. He was willing with all his might for Thaddeus to refuse. This spectacle would not end well for Thaddeus; Seba knew it in his heart.

But Thaddeus gulped the rest of his coffee and slammed the cup on the table. "Of course I can do it. Just name the day."

Seba wasn't sure if was Demetria's name or the promise

of six months' wages. It didn't matter, because now that Thaddeus had agreed, Seba knew he would never back down. Demetria seemed to have that power over Thaddeus—and over many of the boys in the village. She never had an angry or negative word for anyone or anything. When she played the lute, it was as if angels from above were floating from the lute's strings into the listeners' skin, filling them with light and hope and love. She was an excellent student; but unlike her sister, she was not a showoff. She answered questions correctly if Brother Tim called on her, but never volunteered an answer or interrupted. Seba remembered the lesson on the school's roof, when Demetria seemed embarrassed to help Brother Tim demonstrate the clepsydra. She was a sweet soul, and obviously enamored with Thaddeus. If she thought Thaddeus could accomplish the task, Seba knew his friend would do everything in his power to make it so.

After that evening, the villagers could talk of nothing else. Most of the women in the village were appalled that Thaddeus could be goaded into an impossible task, but some of the younger girls were very excited to see their own Heracles in action. Several of the more practical men were unconvinced that it should be attempted.

"Now, if you gave him two days to do it, that would be more reasonable. No one else could do it in two days, but perhaps Thaddeus could. One day is absolutely ludicrous."

"I agree—it would be difficult for two men to stack all that firewood in two days, working all day and all night. One day is just out of the question."

The day was set. An unusual dry wind brought clear skies for a few days, slightly evaporating the dampness of the late autumn mist from the wood. It would be a clear day for what everyone in the village was calling the Firewood

Challenge. There were very few in the village who believed that the feat would be successful—except, perhaps, for Thaddeus himself.

Despite the cold, Seba walked across the rooftops to Thaddeus's house on the eve of the great Firewood Challenge. He knew Thaddeus would also be on the roof, thinking about the challenge—or more likely, thinking about Demetria.

Thaddeus was lying on his back on the stone roof, looking up at the stars making a rare late November appearance. He looked over at Seba and said, "It's been cloudy and misty for weeks. Do you think it's a good sign that the stars came out tonight?"

Seba looked up and saw the constellation of Orion, the great huntsman. "Absolutely."

Thaddeus smiled. "I sure hope so."

"How are you feeling about tomorrow?"

"As good as can be. Over the years, I've probably stacked as much for my own family in the same amount of time."

"You're not just doing this to prove Nikos wrong, are you?"

"Of course I am! But you know my family needs the money, too. Besides, I'm pretty sure his family is the reason why my family is in this situation."

"What do you mean?"

Thaddeus sat up. "Do you remember the day my father broke his back?"

"Yes, it was the summer before the Ottomans took my father away."

"Well, Nikos's father was standing next to the cart, talking to your Uncle Phillip right before the cart began rolling down the hill."

"You never told me that."

"I can't get the vision out of my head—Nikos's father was laughing when that cart started rolling, and I can't shake the feeling that he had something to do with it."

"You think he did it on purpose? To hurt your father?"

Thaddeus shook his head and made a fist. "I don't know. Maybe he knew my father would go after it. He was the one charged with the responsibility of getting the cart of mastiha safely back to the village, after all. It's possible that Nikos's father was just trying to embarrass my father. But if he pushed that cart on purpose, then he is to blame for all my misery."

Seba didn't know what to say, so he remained silent.

"The whole family is rotten," Thaddeus continued. "His father did that to my family, and now Nikos is just making it worse by trying to turn my life into a living hell. I hate them both!"

Seba understood how Thaddeus felt. It was exactly how he felt about Ahmed and the Ottomans. He wasn't going to argue with Thaddeus about Nikos or his father.

"Seba, just think of what this would mean for my family. If I bust my hindquarters like an ox for twenty-four hours, I'll be able to breathe a little easier for the whole winter— and I may even get a little revenge for what happened to my father."

Seba didn't think revenge was the best motivation for this kind of challenge, but he decided not to dampen his friend's confidence. "Well, if anyone on this island can do it, it's you, Thaddeus."

"Thanks, my friend. I know most of the villagers think I'm going to fail. I appreciate you supporting me."

"That's what friends do, right?"

13 THADDEUS

It had been decided that the Firewood Challenge would start at sunrise, which on this chilly morning in November was just after the church bells struck seven o'clock. The embroidery and harvesting had been completed for the season. Now was the time for the cleanup around the skinos trees, which was the most tedious and ill-favored part of cultivating mastiha. The villagers were happy to have an excuse to delay their work in the groves, and they enthusiastically encouraged Thaddeus in his Heraclean endeavor.

Nikos was there, preening like a peacock, his opinion about Thaddeus's ability to complete the task made obvious in his giddy behavior. He didn't look like someone who was going to part with six months' wages.

Thaddeus would have until sunrise on the next day to complete the task. He was dressed in a brown cotton shirt and canvas trousers, and looked anxious to begin. As the church bells rang for the seventh time, Nikos raised his hands and said, "One, two, three—go!"

Thaddeus attacked the first fifteen-foot pile of firewood with a ferocity that Seba had never seen from him, and everyone in the village cheered. A few of them began to peel off toward the open gates, and Seba realized that this challenge was not an event like the ancient Olympics. It was more like a marathon. Seba knew well the story of Phillipides's historic twenty-six-mile run from the battlefield at Marathon to the center of Athens. The heavily outnumbered Athenians had defeated the Persians at Marathon in 490 B.C. Over time, Phillipides's extraordinary solo run became more famous than the battle, and the Athenians cheered for him and their victory at the finish line. Seba knew the same would apply to Thaddeus's Firewood Challenge.

Most of the villagers stayed and talked for a few minutes, drinking little cups of coffee that Sotirios had provided for them in honor of the occasion, and then ambled off to the skinos groves to tend to the trees and prepare them for the winter. Thaddeus was working feverishly as they left, already covered in sweat after just a quarter-hour of exertion.

Many hours later, when Seba and the other villagers returned to Sessera after a long day looking for errant tears, clearing the table of the white powdered lime beneath the trees, and picking up sticks and twigs, everyone paused to see the east village's piles of firewood before entering their own homes for dinner. Thaddeus's pace had not slackened; he looked like a man possessed, but the piles of firewood were still dauntingly high. Seba felt a tightness in his stomach as he viewed the mountain of firewood. Thaddeus had worked for twelve hours, and was nowhere near the halfway point of stacking it. There had been twelve homes to be supplied with neatly stacked firewood; seven homes remained, and more than half the allotted time had already elapsed. Thaddeus would have to work all through the night with no break—and even then, it did not appear that he could possibly finish. Seba wanted to ask him if he had eaten, but he was afraid to interrupt his friend. He saw earthenware water jugs next to Thaddeus's nearest ten-foot high pile of firewood, several already empty; Seba was relieved to know that at least he was drinking.

Just then, he saw Demetria come from the narrow alley leading to her house, carrying another earthenware jug. She timidly placed it near the others. "I've brought you some goat's milk to give you energy," she said. "I know you can do it, Thaddeus."

Hearing her voice, Thaddeus hesitated in his work—but only for an instant. Without looking at her, he said, "Thank you, Demetria. Now I know I will finish on time." Then he pivoted again, lifting a heavy log in each hand.

Watching them together, Seba reflected that Thaddeus would be lucky to marry Demetria, if it worked out for them. She was everything her sister was not: demure and reserved, only speaking when it was really important.

As Seba stared at Demetria's quiet beauty, he felt something brush by his ear, and he slapped it away—then heard a shocked voice: "Ouch!"

He turned to see Xenia, holding a hand to her temple where he had slapped her.

"I'm sorry, Xenia," he said. "You startled me. And I'm trying to be quiet so I don't distract Thaddeus."

"I know," she said angrily. "That's why I was leaning in to whisper to you. Why are you always so obstinate?"

"I said I was sorry," he said. "Now what were you going to tell me?"

Xenia looked surprised. Seba realized that this was the first time he had ever asked her to speak. In a flash, her demeanor changed, and she was her friendly talkative self again.

"Well, I was going to say that if Thaddeus beats Nikos at this challenge and earns those wages, my father just might let my sister marry him."

"Shhh! Keep your voice down and don't distract him," Seba whispered. He couldn't believe she was talking about marriage again.

"I know. That's why I'm whispering, silly. I'm not stupid, you know. In fact, I'm probably one of the smartest girls in this village. If you would ever stop and talk to me for more than thirty seconds, you would know that."

"It seems like all you ever talk about is marriage, Xenia. And I'm not interested in that."

"Love is what makes the world go around, isn't it? And love leads to marriage, or to hear my *yia-yia* talk, marriage leads to love. Either way, it's one of God's beautiful blessings."

"If you say so."

"I do." Xenia giggled and looped her hand around Seba's arm. "I just said, 'I do,' to you, Seba—isn't that sweet? I'm sure we'll be saying those words to each other someday."

Seba loosened his arm from Xenia's and looked away so she wouldn't see him roll his eyes. Xenia shrugged, utterly unfazed. With thick braids flying behind her, she yelled, "We know you can do it, Thaddeus! You're Sessera's Heracles!" Then she sashayed off toward her home, grabbing her sister's hand on the way.

Seba couldn't sleep that evening; he was afraid that Thaddeus would not complete the challenge and would spend the rest of his life being goaded by Nikos. He tried to shake off the horrible thought, but it kept reappearing. Seba tossed on his straw mattress all night; when he heard the first nightingale's coo through the small window by the kitchen, he knew that the pre-dawn light would be peering over the mountains within the next hour.

He could hear that Mama was already awake, as she always was every morning, kneading the dough for their breakfast bread. She had stirred the embers in the hearth upon waking, and the fire was crackling as it came to life. Seba jumped out of bed, wriggled out of his nightclothes and pulled on his working clothes. He could not contain his uneasiness. Papouli, who was sleeping soundly after a night of drinking in the village square, would be asleep for at least another hour.

"Good morning, Sebastian. Worried for your friend, Thaddeus?"

Seba's head nodded quickly up and down. He couldn't contain the feeling of electricity coursing through his limbs.

"Do you want to take him something to eat?"

"I don't think he can stop. He still had so many logs to stack when I left him yesterday—he wasn't even halfway through. He had to work in the dark all night. I don't know how he could have managed it."

"Sebastian, the Lord works miracles every day and every night. Did you ask the Lord Jesus Christ to answer your prayers for your friend?"

Sebastian stopped, all of the energy draining out of him. How could he have forgotten that? Had he been so preoccupied last night that he didn't even think to pray for a miracle? What if Thaddeus failed just because Seba forgot to pray? His faced flushed with shame.

"I couldn't sleep last night, so I prayed to God, the Holy Spirit, Jesus Christ, the Virgin Mary, and every saint that I know, to give our Thaddeus strength and help him complete the task," Mama said. "The east village families will be blessed by his work, and God smiles when His children help each other."

Seba hoped that Mama's prayers had been strong enough to make up for the fact that he had forgotten to pray.

"Here, take this barley bread that I baked yesterday. I soaked it in goat's milk. Even if Thaddeus can't stop to eat it now, he can eat it when he's finished. It's only a few hours until seven o'clock." She placed the softened slices of barley bread in an earthenware bowl, poured a thick drizzle of Mrs. Lampros's wildflower honey over all of them, covered them with a cloth, and handed them to Seba. "Sebastian, you should eat something as well. Here, have a slice."

Seba shook his head no. "I'm too nervous. I can't eat."

"You will need your strength to work in the groves all day, Sebastian. You have to eat."

"I'll get something later, before we go out to the skinos trees. I'm sure there will be plenty of food in the east village. Yesterday there were jugs of water and goat's milk, and I bet people will be bringing more this morning."

"Well, that boy certainly deserves it. He has turned into quite a fine young man." She smiled sadly. "I guess your father was right—a stubborn boy can grow into a responsible man, after all."

Seba shared Mama's sadness, remembering the day his father had defended Thaddeus and Nikos long ago, but he didn't have time to dwell on it. He tucked the bowl under his arm and ran out the door.

It was still dark when he reached the east village, and there was no one else out there with Thaddeus. He was moving much more slowly than the day before; what amazed Seba, however, was that he only had one more ten-foot pile of firewood to go. He had made up the difference overnight somehow. Was it Mama's prayers? If so, Seba vowed never to forget his evening prayers as long as he lived.

Thaddeus looked up when he heard Seba's footsteps.

"Who's there? Is that you, Nikos? Just get out of here. Can't you leave me alone? It's not fair if you keep distracting me."

"It's not. It's me, Seba."

"Oh, thank God. Nikos has been out here every few hours throughout the night, telling me that I'll never finish. I think he was trying to break me down, but he made me so angry that I worked twice as fast as I would have." He continued to move logs to the last home's stable as he spoke.

"I don't want to distract you either, I just couldn't sleep and I wanted to help if I could. I have barley bread soaked in goat's milk with honey, but I don't want you to stop when you're so close."

Thaddeus kept grabbing logs and stacking them. "I haven't had any food since yesterday, but I'm afraid if I stop to eat, I'll lose my motivation. I'm starving, though. What do you think I should do?"

"I don't know. Food will give you more energy, I think. And if you can speed up just a little, you're definitely going to finish."

"Well, Nikos hasn't been here for an hour or so, and without his constant needling, I feel like I'm slowing down. Maybe a little food will help."

"It's got tons of honey on it. Papouli says honey is like a liquid jolt of energy, so it should work the same as wanting to kill Nikos."

"Will you bring it over here, then? I'll stack with one hand and eat with the other."

Seba walked behind him and held the bowl. Thaddeus grabbed the bread with one hand and shoved two pieces in his mouth at once. As he came back to the pile to grab more logs, he scooped up the other two thick slices and they were gone in an instant. Honey dripped from the back of his hand, and he licked it off as his other hand continued to stack the lumber.

With a mouth full of milk-soaked bread, he said, "Glllll."

Seba knew that was a call for milk, or *gala*. He ran several houses down the alley and grabbed the earthenware jug that Demetria had left for Thaddeus. He handed it to Thaddeus's outstretched fingers.

Thaddeus took the handle and poured the whole jug of milk down his throat, much of it spilling all over his sweat-soaked shirt. It was the same shirt he had been wearing yesterday morning, but it was so sodden that it looked like he had been swimming in it.

"*Efcharisto.*"

"*Parakalo.* Now use that honey energy and get to work!"

Thaddeus jumped into action. The food and milk had the desired effect. And this time, Seba remembered to pray for his friend as he began to move more quickly to stack the wood. *Please, God, let him finish and be successful. His family needs it, he needs it, and he deserves it. He's the best friend I have in this village, so please, please, please help him win.*

Seba stayed to give his friend moral support, so he witnessed Nikos's next attempt at treachery. Nikos sauntered up to Thaddeus as the final hour was winding down, and he stood in front of the place where Thaddeus was stacking the wood, taunting him. "You'll never finish."

"Not if you don't get out of my way. Move!"

Seba interjected, "Nikos, stop. You're cheating!"

Nikos strode off to the side, but he was muttering insults

to Thaddeus the whole time.

The villagers gathered as the sky began to brighten. Thaddeus looked as if he were going to drop from exhaustion, but he kept going, and the ten-foot pile became a five-foot, then a four-foot pile. It was going to be close. Seba noticed that Demetria and Xenia had a front-row spot; Seba backed into the crowd so as not to attract Xenia's attention. He was afraid she would call Seba her future husband in front of all the villagers.

It had been a few minutes since the church bells had rung once for six-thirty. Seba knew there were only about fifteen minutes left for Thaddeus to finish the challenge. The crowd of villagers were talking—some encouraging Thaddeus, and others whispering that he might not finish. As the last minutes clicked down, Seba could see that there were only several hundred more logs to go. The crowd started yelling, "Her-a-cles, Her-a-cles, Her-a-cles!" It was just what Thaddeus needed to hear. He began grabbing four and five logs at a time, throwing them into the growing stack. Nikos was pacing back and forth, acting like he was a timekeeper, but really just trying to get in Thaddeus's way so he couldn't finish.

The villagers were clapping and cheering, and the atmosphere was festive; but Seba was concerned that there might not be anything to celebrate, especially if Nikos continued to impede Thaddeus's progress. Seba wanted Thaddeus, and not Heracles, to get credit for his impending victory—and so, for once in his young life, he spoke up in public, stomping his feet and yelling, "Thad-de-us, Thad-de-us, Thad-de-us!"

Xenia's braids whirled around and she looked at Seba in shock. Then she smiled broadly at him and took up the charge, shouting at the top of her lungs, "Thad-de-us, Thad-de-us!!"

The whole village joined in. There were forty more logs to go, and the church bells began to chime, the first of seven loud gongs. If Thaddeus didn't get the last group of logs stacked before the seventh bell rang, it would be over.

He was grabbing armfuls of logs and tossing them in the stack. There were thirty left, then twenty, and the church bells had rung four times.

Three more chimes to go. Nikos stepped between Thaddeus and the stack of logs, just as Thaddeus managed to grab the last twelve pieces of wood in his arms at one time. He threw all but one of them onto the top of the stack as the church bells rang for the fifth time. As the sixth bell chimed, he clobbered Nikos over the head with the last piece of wood, and threw it on the stack as the seventh bell chimed. Thaddeus had done it!

14 FORTUNE TELLING

Riding high from his victory, Thaddeus became an overnight celebrity in Sessera. It now appeared that Demetria might have competition for her man, and Thaddeus went from a donkey to a winged Pegasus in the matter of one day. Nikos put on a happy front, even taking credit for inspiring Thaddeus's performance, but Seba knew that deep down he was furious. Seba was glad that Mama's prayers had worked, but he wondered what it meant for him now that Thaddeus's life was going to change. Would Seba still be Uncle Phillip's special apprentice? Would Uncle Phillip prefer to work with Thaddeus? Would Seba lose his chosen spot on the council?

Seba was happy for his friend—and happy that Xenia was too busy celebrating to try and plan her imagined wedding day with Seba. Papouli was happy, because he was spending more and more time with Mrs. Lampros, and Mama was happy cooking all of Seba's favorite foods to keep his belly warm and full for the winter. It was a little disconcerting for Seba that Uncle Phillip had not mentioned anything further about Seba being his apprentice. He had seen Uncle Phillip a few times in the village square, and had worked side-by-side with him to clean up around the skinos trees after the harvest, but Uncle Phillip did not mention any jobs that he had for Seba or any training that was required. Was Thaddeus going to take his place now?

One evening Mama prepared a warm meal of roasted winter squash and fennel with grilled rectangles of cheese slathered in olive oil and fresh herbs. She had made the cheese from milking their goats, Myra and Sheba. Mama said that Myra was well-named, because Myra was Hebrew for "flowing one," and Myra always gave the most milk. Sheba, her sister, was named for Bathsheba, who was King David's wife in the Bible. Her name meant "promise," so Mama said that she would be giving lots more milk one day as well—that was her promise. Seba was thankful for their contribution to his full stomach. The cheese was crispy and brown on the outside, salty, white, and gooey on the inside. Mama seasoned the squash and fennel with crushed coriander seeds, cinnamon, and cloves, and topped the dish with wild arugula that would hopefully continue to grow throughout the colder months. As long as a hard frost did not reach the tender leaves, the arugula would provide a spicy freshness to their meals until the sun's heat returned and the spring crops were planted. This was one of Seba's favorite meals, especially now, in early December, when the only break from the dark, dank air was a roaring fire and a hot bowl of food.

Seba helped Mama clean the dishes and walked toward the stairs to the roof. Even though he had moved his bed next to the hearth, he still liked to be outside and alone if it wasn't too cold. It gave him a feeling of freedom that he couldn't find anywhere else on the island. The groves were full of people all day, the village was noisy and busy once they were locked inside the thick stone walls, and although he loved Mama's food, he didn't like her pestering him about getting married or asking Uncle Phillip for more responsibility on the mastic council. He intended to meditate with the Holy Spirit, as Brother Tim had suggested, and to thank God for rewarding Thaddeus, whose family really needed the extra money.

As his foot hit the second rung of the ladder, his mother called out, "Sebastian, your Papouli was supposed to return these honeycombs to Mrs. Lampros on his way to the kafenion this evening. Can you take them to her? She needs them for the bread she's baking tomorrow, so it can't wait." Seba thought about protesting, but he was so content (and his stomach so full) that he nodded his assent; the Holy Spirit would wait for him, he was sure.

Seba grabbed the two clay pots full of honey in the comb, secured the lids with twine, and climbed down the home's second ladder that connected the kitchen to the ground floor. Mrs. Lampros lived just off the square, and Seba wondered how she ever got to sleep with the loud laughing and talking of the men outside her windows every night. Maybe she was baking bread during that time. Seba would have loved to live in that house, listening to the talk of the day: politics, trade, stories of Portuguese raiders and pirates, the taxes that other Chians outside the *mastichochoria* had to pay.

It was a short walk to Mrs. Lampros's home. The winding, narrow alleys were mostly quiet, as the village families were inside, keeping warm by their fires.

He knocked on the door, and the sprightly Mrs. Lampros, black hair streaked with silver and a bit of white, answered. She wore an apron covered in flour, but Seba noticed that there was no flour on her skirts or her sleeves. How did she do that? Whenever Mama and the other village women baked, they were covered from head to toe in flour. Papouli always said that Mrs. Lampros was immaculate, and she definitely was today.

"Oh, Seba, I'm so glad you brought this. I almost made your grandfather go back for it when I saw him sit down at Sotirios's cafe to order a coffee." She pointed to the tables and chairs scattered around the open door to Sotirios's kafenion. The warmth from the fire spilled out into the area, and men were huddled in their wool coats and hats, trousers and boots, both inside and outside Sotirios's coffeehouse. They were smoking tobacco from clay pipes and drinking coffee, tsipouro, and wine.

"This bread was going to be mighty tasteless without the honey! My yeast would have revolted! I had a few drops left, but not enough to make any good loaves." She smiled. "You are a godsend, Seba! Please thank your mother for me, and give her this onion and orange-cured olive bread. I know it's her favorite." She turned and grabbed two round loaves from a wooden box, and handed them to Seba. "I certainly wasn't going to give them to your grandfather—they would have never made it back home." She laughed, a cheerful and snappy sound, as if she didn't have a care in the world. He thanked her, took the loaves from her floured hands, and said goodbye.

He thought about going right home with the bread, but the pull of the men talking was too great. How did Mrs. Lampros concentrate on her baking with those men talking all night in the square right across from her home? As he exited her doorway, he saw the men gathered around one of the tables in the square, nearest to the kafenion's front door. Sotirios shuffled passed him and nodded for Seba to push through the crowd. When he did, he saw Thaddeus sitting at the table, hands clamped around a small coffee cup, peering into it as if it held the meaning of life.

Uncle Phillip sat opposite Thaddeus at the table, speaking with authority. "You must only drink from this side," he said. "Do not turn the cup."

Thaddeus looked confident, and quickly lifted the cup to his open mouth, as if to down the entire contents in one gulp.

"No, my boy. Drink slowly. There's no need to rush," Uncle Phillip said. "Heracles never rushed, and neither should you."

It made Seba glad to see Thaddeus treated with such attention and respect. He was proud, and it had been hard for him to bear being the object of charity since his father's injury. His new renown seemed to Seba like a small sign that justice was attainable, even in a small Greek village under the rule of the Ottoman vipers.

Thaddeus took a small sip and put the cup back down with a sharp clatter. It was almost imperceptible, but Seba noticed that both of Thaddeus's hands were shaking with anticipation.

"There is an art to reading the grounds, and as everyone knows, art is not to be hurried," Uncle Phillip said. "Do we embroider the skinos in the early spring? Of course not! Patience is rewarded in all things. As Saint Paul said in his letter to the Romans, 'If we hope for what we do not see, we wait for it with patience.'"

Thaddeus took another few small sips, then held his cup up to Uncle Phillip expectantly.

"Yes, perfect, Thaddeus. Now that there is only about one sip's worth in the cup, swirl it around vigorously to loosen the grounds. Take the final sip, and then make a wish."

Seba leaned in even closer to the table. Thaddeus looked up and winked at him.

Uncle Phillip said, "Now pick up your saucer and turn it over on top of your cup to cover it. Hold it tight—the seal must be kept."

Thaddeus covered the cup with the saucer and pressed down firmly. His face beamed like a little boy's.

"Now hold them up, chest level, like this." Uncle Phillip demonstrated, holding his hands directly in front of his heart.

"Make three horizontal circles clockwise. You are moving the sediment around, so it touches the entire inside surface of the cup."

Thaddeus made a circle, almost violently, as if he were Poseidon waving his trident.

"*Apapa*! Thaddeus, don't break the cup!"

The men around the table chortled and took swigs of their drinks. Thaddeus held the cup and saucer steady in front of his heart.

"Now flip it—lightning quick—onto the table. With some *oomph*!"

Thaddeus's cup and saucer hit the table with a thud. Shoulders hunched over the table, his golden brown eyes peered up at Uncle Phillip, waiting for the next move.

"Now we wait. At least ten minutes. We'll find out if you have the patience of Saint Paul."

Ten minutes passed. Thaddeus looked like he was ready to jump out of his skin as Uncle Phillip gently lifted the cup from the saucer and turned the handle toward himself.

"Were you looking for a reading on love, my friend?"

Thaddeus turned the color of a fully boiled spiny lobster,

and he squinted, trying to understand what was happening. No words drifted up from his throat, but he shook his head yes.

"The coffee knows. First, we look to the handle side of the cup, which speaks to love. What do you see?"

Thaddeus leaned over the cup, and Seba leaned in as well. The inside of the cup next to the handle bore a sludge of coffee grounds that were wide at the bottom, becoming gradually more narrow at the top. There were also a few lone grounds that appeared to be spurting up from the narrow part.

Thaddeus took a guess. "A volcano?"

"Yes—I see you have brains as well as brawn. This means that your emotions will be out of control, and you will feel impatience. As you seem to be no stranger to impatience, this is not a surprise."

The crowd of men who were listening clapped enthusiastically. Thaddeus smiled meekly. Seba knew he was thinking of Demetria. Seba felt a little sorry for him; he had the same expression as a young lamb prior to the spring slaughter.

Phillip saw the look on Thaddeus's face, and stood up, stomping his foot for effect. "Impatience in love is not a bad thing! Do you want the meekness of tepid water in a stagnant pool when you are in love? No! We are Greek, for heaven's sake! We have the passion of the gods within us, and the fire of the Holy Spirit! This is auspicious and wonderful news, just as it should be. Now, looking to my left, your right, the grounds tell something of the present time. What do you see?"

Thaddeus stared at the side of the cup and looked at Seba, leaning his head toward the cup, inviting Seba to peek. Uncle Phillip nodded, and Seba leaned in.

It was as clear as if Seba had drawn it in the dirt with a stick. A beautiful almond-shaped eye, bright and happy, with the white of the cup gleaming through the black iris like a sparkle on the pupil.

Seba couldn't help himself from blurting out, "It's an eye!"

"I agree, my son! Not menacing like the witch's *mati*, but rather a watchful eye, I would say. Very auspicious indeed."

Peering into the cup, Seba wondered if this reading was for him as well as Thaddeus. Was that his father's eye looking back at him from inside the tiny coffee cup?

The entire table was spellbound, even though many of the older men probably knew the symbolism of an eye. Thaddeus looked confused. "What does it mean?"

"Someone is thinking of you."

Seba inhaled sharply and Thaddeus turned an even deeper shade of splotchy red. Now he looked like a spiny lobster that had been left on the fire too long. "Go on," he choked.

Uncle Phillip took pity on Thaddeus, and didn't press him about who might be thinking of him. Some of the men in the village were disappointed, but Uncle Phillip was known to be a merciful man.

Seba had the most unusual feeling that it was his father who was thinking of him. How could that be? He had never had this feeling before. Did it signify something important?

"Now to my right, and your left, Thaddeus, is the telling of the future. Do you see the symbol? I have an idea what it looks like to me, but this is your reading, so we must be sure. What does it look like to you?"

Thaddeus squinted. "Like a wheel," he said. "A wheel with several spokes coming from the center."

"*Eureka!*" Uncle Phillip clapped his hands together. "I

think you could have a future in reading the grounds. You're quite good, my boy—and fortune-telling is something that even Heracles never managed, for all his mighty labors."

Thaddeus sat up a little straighter, and the men around the tables raised their mugs and glasses in agreement.

"What do you think a wheel means, Seba?" Uncle Phillip's eyes were dancing.

Seba thought of the wheels on the carts carrying mastiha from the groves to the village. "He's going somewhere?" he asked. He was still wondering if there might not be a message for him in the grounds, too; he had been thinking of his father, and his father had gone somewhere.

"The wheel is a symbol of change, and since it is on the side of the cup that tells the future, it means there is change in store for our friend Thaddeus."

Thaddeus's eyes widened. "Wow. This cup seems to know a lot more than I do."

Another roar of laughter from the crowd. Seba understood for the first time that this was pure entertainment—like Papouli's storytelling, but more interactive.

Uncle Phillip shook his head in amusement. "Now, the bottom of the cup represents home, and is sometimes the hardest to read. The inside of the cup closest to you represents money, and you'll notice that most of the grounds on that side are sliding down to the bottom as if they are one and the same. I know what I see—but again, this is your reading. Why don't you take a look?"

Thaddeus turned the cup around so he could see the last side of the cup. He looked for a moment, shrugged, then slid it toward Seba.

Seba looked into the cup and couldn't make out any

shapes. He stared so hard that his brain seemed to sizzle from exertion. Just as he was about to give up, he heard the loud clang from the adjacent church tower, ringing the late evening hour.

"A bell! It's a bell!" The grounds on this side of the cup had a large symmetrical curve on either side, which fell into a perfect wide open bell shape at the bottom of the cup. Seba couldn't believe he hadn't noticed it.

Thaddeus and Uncle Phillip said simultaneously, "Yes!"

"And a bell means that unexpected news is coming to your home, Thaddeus," Uncle Phillip continued. "And it will be with regard to money. Your family may expect money in the near future."

Thaddeus smiled broadly, showing all of his teeth. Seba was sure that the grounds were speaking of justice for his friend; Thaddeus would not be stuck being a donkey. It was what he had always dreamed of—somehow escaping from slavery so he could marry Demetria and become an important member of the village, maybe even equal to Nikos's family. Seba was happy for him. Everything was finally going right for Thaddeus. He had bested his rival and showed the villagers his strength and perseverance. Thaddeus seemed to have everything now.

Still, Seba couldn't help but feel sorry for himself. The more he thought about it, the more he realized that those coffee grounds weren't talking to him—only to Thaddeus. Seba's father was gone; his hopes of building ships, or even of working at the shipyard, were gone. He had signed on with Uncle Phillip for a life of working the land. He would coax the Tears of Chios from the skinos trees, just like his mother's ancestors before him. It was that simple. The legacy should have made him feel proud and grateful; but instead, he felt empty.

Breaking into Seba's thoughts, Sotirios said, "Thaddeus, I'll make that fortune come true for me right now—I need you all to pay me so I can close up and get home. The coffee is arriving early tomorrow morning from Constantinople, which means I need to be ready for the shipment. Give me all the cups and saucers. I don't care how long you sit here, but I need to wash up and get to bed."

There was groaning all around, but everyone jumped up to help take the dishes back to Sotirios's kitchen. Uncle Phillip said, "I've got a few bottles of retsina that I can bring out, if anyone wants to stay."

A chorus of approval rang out in response.

Seba was still carrying the loaves of bread from Mrs. Lampros, and as he helped carry a few of the mugs back to Sotirios's kitchen to be washed, he saw a small pot of avgolemono on Sotirios's stove. Standing there staring at the pot, thoughts of his father flooded his brain, little vignettes that morphed and changed. His father's reassuring smile as he stirred the lemon soup so many years ago; his hands drawing angles and figures on the large drafting table at the shipyard; and then, his father's eyes on fire as he threw him overboard.

Suddenly the smell of eggs, chicken, and lemon overwhelmed him, and he felt the bile rise up from his insides. He ran out the back door of Sotirios's kafenion and vomited in the alley. He spit the saliva that was flooding into his mouth out onto the street. His arm was shaking uncontrollably as he wiped his mouth with his sleeve. In fact, his whole body was quivering, though he didn't quite know why. He walked back into Sotirios's kitchen, confused and upset. He looked at that little pot on the stove and was hit with another wave of nausea. He understood that he would never eat avgolemono again; not until he saw his father, alive and well and stirring it over a fire.

15 CELEBRATION

A few weeks later, lying on his straw mattress by the flickering ochre flames in his hearth and waiting for the winter sun to peek its pale face over the mountains, Seba's thoughts remained on the coffee grounds. How could some shapes in a coffee cup know about Demetria and Thaddeus? How could they tell that their fortunes were going to change? Thaddeus had seemed so pleased about the coffee grounds, but it had been several weeks and there was no news regarding money, Demetria, or a change in Thaddeus's future. It reminded Seba of one of Papouli's favorite sayings from the Greek historian Plutarch: "Glory is nice, but uncertain."

Seba thought Plutarch should have also added, *and short-lived.*

However, he didn't have much time to spend considering the coffee grounds or any other weighty topics because it was a time for celebration in Sessera. The villagers celebrated the annual feast of the birth of Christ, which all Greeks on the island of Chios celebrated for twelve days between Christmas Day and the feast of the Epiphany, when the Magi brought their gifts to the baby Jesus. During those twelve days, the villagers attended church each morning and evening, working only a few midday hours in the skinos groves. The villagers' job in the winter was to provide nutrients to feed the trees during the wet season. They gathered all the fallen leaves from the skinos trees and mixed them with the soil to form a layer of compost over the lime-dusted tables surrounding the trees. It was as if they were tucking in the gnarled trunks and branches for the winter, keeping them cozy, fed, and warm.

Uncle Phillip had taught Seba and all the village children that the soil of Chios was magic, made from ancient volcanic rock that mixed with the leaves and crushed-up twigs of the skinos trees over thousands of years. Now, that soil provided all the food the trees needed over the winter to prepare them to produce the beautiful tears the following summer. Spreading the topdressing was a messy job, especially in the cold and misty rain of December, but the villagers had been feeding these trees in this way for generations. Just as the Christians prepared the way for the nativity of Christ, the *mastichochoria* prepared the way for the mastic tears.

Seba turned fifteen on December 30, which was always a celebratory time for Sesserans during the Christmas festivities. He had grown several inches since his last birthday, and although his facial hair did not compare to Brother Tim's bushy beard, the sable-colored growth on his chin made Seba feel like he was leaving boyhood behind. Mama baked him his favorite cake, a sweet yeasted bread filled with raisins, pistachios, and dates, and Papouli had invited Mrs. Lampros for supper. That evening, Papouli sang and danced while Seba played his seven-holed wooden *floghera,* and Mrs. Lampros played the kithara, a seven-stringed lyre with a wooden base. It had belonged to her late husband. For a long time after he died, Mrs. Lampros had refused to touch the instrument, saying that it made her sad to think her sweet husband would never play it again. However, Papouli's love of music and dance had moved her to dig it out and dust it off. Papouli had that effect on everyone he met.

Even Mama danced with Papouli, father and daughter moving in perfect harmony with energy and enthusiasm. Mama's face was flushed and she threw her head back and laughed when Papouli spun her around like a top. Even Artemis the cat climbed up the ladder from the ground floor, curious to see the spectacle for herself. She sat in the corner grooming herself, as if she were the queen who had commissioned these entertainers just for her amusement.

When Mrs. Lampros launched into the *tripatos*, Papouli jumped up and down, clapping his hands, and then ran to Seba. Grabbing the floghera from his hands, he shoved Seba toward his mother and picked up the melody with Mrs. Lampros, adding the floghera's sweet, piercing tone to the kithara's lively twang; his toes tapped while he played. Mama grabbed Seba's hands, whirling him around while they danced the three steps until they were so out of breath that they fell into the kitchen chairs, faces red and beaming with joy. It was one of the happiest days that Seba could remember since before That Day.

As the fire dwindled and they had sung and danced every traditional Greek folk song and hymn celebrating the birth of Christ, Papouli brought out a bottle of tsipouro and poured a cup for each of them. Holding his cup high in the air, he said, "To Seba, may you live to a hundred years and may you always be happy for your name!"

They all held up their cups and Mama and Mrs. Lampros replied in unison, "And may you receive everything you desire!"

Seba nodded his thanks and took a big draught of tsipouro. It burned his throat, but he didn't care, because he was now a man and it felt good to be alive. Papouli, Mama, Mrs. Lampros, and Seba talked long after midnight, so late that Seba saw a sliver of the moon rise through the small window by the hearth. Papouli walked Mrs. Lampros to her home as Mama prepared for bed. That evening, lying on his mattress before the glowing red logs in the hearth, Seba treated himself to one of mastic tears from the pouch that Uncle Phillip had given him, inhaling the heavenly aroma before crunching through the crisp exterior to reveal the minty and healing flavor of the mastic gum. It was the end of 1765, and Seba felt as if 1766 would bring many changes and many blessings into his life. He prayed to the baby Jesus, thanking him for the joy and mercy He had bestowed on Seba's family.

December 31 brought even more excitement to the village; it was the day of the festival of *Kalo Podriko*. The villagers gathered for the evening meal together in Sotirios's kafenion after the worship service. The entire village of Sessera smelled of grilled meats, baked breads, and every kind of winter vegetable available on the island. They ate sweet breads and cakes filled with dried fruits and honey, stuffing themselves until there was room for no more. Even Sotirios, who usually nibbled at food like a small bird, loosened the drawstring holding up his woolen trousers. It felt like every person in Sessera was part of Seba's extended family—and in a sense, they were. They looked out for one another and did their best to care for each other, offering medicine, food, a listening ear, or whatever would lift up a neighbor who needed something. They all made sacrifices for each other and did it willingly, knowing that if they were in need, there was an army of fellow Greeks who would lend a hand without question.

After the meal, which seemed to last for hours, an assembly of musicians played the traditional folk dances as the villagers, dressed in their most colorful clothes, linked arms, sang, danced, clapped, snapped, tapped, and enjoyed the revelry. Despite the cold December air, Seba was warm in the glow of the villagers' merriment. Papouli's face was red with exertion from the dancing. Thaddeus was sweating, too, and dancing with Demetria every chance he got. Brother Tim was particularly jolly that evening, dancing with Mama, Mrs. Lampros, and the other older women of the village. Seba laughed to watch him comically push his spectacles up on his nose with the back of his hand as they slid down in response to his fancy footwork. Seba was not one to dance, but he loved watching all of the villagers twist and turn through the steps as they and their ancestors had done for generations.

"It's a beautiful night, isn't it?"

Seba turned to see Xenia standing next to him in a bright red skirt with a gold sash, under a pale green woolen wrap. Her curly brown hair had escaped her tight braids, probably from all the dancing, and her face was flushed pink. She smiled broadly at Seba.

The night *was* beautiful. Seba had a full stomach, he had enjoyed a wonderful birthday party the night before, the entire village was celebrating the birth of Christ, and a new year was almost upon them. He looked at Xenia and found that he couldn't bring himself to be mad at her. "Yes, it is," Seba said contentedly.

To his amazement, Xenia stood next to him and watched the dancing, but didn't say a word. Seba had prayed that Xenia would stop talking, if even for just a few minutes, and it appeared that on this festival of Kalo Podriko, God was answering his prayers. He didn't know what caused him to do it, but he looked at Xenia and said, "Would you like to dance?"

The broad smile she had been wearing widened even further, all the way up to her eyelashes. "Yes, very much!"

Seba had watched Papouli dance with Mrs. Lampros for hours the night before, so he took Xenia's hand and jumped into the circle alongside his grandfather. They danced and sang the traditional Christmas *calandas*, Seba holding Xenia's hand as they and the other villagers moved through the village square in a circle.

When the band stopped playing, Xenia excused herself, saying she needed a drink of water. Papouli walked over to Seba and put his hand on his grandson's shoulder. "See, I told you girls don't bite."

Seba laughed, feeling happy to be alive.

As midnight approached, Uncle Phillip reached into a box that sat outside Sotirios's kafenion and handed out a pomegranate to each family.

"These pomegranates are a symbol of the bounty that God bestows on us. Take these pomegranates to your homes and celebrate the ritual of Kalo Podriko! It will bring God's blessings and good luck to each of us in the coming year! Blessings to all of you, and *Kalinixta!*"

Each of the families took the pomegranate back to their homes to celebrate the ritual of Kalo Podriko. As was the custom, Seba was in the lead as they entered. He was considered the "first footer," the lucky one of the family, who was to open the door and step through the threshold just as the village bells rang midnight. In addition to the "first footer," the ritual required a second person, who had to be of a clean and fresh spirit, and who had the job of smashing the pomegranate into the top of the door frame to ring in the new year exactly at midnight. Although the church bells usually stopped ringing at nine o'clock, Brother Tim had solicited a few of the young boys in the village to continue to ring the church bells on the hour all evening, until midnight and the beginning of the new year. As the church bells began to chime, Seba opened the front door and stepped inside with his right foot. At that exact time, Mama reached up with the pomegranate in her right hand. Because she was only five feet tall, however, she couldn't reach the uppermost part of the door frame. Papouli picked up his daughter and raised her above his head. With great force, she crushed the pomegranate above the front door with all her might just as Seba's foot crossed the threshold. Hundreds of tiny red pomegranate seeds fell to the ground in front of their home; the ruby-colored jewels scattered across the ground, symbolizing good luck and the raining down of God's blessings on the family that year.

Seba's heart felt so full that it might burst out from his chest. He looked at his mother and grandfather, laughing as they popped the remaining pomegranate seeds into their mouths, and thought that he couldn't love them any more than he did right at that moment.

The following day, the first day of the new year, the celebration continued. It was the Feast of Saint Vasilios, the time when they celebrated the generosity of the bishop who saved the community of Kappadokia from devastation during a time of severe famine. Despite the famine, the ruler of the area continued to demand payment for taxes. Saint Vasilios asked each family to give him a piece of jewelry to try to assuage the ruler's anger. Each family complied, giving Saint Vasilios a coin or trinket. Saint Vasilios intervened with the ruler and convinced him to waive the taxes; then the saint baked each family a cake, hiding a piece of jewelry in each one. He returned the citizens' treasures to them to reward them for their faith. In commemoration of Saint Vasilios's generosity, each year on New Year's Day, the matriarch of the family baked a sweet bread or cake that included a coin or piece of jewelry inside.

Mama's Saint Vasilios cake was an olive oil and yogurt cake flavored with orange and lemon peels. Seba loved this olive oil cake almost as much as his birthday cake, and he felt blessed that he always had the good fortune to enjoy them two days apart in the winter. As was the tradition, when the cake was ready Papouli rotated it on the kitchen table three times, saying, "We humbly thank the Lord for His blessings. In the name of the Father, the Son, and the Holy Spirit, we are grateful for the Sacred Trinity."

Papouli made the sign of the cross over the cake with a knife and cut one slice. Holding it in the air, he said, "This slice is for Jesus," and he set it aside. He cut a second slice: "This slice is for the Virgin Mary," and he set it next to the first slice as Mama made the sign of the cross. Papouli cut a third slice, held it up, and said, "The third slice is for Saint Vasilios," and set it next to the other two slices. Papouli cut a fourth slice for their home, a fifth slice for the poor stranger, and the remaining slices for himself, Mama, and Seba. As they bit into their slices of cake, Seba felt something hard. Reaching between his teeth, he pulled out a silver coin. It had the same marking as the seals on the fabrics from the English ships of the Levant Company. He recognized the *tughra* of Sultan Mustafa III, and knew that this was a valuable coin. He looked at Mama, who shrugged her shoulders, and then to Papouli, whose eyes were sparkling with amusement.

Seba asked, "Where did you get this?"

Papouli said with a grin, "Your old grandfather can't tell you all his secrets, can he?"

Seba, still confused, said, "Can I really keep it?"

"Yes, of course! You received the coin, and it will bring you luck this whole year."

Seba jumped up and ran to the other side of the table, throwing his arms around his grandfather. "Thank you, Papouli!"

The next day brought more festivities and more food. The Sesserans made the most of all of the twelve days between celebration of the birth of Christ and the celebration of the Epiphany. That evening, after Seba, Mama, and Papouli had eaten a meal of smoked lamb sausages and cabbage rolls stuffed with oregano, basil, parsley, chickpeas, mushrooms, and cracked wheat, Papouli was entertaining them with his usual antics. He was standing on a kitchen chair, reciting from the *Iliad*. Because he was reciting a passage about courage and truth, Mama allowed it, saying that if Papouli wasn't going to recite the Sermon on the Mount, then Homer's poetic discourse on courage was an acceptable alternative. She said Homer's words reminded her of the Old Testament.

Channeling Odysseus while gesticulating in wild dramatic fashion, Papouli reached the climax of his discourse, shouting, "Hateful to me as the gates of Hades is that man who hides one thing in his heart and speaks another!" He stomped so hard that one of the chair legs gave way, sending Papouli and the chair clattering to the ground.

He lay motionless on the floor, his eyes closed. Seba ran to him, gasping. "Are you all right, Papouli?"

Papouli opened his eyes, jumped up to both feet in a flash, and bowed, as if he had planned the whole thing. He slapped his chest and said, "I'm as fit as a fiddle—I feel so good I could even scale the watchtower!"

Seba reprimanded, "You scared us! And by the way, no one can scale the watchtower. It's forty feet high, with no footholds, and the window for the guards is at the very top. It's impossible!"

Papouli laughed. "Yes, but I had you going, didn't I?" He grabbed Seba's shoulders and tried to get him into a playful headlock. Seba let him and the next moment they were wrestling on the floor in front of the hearth. Mama gave an exasperated sigh as she walked to the front door and invited someone inside.

She turned and said, "*Baba*, Mrs. Lampros is here with her spinning wheel. It has a loose leg that she'd like you to repair for her. I told her that she has perfect timing, because you were about to repair a broken kitchen chair." Mama smirked at Papouli and waved her hands to invite Mrs. Lampros inside.

Mrs. Lampros was wearing a light brown dress with dark green and bright yellow embroidered flowers. She carried the spinning wheel in both hands, and on her arm hung a woven basket full of loukoumades glazed with honey.

Papouli attempted to look respectable by running his hands through his wiry hair and brushing the hearth's ashes from his trousers. He needn't have bothered, because the look on Mrs. Lampros's face when she saw him was so amused that Seba almost laughed out loud. Mrs. Lampros didn't care what Papouli looked like, whether his clothes were dirty, or if he had been wrestling with his grandson just moments before. It was obvious that she loved him.

"Vaios, I come bearing gifts. If you will use your talents to fix my spinning wheel, you can have this whole basket of loukoumades." She put the basket on the table and smoothed her dress.

"Of course, Barbara. I would be happy to save the day. A spinning wheel is a necessity, especially in the winter months—there can never be too many layers of wool. However, I think I'll need something more than these delicious loukamades as payment."

Mrs. Lampros blushed a deep shade of red, and Mama looked at Papouli skeptically. But he only smiled and said, "How about a song while I work? You have a lovely voice, and as you know from the other evening, my grandson is quite skillful on the floghera."

Mama breathed a sigh of relief, and Mrs. Lampros tried to decline. "Oh, Vaios, you don't want to hear my caterwauling. My old voice is hoarse from all the singing we've been doing for the last eight days. It probably sounds like a forlorn donkey."

"Nonsense! If you want your spinning wheel fixed, I'll need a song. And just to be magnanimous, I'll let you choose the tune."

Mrs. Lampros looked at Seba and said, "Well, young man, shall we?"

Seba took the flute down from the mantel above the hearth and blew a few melodic phrases. Papouli smiled happily, as if this day couldn't get any better.

Seba agreed that Mrs. Lampros probably had one of the most beautiful singing voices in all the village, even if she was hoarse from all the merrymaking. Nodding conspiratorially at Mama, he started playing the ancient love song, "My Jasmine." Everyone in the village knew it, and it was one of Papouli's favorites. He felt a little guilty putting Mrs. Lampros on the spot by making her sing a love song for his grandfather, but then, remembering the way they had looked at each other, he guessed she wouldn't mind. She sang it perfectly:

Το γιασεμί στην πόρτα σου
γιασεμί μου
ήρθα να το κλαδέψω
ωχ γιαβρί μου
και νόμισε η μάνα σου
γιασεμί μου
πως ήρθα να σε κλέψω
ωχ γιαβρί μου

Το γιασεμί στην πόρτα σου
γιασεμί μου
μοσκοβολά τις στράτες
ωχ γιαβρί μου
κι η μυρωδιά του η πολλή
γιασεμί μου
σκλαβώνει τους διαβάτες
ωχ γιαβρί μου"

This jasmine outside your door
My jasmine
I came to prune it
Oh, my love
And your mother thought that
My jasmine
I came to steal you
Oh, my love

This jasmine outside your door
My jasmine
Smells divine
And its abundance
My jasmine
Enslaves all who pass
Oh, my love

After repairing the spinning wheel and entertaining the women with his stories, Papouli insisted on walking Mrs. Lampros back home, even though it was only two minutes away. When he returned, Papouli's face was flushed with gladness, and he said to Seba, "That woman is amazing. And her singing—it comes directly from the heart. It's as if the words and music are jumping right into my skin. She's something special, that woman."

Seba loved seeing Papouli so happy. His contentment filled the whole house. This must have been what Thaddeus was talking about when he said he wanted to start a life with Demetria. Seba remembered how he had danced with Xenia on the evening of Kalo Podriko, and smiled.

16 A SACRED NUMBER

The festival time was over and the villagers were gearing up for the new growing season of mastiha. It was mid-February, and the weather remained gray and misty. Seba was eating a breakfast of hot spelt and lupine cereal with goat's milk, peaches, and sour cherries. Over the summer, Mama had strung the ripe peaches and cherries on a thick cotton thread and hung them across the arch spanning the narrow alley of Seba's home. The soft-textured fruit had dried in the sun's heat, their sugars coalescing into orange and red jewels that tasted like candy. As a burst of sun-dried cherry washed across Seba's tongue, he heard a knocking on the front door. Mama said, "You're not expecting Xenia, are you, Sebastian?"

Seba shook his head no. He hadn't thought about her since the night they had danced at the Festival of Kalo Podriko.

Mama ran to the door and swung it open. She waved her arm with a flourish when she saw that it was Uncle Phillip.

However, she stepped back, puzzled that Uncle Phillip had not come alone. Thaddeus and Nikos were standing behind him, Nikos rubbing his hands together to keep warm and Thaddeus's hands shoved in his threadbare trouser pockets.

"Phillip, what a special surprise! Would you like some breakfast and hot coffee? I have water boiling on the fire and the briki is ready."

"Yes, Agnete, coffee would be perfect. Do you have enough for my strapping young associates?"

Seba could tell that Mama was caught off guard, but he knew that a Greek mother will never pass up the opportunity to feed someone.

"Yes, of course. Anything for you, Phillip. Do you boys drink coffee as well?"

Thaddeus looked as perplexed to be there as Mama was to see him. As for Nikos, he seemed slightly perturbed to be associated with Thaddeus, although obviously pleased to be out with Uncle Phillip. This was probably the closest the boys had been to each other since the Firewood Challenge. Seba wasn't concerned for them, however; he was more embarrassed that his friends caught him eating breakfast without coffee. Now that he was fifteen and a man in all his bearded glory, he was expected to be drinking coffee with every meal. All of the men in the village drank coffee all day long and late into the evenings. It was a symbol of manhood, and as ubiquitous in the village as lemons and stray cats. When Uncle Phillip, Nikos, and Thaddeus arrived, Seba had been drinking water with a bit of lime squeezed in it. The limes seemed to last longer over the winter than the other citrus fruits, and lime juice was his favorite. He was waiting for Nikos to make a comment about Seba eating baby food cereal and drinking juice, but his thoughts were interrupted by Thaddeus's enthusiastic response.

"Yes, Mrs. Krizomatis, thank you very much!" Thaddeus was channeling Heracles even more than usual this morning, and Mama was beginning to warm to the boys' presence.

"Well, aren't you just a lovely young man?" She busied herself at the hearth, pouring boiling water into the briki with the coffee grounds. "I guess that means you don't need honey in your coffee—you're already as sweet as sugar."

Seba couldn't decide whether to puke into his cereal or laugh out loud.

"Mrs. Krizomatis, everything smells wonderful here, and I would love a cup of that heavenly coffee you're making." Nikos even bowed a little, and Seba choked down the urge to snort his disdain. "I see you practice the hospitality of the Old Testament—*You shall love the stranger, because you were strangers in the land of Egypt.*" Nikos gave an oily smile. "I believe that's from Deuteronomy 10."

Now Mama was really caught off-guard. Beaming at Nikos, she almost dropped the spoon containing the coffee grounds into the scalding copper pot.

"I see that Brother Tim has been teaching you well, Nikos. *Stand firm, then, with the belt of truth buckled around your waist, with the breastplate of righteousness in place.*"

Before she could cite to the verse, Nikos replied, "Ephesians 6:14."

It was as if Thaddeus no longer existed for Mama. If she could have adopted Nikos on the spot, she would have.

Nikos, looking perfectly angelic, smiled back. Thaddeus gave Seba a quizzical look. Seba shook his head and looked down at his cereal. Nikos was obviously up to something. He had never paid any attention to the worship services in the village church on Sundays, and he often whispered under his breath during Brother Tim's school lessons. Knowing Nikos, Seba guessed this overt display of Bible knowledge was simply a ruse to get something he wanted. Nikos's new angelic persona had certainly worked its magic on Mama, though.

Seba scarfed down the rest of his breakfast; he didn't even get to enjoy the sweet taste of lime juice as he poured the whole mug down his throat.

Uncle Phillip said, "You are as gracious as ever, Agnete. I hope you will indulge me to borrow your son for the day. I have some important business for these three gentlemen."

This was turning out to be a stellar day for Mama. She squeezed her hands together in front of her heart, her face aglow like Virgin Mary on the day of Jesus's birth.

"Well, that's very exciting, Phillip. May I ask what kind of important business?"

"I'd love to tell you, Agnete—but not right now. I don't want to spoil the surprise for these fine young men."

"I understand. And boys, I hope you appreciate how lucky you are to have Phillip all to yourselves today. He is the most important man in Sessera, and if he is choosing you for a special project, you can be sure that it means you have shown yourselves to be worthy in his eyes—and in the eyes of the Lord, who has blessed us with His wisdom and bounty."

As they sat at the table drinking thick, dark coffee from small stoneware cups, Uncle Phillip said, "Seba, like you and your mother, I am no stranger to the grief that comes from the loss of loved ones. Just as your sister was killed by an Ottoman viper at the tender age of three, and your father was taken from you when you were only nine years old, I also have known this grief. Many years ago, when your mother was just a child herself, I fathered many children with my wife, Halia."

All three boys raised their eyebrows; this was news. It was well known in the village that Uncle Phillip had no children. The villagers never talked about it, but Seba had always assumed that either Uncle Phillip or Halia were barren and couldn't have children. "I...didn't know," he stammered.

"Although this village is small, the men and women of Sessera are respectful, and have not discussed the pain that Halia and I suffered many years ago," Phillip continued. "They died in infancy, one by one, each living only a few weeks or months before succumbing to fever and phthisis. We prayed. We went to every healer on the island. But none of the fifteen children my wife bore survived beyond one year."

Mama reached out her hand and placed it on Uncle Phillip's arm.

"It was not your fault," she said to Uncle Phillip. Although she was not speaking to Seba directly, he felt a surge of heat move through his body. Her words communicated directly to Seba's heart for the first time since That Day. A deep yearning for his father enveloped him. At that moment, he believed that if he became very still and focused on his father, he might be miraculously transported to Constantinople to free his father from the Ottomans.

Seba was jolted back to his kitchen by Uncle Phillip's clear voice. "Thank you, Agnete. Nevertheless, it was at that time we determined I was to be the father for every child in the village." His gaze slowly circled the table, stopping for a moment on each boy's expectant face. "And now, young men, it appears that the Lord has blessed us in the form of a trinity for the next generation." He pushed himself back from the table and stood. "Time to go. A million thanks for your hospitality, Agnete."

As Phillip and the three boys exited Sessera, Seba noticed the low clouds and cool air. It was a typical January day, when the mist over the sea pushed into the low valleys of Chios.

Uncle Phillip led the three boys up the trail to the skinos groves, but as they continued past the last skinos tree and the small field chapel, Seba realized he had never walked the narrow footpath that continued up into the mountains. There was a hum of electricity in the air despite the shrouded sky; Seba felt excited, as if something new and special were about to happen. Neither Thaddeus nor Nikos spoke. They hadn't even punched each other or traded barbs the whole time they were walking, which was unusual. As they walked, Uncle Phillip, ever the teacher, pointed out native birds and plants, explaining how God had made them especially for the people of Chios.

At one point the mountain became very rocky and steep, and they had to climb with hands and feet, moving vertically up the steepest part of the hill. They were almost totally encompassed in the clouds, and could not see more than a few feet in front of them. Uncle Phillip seemed to know exactly where he was going, however, and he moved as nimbly as any of his younger companions. The sun was a watery orb behind them, and Seba knew that it was only a matter of time before the marine layer would disappear as quickly as it had formed.

Seba remembered a book that he had seen in Brother Tim's classroom, entitled *The Clouds*. Brother Tim's face had lit up like a candle when he realized Seba's interest in the subject. "Oh, Seba, it is a wonderful play written by the great Greek playwright, Aristophanes—our very own

Father of Comedy. As you may know, he was a contemporary of Socrates and Plato, living in Athens during the time of great thinking in Greece."

Seba had nodded his head and said, "Why is it called *The Clouds*?"

"I hesitate to spoil it for you because you really must read this yourself. But suffice it to say that the clouds in this play are goddesses—a metaphorical symbol of a certain way of thinking which enables man to see the world in any way he chooses."

"You mean we have control over how we see the world?" That didn't make sense to Seba at all. As a mastic slave to the Ottomans, he felt like he had no control over anything.

"Yes, exactly—your perspective drives your reality. Discernment is the key. Just as Saint John advised: *Dear friends, do not believe every spirit, but test the spirits to see whether they are from God, because many false prophets have gone out into the world.* Aristophanes used comedy to state a different version of the same idea. It's fascinating and inspiring, don't you think?!"

This was one of the many reasons why Seba and Thaddeus enjoyed spending time with Brother Tim. Seba had been intrigued, but hadn't managed to read *The Clouds* yet. It didn't prevent him from thinking about the goddesses trying to shape the thoughts of the mind or false prophets trying to trap the unwary with fear and anger.

And so, on this morning, Seba was thinking about whether these clouds would allow him to see the world as he wished it was—with his family together and his father safe. He wondered if there were any dolphins in *The Clouds*. His father had told him to always watch the dolphins.

As Uncle Phillip and the three boys reached the top of Mount Phaneros, they came to an open space that resembled a small outdoor shrine, with several large boulders situated in a circle and a stela in the center. Seba looked down at the swirling gray mist hovering over the valleys and saw that the clouds were thinning with the strength of the sun. Uncle Phillip told the boys to each find a seat on one of the boulders and to pray to God for clarity, understanding, and revelation of His purpose for them.

On a large rock facing southwest, Nikos closed his eyes, swung his arms around in a large arc, raising his hands together above his head, then lowering them in front of his heart like Father Jacobos during the Sabbath worship service. Seba immediately thought of the Pharisees of the Bible who did everything for show. Jesus had seen right through them, just as Seba saw through Nikos today. A verse from Luke 11 came to mind: *Now then, you Pharisees clean the outside of the cup and dish, but inside you are full of greed and wickedness. You foolish people! Did not the one who made the outside make the inside also?*

Thaddeus growled his discontent and chose a boulder as far away from Nikos as possible. Seba chose a third between them.

Uncle Phillip stood and raised his arms high above his head, saying, "Lord and Savior, reveal to us Your plans and how You would use each of us to praise You and carry out Your will."

Seba didn't know if God was responding to Uncle Phillip or if Uncle Phillip simply knew the exact timing of the winds on Chios, but in that very moment, the last of the clouds disappeared and the sun shone bright, its rays pulsing out little rainbows on everything below.

Seba heard Thaddeus gasp, and knew that he noticed it, too. Maybe Uncle Phillip's power stretched beyond the thick walls of the village after all.

"Three hundred years ago, the Ottoman Empire granted us the right to manage our own affairs without interference. We are the only Greeks in the Ottoman Empire with an *ahdname*, a bilateral agreement with the sultan himself. Without this mutual respect, we would have no power to manage our own affairs. It is because of this fellowship that the Ottomans treat us as equals in the mastic trade."

Seba heard Uncle Phillip's words, but something about them seemed off. His thoughts traveled back to That Day, specifically the vision of Ahmed with his silk gloves and nasal voice. "Respect" was not the word that came to mind when Seba thought of the Ottomans' treatment of the Greeks.

Uncle Phillip continued, "We carry on a time-honored tradition that dates back to the time of ancient Greece. Homer himself may have sat on this very mountain, composing the words to the *Iliad* and the *Odyssey*. We are a chosen people, and we provide a valuable resource to all the world. In the past, the mastiha-growing families settled into communities, surrounded by thick stone walls to protect them from outside invaders. And yet those raiders continued to attack, targeting one village at a time. The walled communities soon realized that if they worked together, they could better protect each other and their mastic heritage. Our ancestors shared their knowledge of the land and their tools, and supported each other when storms and pestilence attacked their livelihood. In partnership, with the blessing of the Ottoman Empire, we continue to share our experiences, discuss challenges, determine how best to bring our harvest to the world, and pay our taxes to the sultan. We are the only Greeks in the empire with this special position of self-governance."

Uncle Phillip raised his arms to the heavens. "And now,

O God, we ask that You bless each of these young men as they begin their journey of apprenticeship in the way of the mastiha. Arm them with Your power, guild them with Your goodness, and answer them with Your wisdom."

Seba had intentionally chosen a seat facing Constantinople, far to the northeast, where his father was likely slaving away building ships for the Ottoman merchant fleet. He couldn't reconcile Uncle Phillip's statement about the Ottomans treating them as equals. He understood that the villages had more power by working together than producing their mastic alone, and he knew from talk at the shipyard many years ago that the other residents of Chios did not enjoy the privileges of the mastic villages. Up on Mount Phaneros, he understood why Sessera and the other villages had been constructed in the wide valleys, where they were hidden from any ships or invaders who might be scanning the North Aegean islands for targets. From this vantage point on the mountain, he understood that these valleys contained the most important treasures of the Ottoman Empire.

Seba's hands were clammy and his heart was racing. Despite the cold January day, his feet were soaked in sweat inside his boots. His lower legs felt trapped; the feeling was so strong that he reached down and ripped off his boots. He hoped that if Uncle Phillip noticed what he was doing, he would think it was an attempt to commune more closely with God. He sat on the rock, cross-legged and barefoot, facing the sun, and closed his eyes. After the boys prayed, Uncle Phillip regaled them with the recent history of the *mastichochoria*.

As Uncle Phillip described it, the Ottomans needed the people of Sessera and the other villages, because no one else knew how to get the most from the skinos trees. If the

Ottomans tried to cultivate the mastiha, they would embroider too much, or they wouldn't give the trees the right amount of nutrients, or they wouldn't prune them or plant new trees, and the sultan's harem would have no mastiha. They weren't donkeys at all—they were specialists, and were treasured by the Ottomans for their skill and their traditions. That's why they weren't required to send their oldest sons to the Ottoman army or pay taxes on the land or the crops they produced.

Uncle Phillip asked them to stand. "The future is in your hands, and your journey will not be easy. Working for the council means long hours, as our business continues after we tend to the trees. You will no longer have time for school, games, or any childish pursuits. For your efforts, however, you will be rewarded as the most important men in Sessera and likely all of the *mastichochoria*, supported by me and the other council members as you embark on the road to fulfilling your birthright and your legacy. What is your answer?"

Nikos was the first to respond. He stepped toward Uncle Phillip with his hands clasped in front of him. "Yes, sir!" he said, histrionics on full display. Uncle Phillip took Nikos's hands in his own and raised them up in a triumphant gesture, then pulled Nikos into a great bear hug.

Next was Thaddeus, whose face was practically glowing with the prospect of leaving donkeyhood forever. His face bore a dreamy expression as he stepped forward and said, "Yes, I will." Uncle Phillip, still with one arm around Nikos, took a step toward Thaddeus and threw his other arm around Thaddeus's broad shoulders.

Uncle Phillip looked expectantly at Seba. Seba knew that Uncle Phillip wanted his response to be even more enthusiastic. Beyond Uncle Philip's head, however, was the

Strait of Chios, and beyond that, the Ottoman Empire, including Constantinople.

Seba was having trouble reconciling Uncle Phillip's words with his own experience aboard the *Dame*. Ahmed did not respect his father, Mesich, or even the English sea captain. Did Uncle Phillip really hold a higher station than them? If Seba agreed to Uncle Phillip's offer of apprenticeship, would it be a betrayal of his father? From his vantage point at the top of Mount Phaneros, Seba could see the path the *Dame* had traveled — north through the Strait of Chios, and around the point at Çeşme, toward the Ottoman capital. If Seba said "yes" to Uncle Phillip, his dreams of leaving the island would be dead; and he wasn't sure if Uncle Phillip's impression of the Ottoman Empire was accurate. Something about Uncle Phillip's words did not ring true.

On the other hand, he had just turned fifteen, so what did he know? Being invited to work for the mastic council was a great honor, and according to his mother, it was his destiny. The blood of his mastiha-growing ancestors coursed through his veins. Thaddeus and Nikos obviously thought they were being offered a rare privilege that would change their lives. How could Seba possibly refuse?

He gulped and said quietly, "Yes, sir."

It was perhaps not the enthusiastic response that Uncle Phillip had expected, but it was acceptance. Now the deed was done and there was no going back. Uncle Phillip, with Nikos and Thaddeus in tow, stepped toward Seba; the four of them stood shoulder-to-shoulder, heads touching, bent inward, in a small circle.

"This is a fortuitous day, my young men—one that the people of Sessera will talk about for many generations to come. I welcome you as apprentices to the mastic council of

Sessera!"

The three boys walked down the mountain behind Uncle Phillip, lost in their own thoughts. Seba had made his decision. His mother would be proud of him; she would probably start crying as soon as she heard the news. Papouli would congratulate him and tease him, saying that Uncle Phillip was abandoning his old friend for the younger generation. Mrs. Lampros would probably bake him a special honey cake to celebrate the occasion.

After all, there were kings and queens who clamored for the mastiha that only the Chians could produce. Seba had signed on to continue the tradition that his Greek ancestors had passed down over a thousand years ago. The healing properties of mastiha were known throughout the world, and those little glittering tears traveled around the globe, bringing with them a magical relief from many ailments and an exotic flavor that came from one tiny island in the Aegean Sea. This bright day on Mount Phaneros signaled a new beginning, but Seba's heart was heavy. Deep inside, he said goodbye to that fragile glimmer of hope he had kept alive for six years: the hope of traveling the sea to find his father.

17 THE TOWER

The days following the ceremony on Mount Phaneros were a whirlwind of activity. Seba, Thaddeus, and Nikos were invited to several of the council meetings, in which the men spoke of concepts and details so unfamiliar that they sounded like a foreign language. Production figures, soil analysis, and merchant names flew around the room like a colony of darting bats. The boys were overwhelmed with the level of detail, pace, and machinations that surrounded cultivation and production of mastic. The council members welcomed them into the fold, and although Seba and Thaddeus kept their distance from Nikos, they all managed to enjoy their new status as Uncle Phillip's heirs apparent. Seba, who generally disliked the taste of alcohol, drank more tsipouro with the councilmembers than he could remember, as the men on the council welcomed the three apprentices into the fold.

Nikos took well to the complicated accounts, figures, and projections that the boys were given to study. Whereas Seba found the discussions about weights and measures, gold, competition, pruning practices, and other details tedious and boring, Thaddeus seemed downright terrified by the amount of information he was required to retain. His moods swung from delight with the opportunity to improve his financial circumstances to devastation that he wouldn't be able to keep up with the math. Seba also worried that Thaddeus was afraid Nikos was trying to sabotage him, just as he believed Nikos's father had sabotaged Thaddeus's father so many years ago.

One day, while Nikos was going over production figures with the other council members and Thaddeus was being tutored on the different methods for applying topdressing to the skinos trees, Uncle Phillip received a message that there was an issue at the watchtower that needed his attention. "Seba, you're going to be dealing with this someday," he said. "Why don't you come with me? This is exactly the type of project I said I needed you for when we spoke some time ago in the village square. Now that you've pledged your loyalty to me and the council at Mount Phaneros, I know I can trust you. It will be a good learning experience for you to see how our central tower operates."

Seba was ecstatic. The central watchtower in Sessera was off-limits to all but a handful of the villagers. It was a military enclave in the heart of the village, housing most of the village's weapons and overseen by three highly trained guards. They lived in the watchtower for months at a time, taking turns to be on watch for eight hours a day, so that someone was always on alert to receive messages from the other villages' watchtowers or report any suspicious activity on land or sea. It was a lonely and difficult job, but Seba had always been told that it was a great honor to be a guard for the mastic villages. Unlike the Ottoman guards who controlled the gates of Sessera, the watchtower guards were Greek men of the *mastichochoria*. They were sent away to be trained by the Ottoman army for the sole purpose of guarding the mastic villages, and their lives were so lonely that they rotated in and out of service to prevent boredom, insanity, or both. They were paid well—almost as much as those who served on the council—and the watchtower guards were revered by the villagers who depended on them for their safety, indeed for their very lives.

Sessera's stone tower was nearly forty feet high, with no door on the ground floor; the only way in or out was through one of the three narrow windows that faced north, southeast, and southwest. The watchtower stood alone in the central square, with the closest building more than thirty feet away. The military guards accessed the tower with a rope ladder dropped from one of the windows down to the ground level, or, in the event of an emergency, with a wooden ladder stretched from a tower window across to the top of one of the village rooftops. The guards usually cooked their own meals in the tower; occasionally Mrs. Lampros or even Sotirios would bring them meals in a basket, which would be hoisted up on a rope lowered down from the window.

"Are we really going up into the watchtower?" Seba felt like he was being invited into Jerusalem's Holy of Holies. Maybe Uncle Phillip really did have a higher station with the Ottoman Empire.

"If you are going to be my apprentice on the council, you'll need to understand this important part of our village." Uncle Phillip stopped and looked sternly at Seba. "You may not share what you're about to see with anyone. There are raiders and spies who would love to know how our watchtowers operate. They would torture you to gain one little detail that would give them an advantage in an attack on our village. You must guard the secrets of the watchtower with your life, as I have for many decades. Do you promise to keep this secret?"

"Yes, sir."

They walked quickly to the central tower. When they arrived, they saw that one of the guards was hanging his head out the north-facing window. "Come quickly, Phillip!" he hailed. "We need to speak with you immediately!" Noticing Seba standing below, the guard added, "Alone."

"This is my apprentice, Sebastian Krizomatis—the council's newest member," Phillip called. "Anything you need to say to me, you can say in front of him. I vouch for him. And one day you will likely be taking orders from him as well."

The guard looked slightly irritated, but laughed anyway. "I'll be long dead before that happens, but you're the boss." He tossed a rope ladder from the window and Uncle Phillip grabbed onto it, pulling himself up rung by rung. Seba waited until Uncle Phillip reached the top, and then he put both hands on the ladder and quickly followed. Even at his advanced age, Uncle Phillip made the climb look easy; but the rope swung and twisted as Seba neared the open window. The guard held out a hand to pull him inside.

He entered a wide open space, a square about twelve feet on a side. His throat tightened; he had never seen so many weapons in one place—and some appeared to still have blood on them. There were enormous broadswords, in and out of sheaths; daggers; lances; maces; axes; three crossbows; and at least ten longbows, with enough arrows to take down an entire shipload of raiders. There were sealed pots of caustic quicklime, and in one corner a pile of guns leaned against the wall like so many tree branches.

Seba thought there must be more weapons in this tower than there were villagers in Sessera who could wield them. He was terrified.

There was a hearth in the center of the tower, obviously used for cooking; but Seba also knew that the fire was kept going at all times in order to signal the other villages' watchtowers when danger was spotted. Three straw mattresses lay in the western corner of the tower, along with several rugs and blankets strewn about.

Seba began to feel sick. Although the chamber pot in the corner was covered with a wooden plank, the smell of urine and feces was overpowering. Nearby stood a number of earthen crocks carefully sealed with wax; the words painted on the sides identified the contents as quicklime. The crocks stood ready to be poured out onto attackers at a moment's notice, to blind and scald and poison. Seba guessed the chamber pots were probably used on attackers as well. His eyes watered and he tried to hold his breath.

His thoughts were interrupted by Uncle Phillip asking, "What's so important that you needed me to see your bachelor's quarters in all their squalor?" His voice was light, but Seba could tell that he was concerned. The guards were professionals and did not call for assistance for trivial matters.

"Come see for yourself. Something is wrong with the mastiha."

Uncle Phillip's eyebrows went sky-high. "Show me."

One of the guards kicked a rug out of the way and pulled on a large iron ring on the floor. A trapdoor opened to a set of stone steps below, leading down into darkness. The guards grabbed torches hanging on the stone hearth, lit them, and walked down the steps, followed by Uncle Phillip and Seba. The space below was as black as a starless sky; there were no windows. The torchlight was nearly swallowed up by the inky blackness, but Seba didn't need any light to know what was in that space. His nose told him what it was.

As they all reached the ground level, Seba looked around in the dim light and saw what he had smelled. Whereas the terrifying weapons stash of the upper floor smelled like dead animals, urine, and feces, the lower windowless area below the trapdoor was filled with the heady smell of the best mastiha.

He looked at Uncle Phillip inquisitively.

"And now you know our secret," Phillip said quietly.

"I don't understand."

"This is where the excess mastiha from each harvest is stored."

"Excess mastiha? I thought we sold everything we harvested."

One of the guards scoffed. "We don't need to discuss it now," Phillip said quickly. "I will explain this tower to you another time. For now, we need to investigate what is happening to our precious tears."

Seba noticed he didn't say "watchtower" this time, and a realization quietly tapped him on the shoulder. Because it *wasn't* a watchtower, not really. Right under the noses of the Ottomans—unbeknownst even to most of the villagers— this tower concealed a fortune in mastiha. There were hundreds of crates of the prized translucent tears, a hoard larger, perhaps, than the one in the sultan's own palace. And in all of Sessera, the five of them in that room might be the only ones who knew.

Seba was trying to keep his wits about him, but the strong smell and the shock made it impossible. So much wealth, piled up for all this time, while so many in the village—including his own best friend—struggled to feed their families. The waste of it appalled him.

He willed himself to stay calm, keeping in mind all of the weapons on the upper level and the fact that the guards did not approve of his presence here in the first place. He pictured himself being split in two by one of the battle axes and shuddered from head to toe, like a dog shaking off cold water.

The guard removed the lid from one of the crates and held his torch over it. The tears were no longer crisp and white, but were turning yellow and sticky.

Phillip said, "What happened?"

"I don't know, sir. That's why we called you. We periodically check the mastiha to ensure that it retains its potency. We spotted this yesterday."

Phillip pulled on his beard thoughtfully. "It appears to me that there is not enough air flow around the crates, and something is growing on our precious mastiha. A fungus, perhaps." Seba looked around; there were crates stacked upon crates, more than he could count. If there had been fewer crates or shorter stacks, the mastiha could breathe in the wooden crates. Seba wondered how many years it had taken for this stockpile to grow.

"What should we do?"

"We'll need to keep the air circulating. Fashion large fans from palm branches or canvas sheets, and increase your shifts to take turns moving the air in this tower."

Seba surreptitiously eyed the guards; they said nothing, but he could tell that two of them were displeased by the prospect of extending their shifts and losing sleep in order to protect the mastiha. And he had the feeling that there was much more to the story that Phillip had omitted.

As they all walked back up the stone steps to the

weapons cache, Seba took a final glance at the crates of mastiha. He was still half in shock. This was more mastiha than he had ever seen at a harvest celebration. How did it all get here? And how long had it been here? The guard motioned roughly for him to move on, making sure that Seba was not tempted to snag a tiny tear from the huge cache that he had just discovered.

Closing the trapdoor, the oldest of the guards said, "When can we expect the supplies to make these fans? You know we can't leave the tower."

Phillip sighed. Seba could see the weight of what he carried. "You'll have everything you need before sundown. I'll send Thaddeus over with the materials. He's one of my trusted apprentices, just like Seba here. Thaddeus is strong and he can carry everything you need in one trip. If you need anything else, you know how to reach me."

The guard held out his hand and they shook.

"And in the name of the Lord our Father, please empty that chamber pot today. It may not just be lack of air flow fouling the mastiha below."

This time all three guards laughed, a genuine sound of levity echoing among them.

Seba felt no levity. In fact, the only thing he felt was remorse and betrayal. This was not the legacy his father had promised for him; and Phillip's version of the relationship with the Ottoman Empire had been a lie, just as Seba had felt on Mount Phaneros.

They climbed back down the ladder, and Seba couldn't contain his anger or confusion. "Why is there so much mastiha in that tower? If we sold even a tiny portion from one of those crates, no family in Sessera would ever be hungry! There's so much in there that it's spoiling! Why aren't we selling it?"

"Sebastian, keep your voice down. You don't understand."

"You're right. I don't understand. This makes no sense!"

"In order to get the best price for mastiha around the world, we have to limit the supply that is available. It keeps the prices high and makes us the most money. It also protects us in years that the harvest is lean."

"Who is 'us'? The Ottomans? You're not protecting any of us! This does not make the villagers the most money. And that whole tower is full, from floor to ceiling! I've never seen so much mastiha, not even after the best harvest we've ever had. That's why it's turning bad. Don't you see?"

"I see perfectly, Seba. You're just a boy—and in time, you'll learn how our council works. The guards will protect the mastiha and keep it from spoiling. It has to be this way."

"Who says? You, and the council? You've done this to our village?"

"Of course not, Seba. The prices are set by the Ottomans, and we've agreed to it in our ahdname, just as I told you when you agreed to join the council."

"Why would you concede to hoarding something that could help us all? It's not right! We can't even have more than a few tears after a harvest, to bake with, or to use as medicine. What if Thaddeus's father could get better with more mastiha? We're keeping this from our own villagers, even though it benefits all of us to sell it!"

"It's not that simple, Seba. The Ottomans set the prices and the production levels, and we don't have a choice. We must go along."

"Or what?"

"Or we lose our privileged position in the empire."

That was it. The niggling that had been festering deep down inside Seba when he thought of the *mastichochoria* had finally erupted.

"Thaddeus was right—we're just slaves to the Ottomans! You work for them, and you don't have any power at all. You say you do, but it's an illusion. A bilateral agreement where one side sets all the terms and the other side has no choice but to obey is *not* equal! It's not even a real agreement—it's a sham. They don't respect you—they're using you! How could you?"

"Seba, calm down. You're too young to understand the way the world works. That's why I've taken you on as my apprentice. When you learn more about the workings of the council, you'll come around."

"You're wrong," Seba said. "Those Ottoman vipers stole my father from me, the best man that I've ever known." Frustrated tears sprang to his eyes. "And you work for them—do their bidding. You're not just an Ottoman slave, you're the king of the slaves, helping them to keep us down. We trusted you!"

Phillip was trying to put his hands on Seba's shoulders to calm him down, but Seba escaped his grasp. Phillip, becoming agitated, lunged forward and grabbed the back of his neck. Seba cried out in pain and anger.

Phillip, his iron grip hinged around the back of Seba's neck, whispered fiercely, "I brought you into the council because you exercised discretion—because you thought before you acted. Your behavior today shows me otherwise. You're letting your emotions control you."

Seba stared right into Phillip's eyes and said nothing. His emotions wanted him to punch Phillip in the face.

"I see that I pushed you too hard, and too soon." Phillip relaxed his grip ever so slightly. "You need time to process this information."

He released Seba, and the two of them stood facing each

other. Seba was seething, but he remained composed.

"Seba, promise me that you'll think about what we saw in the tower. Say nothing to anyone until we've had a chance to discuss it in private. Take as much time as you need, but do not say a word. Can you promise me that?"

Seba needed time to think anyway, so he nodded in agreement. Phillip hurried off to the council office to make a list of supplies for Thaddeus. Seba couldn't stomach the thought of facing anyone at the council, so he turned toward Sotirios's kafenion with an intention to climb to the rooftops and think.

As he began walking in that direction, he heard shouting from around the corner. Thaddeus and Nikos appeared in the square, arguing even more violently than usual.

"You're a liar, Nikos!"

"You have no idea what you're talking about. Even an imbecile like you should be able to understand how the council works."

Thaddeus curled his fingers into a fist, barely holding back his rage. "You're the imbecile, thinking we can't see through your fake piety. And you follow your father and every other council member around like a stray cat, just waiting for one of them to throw you a scrap of meat."

"At least my father can still throw—unlike yours."

Thaddeus gave a roar and jumped on Nikos, pummeling him with both fists. The two tumbled to the ground, both swinging wildly at each other. Thaddeus landed a blow right between Nikos's eyebrows, gashing the thin skin above his right eye and causing a cascade of bright red blood to flow into his eyes. In a flash, Nikos's face was covered in blood. Kicking out blindly, Nikos managed to strike Thaddeus between the legs before he could land another punch. Thaddeus instantly curled up like a fetus in the dirt, barely able to catch his breath. Nikos's sleeve was smeared with a swath of deep red where he used it to wipe the blood from his eyelids. Seba knew that Nikos would have two swollen black eyes by the next morning.

He stood over Thaddeus, still twisted up in a ball and rocking from side to side, wracked with pain. Nikos spat blood and said, "You know what—you're nothing like Heracles—he had brains *and* strength."

With that, Nikos kicked dust on Thaddeus and shuffled away.

18 DARKNESS

The days following the confrontation with Phillip were agony for Seba. They barely spoke; Seba slogged through his daily chores for the council in a haze. He convinced everyone, including his mother, that he was so busy with the council that he didn't have time to talk. No one questioned him. Phillip, for his part, gave Seba plenty of space, going so far as to tell his mother to go easy on him because he was experiencing growing pains as he entered manhood. Phillip seemed convinced that Seba would not divulge his secret, and they never spoke of the tower again. Seba went out of his way to avoid the structure, sometimes walking ten minutes in the opposite direction to the village square through the narrow, winding alleys just to avoid the sight of it.

Seba felt stuck. He had no choice but to continue working for the council, but it made him sick to think of what they were hiding from their fellow Sesserans. He wanted to talk to Thaddeus about it, but if the Ottoman guards found out that he had divulged the village's secret, he feared he would be arrested—perhaps even executed.

In any case, Thaddeus was also too busy to talk to Seba, so the secret was safe. The days of sitting on the roof and fantasizing of escaping the life of donkeyhood were a distant memory for both of them. Thaddeus worked day and night to show Phillip he was worthy of the apprenticeship, but the complexities of farming science and international trade overwhelmed him. Seba and Thaddeus hadn't spoken for weeks, though he occasionally caught snippets of arguments between Thaddeus and Nikos. Neither one had the sense—or perhaps the willpower—to stay out of the other's way. In particular, Thaddeus's hatred of Nikos had grown from a boyhood rivalry into something far darker, something akin to madness. Thaddeus saw Nikos and his father as the reason for all his pain, and Seba could see that it was eating Thaddeus alive.

Nevertheless, the spring growing season was upon them, and the villagers had work to do. The sun reintroduced itself to the wide valleys of southern Chios, and Seba was working on the farthest slope of the mastic groves, clearing branches from under the trees that had just been pruned. There was a pleasant breeze wafting through the skinos terraces, bringing the promise of new life. This was Seba's favorite time of year, when the scent of orange blossoms permeated the whole valley, fulfilling the promise of spring and rebirth. His thoughts turned to the peaches, apples, cherries, and pears that would be ready for harvest in a few months' time. The fruit blossoms were just beginning to appear, and he felt the juices in his mouth as if he were already enjoying the bounty.

His daydream and the perfect pastoral scene were interrupted by a girl's voice crying, "He's dead! He's dead!"

He turned to see Xenia running up the dirt path at a full clip, her brown curls escaping from her thick braids, dragging her sister behind her. Both girls were pink from exertion. The other villagers stopped what they were doing and watched Xenia run straight for Seba.

"Seba, did you hear what happened? It's just horrible!" She looked at her sister. "She's going to die of heartbreak. I can't think of anything worse!"

Seba stood up. "What happened? What is it?"

Xenia was bent over, her hands on her thighs as she caught her breath. Her sister stood adjacent, her beautiful face blank, as if she were in another world. The villagers were now walking to the end of the terrace, worried and whispering to each other.

At last, Xenia had breath enough to speak. "Nikos and Thaddeus were fighting again, in the middle of the village square. They were screaming—it was awful. Nikos said if Thaddeus was so great, he'd accept a dare to swim the channel and back, and prove once and for all that he was Sessera's own Heracles! Thaddeus said, 'I'll do it right now—I succeeded with your first stupid challenge, and I'll do the same with this one.' They both ran all the way to Mount Aeon, just above the shipyard."

Seba's stomach was starting to churn, and he could feel the blood thumping inside his head.

"My sister and I ran after them, yelling for Thaddeus to stop. Demetria was pleading with him, but Thaddeus was like a bull in a rage. He dove right off the highest rock at Mount Aeon, right into that freezing cold water!"

Demetria looked toward the east and said in a monotone, "But I love him."

Xenia put her arm around her sister. Now the villagers were closing in. Seba's legs felt weak, as if they couldn't hold him any longer. He had never seen Demetria like this. He had always believed he could rely on her quiet good cheer; the vacant look on her face now terrified him. He felt as if the sun would never rise again.

"Nikos knew no one could fight that current for the whole eight miles to Anatolia, much less come back to Chios—not even Thaddeus. It's too far to swim, and the current is impossible to overcome. Why would he even suggest such a thing?"

Seba felt his knees begin to buckle, and a hand from behind him steadied him as he fell forward and landed on his knees. This couldn't be happening. The coffee grounds said Thaddeus would find love, money, and a change of circumstances. This was all wrong.

Xenia bent down to put her arms around Seba, but he pushed her away. She wrapped her arms around her sister instead, and her eyes bored into Seba. "I know, it's horrible—he was your best friend!"

Seba's entire body was electrified, as if lightning had struck him on the top of the head. Xenia's voice sounded surreal, like a ghost in a nightmare. Seba shook his head violently. It couldn't be true.

"Look what he's done to my sister! They were going to get married." Xenia's voice broke.

Mrs. Lampros came forward with a wooden ladle full of water. "Drink this, and give some to your sister. She's in shock."

Xenia took the ladle with shaky hands and raised it to Demetria's lips. It was as if Demetria didn't even know where she was. The water poured over her closed mouth and down her chin. Mrs. Lampros dipped the ladle into the wooden bucket of water, handing it to Xenia again. Xenia gulped the cold water, some of which joined her tears to spill down her cheek.

"He almost made it, he almost did! It was a miracle that he made it across to the other side. I can't imagine how cold the water is right now. Nikos was watching from the top of Mount Aeon, just like a statue, frozen there. He never said a word. I don't know how long we all stood there watching because it seemed as if time stood still. At some point, Demetria must have left and come back because I looked beside me, and she had Brother Tim's spyglass in her hand. She must have run all the way back to the village and taken it from the school. Through it, we could see that Thaddeus was bleeding and it looked like he was limping when he climbed up the Anatolian rocks on the other side of the channel. Demetria was yelling for him to stay there and rest, and come back tomorrow. He looked at her from across the water—eight whole miles—and I thought he was going to wait. Demetria was begging him to rest, screaming at the top of her lungs."

Demetria said again, "But I love him." The pain in Demetria's voice was the scariest thing Seba had ever heard.

Xenia pushed the hair back from Demetria's forehead and kissed it, saying, "I know. I'm so sorry." Seba would not have believed Xenia's story if he hadn't seen Demetria with his own eyes. The channel was eight miles across, which means that Nikos dared Thaddeus to swim sixteen miles, from one rocky shoreline across the swift-moving Strait of Chios to the other rocky coastline and back again. There were a few jagged rock formations that jutted up between the opposite shores, but they were more of a danger than a safe haven for someone stupid enough to swim the channel. Eight miles across did not seem like a great distance when looking from the cliffs of Chios across to Anatolia, but it was the current that made it dangerous.

One of the villagers asked Xenia, "Then what happened?"

"He was exhausted and bleeding; he looked back toward us, and he put his hands on his hips. He looked as if he couldn't believe that he had made it. He crossed the eight miles, fought the current, and made it to the other side. We thought he was going to stay and rest. He had just accomplished something great—just like the Firewood Challenge. No one had ever swum across the Strait of Chios, and Thaddeus did it! We were jumping up and down and clapping for him. He should have just stayed there, even for a few hours, just to rest and regain his strength! But then he looked back across the channel at us, and when he saw Nikos standing there like a hunk of marble, he started jumping up and down, like he was trying to grind Nikos under his feet. Seeing Nikos standing there turned Thaddeus into a crazy person. He jumped from rock to rock all the way back down to the shoreline and dove right into the water to swim back. Just the sight of Nikos drove him insane!"

Seba tried to picture Thaddeus making it all the way across the Strait of Chios. He should have been so happy! Who cares if Nikos was standing across the channel from him? Thaddeus had accomplished something that no one in Sessera or any other village would ever even attempt. Seba couldn't manage to swim a few hundred yards to the shipyard when his father threw him overboard, and Thaddeus swam a full eight miles against the powerful current. The rocks were sharp, the current was fierce, as if Poseidon himself were swirling the water with his great trident. Why would he undertake such a stupid stunt?

Xenia was still talking. "On the way back, he managed to swim to that little rocky island—you know, the one that juts up in the middle of the channel. He was scratched and really bleeding by now. We couldn't even see his face because it was covered in blood. Demetria, you thought he was going to make it, didn't you?"

Demetria was a statue, staring blankly as if half-dead, the spyglass still in her hand.

Xenia continued, "We both thought he was going to make it. But as he launched himself off that little rocky ledge, the current grabbed and spun him around like a corkscrew. He looked so small and powerless; I'd never seen him like that before. It was terrifying. No matter how hard he kicked or stroked his arms, he made no progress. There were still three miles between the little island and the rocks on our side of the channel. He had already swum thirteen miles! No one has ever done that, not even close to it. But the current was too strong—it dragged him northward, like a tree branch floating on the water. He was struggling furiously, and then he disappeared under the surface. Demetria was crying and screaming his name, and we searched the water to see if his head popped up again. We must have stood there for an hour, but the current took him out to sea."

A tear emerged from Demetria's eye, and Xenia wiped it away with her thumb. She looked tenderly at her sister. "I know, my darling Demetria. I can't believe he's gone."

Seba couldn't believe it either. Some of the workers started crying, and everyone dropped their tools. There would be no work in the groves until they had prayed to God to protect Thaddeus's soul. Seba couldn't stand. He knelt in the dirt, staring at the ground, as the villagers walked past him, crying and hugging each other.

Xenia released her arms from her sister and leaned down where Seba was bent over in the dirt. "Seba, I'm sorry. I know this is a shock for you, too."

Seba's voice cracked as he asked, "Are you sure he's gone? Were there any boats around? Could he have been dragged up toward the coast at Çeşme where someone might pull him out of the water?"

"Seba, I wish I was wrong. Look at my sister, she's been like this since it happened. We saw his bloody face, and his legs covered in scrapes and gashes. He was exhausted and when he got back in the water to return to us, his strength was gone. I'm sorry, Seba, I really am."

Seba began to think of Thaddeus's family. It would be very difficult for them to feed all of those hungry mouths next winter.

For the following days, the villagers spoke only of Thaddeus—every kind deed he had ever performed for anyone, the diligence with which he worked to support his family, his strength and capability. A dark cloud of mourning enveloped the village, threatening to suffocate all of them. Seba felt like someone had snuffed out a candle and then thrown it in the sea so it could never be lit again. This was a different kind of grief from what he had felt on That Day, when he was only nine years old. Now he was a man, and understood the implications of Thaddeus's death; how the loss affected not only him, but Thaddeus's family, Phillip, the council—even Nikos.

Brother Tim and Father Jacobos led the funeral service for Thaddeus in full Greek Orthodox tradition. Every person in the village packed into the church. Phillip declared that no one was to enter the skinos groves until three days after the funeral. The church bell tolled seventeen times, one for each year of Thaddeus's earthly life, and the low reverberating tones had a mournful sound, as if the bells knew why they were chiming. There was a finality when the seventeenth *bong* rang out, closing the door on a bright life that was nonetheless marred by shadow. Thaddeus's eleven brothers and sisters were at the front of the church with their parents. His father, whose back was crooked to begin with, was doubled over in grief and agony. The siblings' faces were puffy and red, and they sniffled intermittently. Only Thaddeus's mother was stoic, sitting upright and trying to hold space for her children to grieve the loss of their larger-than-life brother.

Xenia's family was seated nearby. Xenia, next to her sister Demetria, was unusually quiet. She dabbed her cheeks with a white handkerchief. Seba almost expected her to be wailing loudly and making a scene, but Xenia seemed different now. Demetria, the quiet one, was sobbing, uncharacteristically oblivious to those around her, unable to contain her grief. Seba remembered the evening she had brought the jug of goat's milk to Thaddeus when he was stacking the firewood. She had just wanted to help her Heracles. Now she would never have the chance. She didn't deserve this pain. No one did.

Seba sat with Mama, Papouli and Phillip's family near the front of the church on the left. On the altar was a silver and antimony vase with a pattern of interlocking doves and vines made of gold. Inside the vase was an explosion of pungent flowering oregano and early spring wildflowers, which filled the church with the scent that felt like home. The altar was draped in a white cloth and covered with hundreds of beeswax candles, which smelled slightly of honey as they flickered and glowed, representing all of the angels surrounding Thaddeus in heaven.

Because Thaddeus's body had not been recovered, a box of his belongings lay on a table in front of the altar, to be buried in his place. Staring at the box, Seba envisioned

Thaddeus at the bottom of the Aegean Sea; then, all unbidden, he had the image of him walking through the back door of the church, covered in seaweed and laughing that it had all been a mistake.

Everyone in the village knew the funeral liturgy. Death was not an uncommon event in Sessera, or anywhere on Chios. Father Jacobos and Brother Timotheos wore their formal robes, and as they went about the service, Seba noticed that Brother Tim's face was as red and puffy as those of Thaddeus's siblings. Still, his sonorous voice never wavered as the two priests chanted, "Blessed are those whose way is blameless, who walk in the law of the Lord." Brother Tim lit the incense and handed the brass censer to Father Jacobos, who alternately chanted and sang the blessing of Saint Paul for Thaddeus's spirit, represented by his earthly treasures: "For just as the Father raises the dead and gives them life, even so the Son gives life to whom He is pleased to give it. The Father judges no one, but has entrusted all judgment to the Son, that all may honor the Son just as they honor the Father. Whoever does not honor the Son does not honor the Father, who sent Him. Very truly I tell you, whoever hears my word and believes Him who sent me has eternal life and will not be judged but has crossed over from death to life."

Father Jacobos handed the censer back to Brother Tim, who swung it over the box. Seba thought that Brother Tim might faint; the overpowering smell of the incense—myrrh mixed with sweet rose—filled the room, giving an otherworldly feeling to the space. Seba felt a whoosh of air sweep down from the rafters, even though the church doors were closed and the stained glass windows allowed no outside breeze to enter the chapel. Was this Thaddeus, visiting him in the smoke and perfume? Seba whispered,

"Thaddeus, is that you?"

Just then two of the candles on the altar went out, and the smoke that rose from them formed a distinct shape in the air. *It must be Thaddeus's spirit*, Seba thought, for the tendrils of smoke looked exactly like donkey ears. It was so obvious, there was no other explanation. As the fragrance permeated the church, the two donkey ears of smoke floated up and swirled together. Seba blinked, and when he opened his eyes, the smoke from the two extinguished candles was now in the shape of a dolphin. What was Thaddeus's spirit trying to tell him?

Brother Tim chanted, "With the Saints give rest, O Christ, to the soul of Your servant where there is no pain, nor sorrow, nor suffering, but life everlasting." Thaddeus's mother sounded a sharp intake of breath then lowered her head. Seba could see her shoulders shaking with silent sobs. She had tried to stay strong for her incapacitated husband and devastated children, but the weight was more than she could bear.

Watching her, and seeing the effect it had on Thaddeus's brothers and sisters, whose heads darted back and forth as they witnessed their stoic mother crumble in her anguish, Seba thought of his own mother. She had lost a daughter to an Ottoman viper and her husband to an entire colony of Ottoman vipers. No wonder she was a little crazy sometimes, trying desperately to control her circumstances—even if that meant controlling Seba in the process. He felt as if he now understood the depth of her pain.

Xenia had said that Nikos stood on the mountain like a chunk of marble, watching Thaddeus struggle and succumb to a watery death. Seba looked around; Nikos's family was sitting behind Xenia's, but Nikos was not with them. Seba's head swiveled around from right to left; Nikos was nowhere in sight. He had sent Sessera's Heracles to his death and didn't even have the decency to mourn his passing. Seba knew that Nikos was low, but he couldn't believe he would disrespect Thaddeus's family or the other villagers by missing the funeral. That was outright blasphemy. Seba resolved there in the church never to speak to Nikos again.

As Seba's gaze returned to the front of the chapel, he saw Brother Tim trying to get his attention. When they locked eyes, Brother Tim gestured for Seba to go the back of the church.

Seba knew it must be important for Brother Tim to send him away during the service, so he jumped up and ran down the side aisle toward the exit doors. He heard a whimpering from the steps to the clerestory level at the back of the church. Someone was obviously too upset about Thaddeus's death to join the others in the pews; Brother Tim must have seen or heard the person, and was sending Seba to provide comfort.

Seba walked up the steep, narrow steps to the church's rear balcony, but stopped when he reached the landing. Nikos was bent over with his knees on the floor, shoulders hunched, weeping into his hands.

Seba stared at him for a moment, feeling nothing, then turned and walked away. He returned to his seat as the last song of the funeral service swelled, drowning out the sound of Nikos's lament.

Ἅγιος ὁ Θεός, Ἅγιος ἰσχυρός, Ἅγιος ἀθάνατος, ἐλέησον ἡμᾶς

Holy God, Holy Almighty, Holy Immortal, have mercy on us.
It was over.

Sessera's Heracles was gone.

19 NEA MONI

The days after Thaddeus's funeral were tense and uneasy. For as much as Thaddeus complained about all the work he did for the village and for his family, no one really understood the extent of his contribution to the mastic community—not only his physical strength, but his gregarious demeanor and self-deprecating humor. The loss was felt more deeply by the villagers of Sessera because Thaddeus's death was unexpected. Sessera's Heracles was supposed to live to a ripe old age and regale the younger generations with tales of his amazing feats of strength. Now he would never have the chance.

On the roof each night, Seba would drift to sleep half expecting to be stepped on by Thaddeus and hearing his wry "eee-ore" as he flapped his hands like donkey ears around his head. Seba knew that it was wrong and unchristian, but he couldn't help thinking that it should have been Nikos.

He wasn't the only one. There were whispers and

murmurs; of Phillip's two remaining apprentices, one was now widely seen as the village pariah. Seba wondered if Phillip would dismiss Nikos just to keep the peace. At least Nikos was shrewd enough to stay out of sight and away from the village square after Thaddeus's death. Many complained that Nikos's absence from the funeral was an unforgivable show of disrespect; Seba did not see fit to set them straight.

Some were calling Nikos a murderer, and wanting him to be punished for his participation in the drowning. One evening when the talk became heated over Nikos's culpability, Phillip finally went on record to quell the grumbling: "Nikos is still just a boy. It was a thoughtless dare, yes—but he is young. He did not think it through. Don't be unfair to Nikos. He is suffering more than anyone!"

Seba wondered how Phillip knew that. Nikos had not been seen for many days. He no longer worked with the others in the skinos groves, and Seba never saw him near the council office; before the drowning, he would often be found deep in conversation with his father and Phillip. Seba wondered if Nikos had been sent away to another village, maybe Vousta or Olympi, to give the people of Sessera time to heal. Seba hoped this was so; he never wanted to see Nikos's face again.

Mama seemed to agree with Phillip's perspective on Nikos. She took both Thaddeus's and Nikos's absences especially hard. She had finally begun to appreciate the boys who had grown into men, and now was grief-stricken that they were gone. She prayed to the Virgin Mary to keep Nikos safe and to bless Thaddeus as he walked the streets of heaven. Seba understood intellectually that he was supposed to forgive Nikos, but his heart wasn't cooperating. It had been walled off by too much loss.

One evening, Seba could not restrain himself from arguing with his mother. "Mama, if Nikos knew that Thaddeus would die—isn't that the same as killing him?"

"Sebastian, you don't know what Nikos was thinking and you don't know what is in someone's heart. Remember the words of Jesus in Matthew 7—*Do not judge, or you too will be judged. With the measure you use, it will be measured to you.*"

"But Mama, doesn't the Old Testament say that justice must be served by taking life for life, eye for eye, tooth for tooth? Nikos isn't being punished at all, and it's not fair."

"Sebastian, I believe you need to speak to Brother Timotheos. Lord knows you listen to him more than you ever heeded my advice. He will tell you that the laws of Moses were distilled by Jesus into two commandments—love God with your whole heart, mind, and soul; and love your neighbor as yourself. Whether you like it or not, Nikos is your neighbor. Ask Brother Timotheos, I'm sure he will tell you the same."

Seba couldn't ask Brother Tim, however, because the monk had been called to Nea Moni, the 700-year-old monastery northwest of the village, just days after Thaddeus's funeral. Seba was all alone—Thaddeus was gone, Brother Tim was at Nea Moni, Papouli now spent all of his waking hours with Mrs. Lampros, and Phillip was busy protecting a storage tower full of rotting mastiha for the Ottomans. Although his father had been gone for six years, Seba felt the loss like it happened yesterday.

Seba's life was now a bad dream that didn't end when the morning came. He didn't care about mastiha, the council, the village, or his future. What was the point of trying to create a legacy if someone like Nikos or the

Ottomans could extinguish it with the snap of a finger?

One week after Thaddeus's death, Mama asked Seba to accompany her to pray for Thaddeus's soul at Nea Moni. Even though he feared a lecture by Mama about forgiveness during the four-hour trek to the monastery, he agreed to join her. Maybe the hard climb up the hills surrounding Nea Moni, and the final ascent to Mount Provateio, would burn the deep despair out of his body.

Mama and Seba walked through forest groves of olive trees, Chian pine, and blossoming citrus. The steep mountains rose up before them to the north and Seba remembered the story of the monastery's creation. The closer they came to the sacred mountain, the more Seba could feel the magic of the place. He desperately needed that magic.

Seba had only been there a few times in his life. There were almost 600 monks occupying the tiny enclave, but their very existence on the mountaintop was peaceful and serene. The monks' east-facing quarters offered a stunning view of Mount Provateio's valley as well as the Aegean Sea and the Anatolian coast. Seba thought it was as close to heaven as he could get with his feet still on the ground.

When they arrived at Nea Moni, Seba's mother greeted some monks who were repairing the hinges on the front gate. After receiving their blessing and stating her business, Mama strode confidently to the tiny prayer chapel by the monastery's entrance to pray for Thaddeus's soul. The chapel was full of skulls and bones of the holy men who had visited Nea Moni over the last 700 years; Seba shuddered as he passed. As he and his mother knelt by the simple wooden altar, Seba said a prayer for Thaddeus and his family. He thought about adding a prayer for Nikos, but he couldn't bring himself to do it. Instead, he asked the Holy Spirit to do its job and mete out punishment like the judges in Exodus. He knew that Mama would be praying there for several more hours, so he pushed himself up from his knees and exited the chapel to search for Brother Tim.

A stone pathway led up the hill from the prayer chapel to a large sanctuary. The tall wooden doors were open wide; Seba knew that the doors were never locked because everyone was always welcome in God's house. Seba was astonished by the ornate gold-inlaid mosaics that covered the floors and walls of the large domed chapel, as well as the elaborately decorated icons of saints and hundreds of images of Jesus, from infancy to the crucifixion. Each saint and each depiction of Jesus or the Virgin Mary was surrounded by a halo of gold, which made them look otherworldly and angelic. There were marble statues everywhere—some the rich red marble of Chios, others traditional gray and white, and even some green and black marble imported from other islands. The sunlight through the domed ceiling reflected off the gold paintings and mosaics so that Seba felt like he was in a room that moved with the light. He held his hand out and leaned on a marble column to steady himself. He had never seen anything so beautiful.

Seba exited the church and wandered the grounds, which had a different kind of beauty than the elaborate decorations inside the large sanctuary. Seba enjoyed the sounds of the chickens clucking, goats bleating, pigeons cooing, and the serene atmosphere created by the cheerful bell tower, refectory, cistern, kitchen, monks' quarters, and barnyard. Seba admired the monks' tranquil way of life nestled high in the mountains. Just as Jesus suggested, they had established a shining city on a hill.

Entering the barnyard, Seba spied Brother Tim walking

toward the *kouzina*, a full pail of goat's milk hanging from each arm. Seba opened his mouth to call out a greeting to his teacher, but stopped when he heard his name, which caused a jolt of electricity to course through his body. It was Xenia.

"Seba! I can't believe you're here. It's like a dream come true." Her cheeks were a splotchy red color, and she smiled wanly through bloodshot eyes. "I've been mourning Thaddeus, and trying to help my sister with her grief. It's been horrible. I feel like nothing is ever going to be the same in Sessera ever again. I prayed for the Lord to send me some comfort, and now here you are. I thank the Lord that He answered my prayers." She wrapped her arms around him, as if he truly had been sent to Nea Moni just for her.

But Seba did not feel the same. The pain that had been building since Thaddeus's death, maybe even since the loss of his father, bubbled up and broke through. He clasped his hands around Xenia's arms and pushed them away from him. "Xenia, I am not the answer to your prayers! I've prayed to God for you to stop chasing me for as long as I can remember. He never answered my prayers—because here you are."

He knew the words were cruel even as he spoke them, but he was beyond the point of caring. Xenia seemed to shrink like the leaves of an unwatered plant. Seba looked at her, trying to recall the feeling he had the evening when he and Xenia had danced at the Festival of Kalo Podriko. But he could only remember the day she embarrassed him by telling everyone he was almost killed by an Ottoman viper. The misery and ugliness of his thoughts swirled around him like a vapor.

What he heard was completely unexpected.

Xenia looked directly into his eyes and after a long pause,

said, "I've been nothing but caring and helpful to you for as long as I've known you, practically our whole lives. All I've ever wanted is to be close to you." Her lips trembled and her voice was low, almost gravelly. It had lost its lilt and energy. Seba stared at her in a stupor.

"And now, the person most dear to me in the world—my beautiful sister—is in agony, her world turned upside down and her hopes dashed. I thought you of all people would understand. You've lost your father and your best friend. I thought you might know how to show me the smallest kindness. Like the night we danced at the festival. But you couldn't even do that for me, could you?"

Seba didn't know what to say. Everything that had happened to him, from his father's kidnapping to Phillip's betrayal, and now the death of Thaddeus, was all wrong. To top it off, Xenia, the girl with all the answers, was suddenly asking him for help when he couldn't manage to help himself.

Xenia lowered her voice even more, as if she was afraid to say the next sentence. "You're so *mean*. It feels like you're plunging a blade into my aching heart and twisting it with all your might." She swallowed hard. "You've never seen me for who I am, Seba, and all I've ever done is try to show you. I know I'm not like my sister—but I'm my own person! I have feelings, hopes, and dreams just like everyone else. I don't deserve to be treated this way—by you or anyone else!"

She buried her face in her hands, still standing in front of him, and tried to hold back her sorrow.

Seba knew he was supposed to put his arms around her and console her. It would be the right thing to do, and it seemed to be what she needed. But today, his arms and legs simply wouldn't comply. Instead, he shook his head and turned away from Xenia, leaving her alone with her tears.

Seba's insides were roiling and he felt an urgent need to run as far away as his feet would take him. He looked up and saw Brother Tim, sitting some distance away on a stone bench with two pails of goat's milk at his feet. It was obvious that he had seen and heard the entire exchange. Seba walked over to him.

"God be with you, my friend. I believe you need the Lord's comfort now more than ever."

"Comfort?" Seba's hands were shaking, and he stomped his foot on the cobbled pathway. "Is that all you can say? God took away two of the best people I knew! First my father, and now Thaddeus."

Brother Tim opened his mouth to speak, but Seba interrupted.

"And don't tell me about my legacy in the *mastichochoria*—I hear it from my mother every day, but Phillip and the council in Sessera are just puppets for the Ottomans." Now that the volcano was erupting, Seba couldn't control it. He pointed back where Xenia had been standing. "And don't tell me you didn't see that—the girl who told everyone I stupidly fell into an Ottoman viper's lair, then followed me around for years trying to force me to marry her, just accused me of plunging a dagger into her heart. What else can go wrong with my life?"

Brother Tim exhaled loudly, the curly hairs in his mustache waving in the rush of air. "I know you are in pain, Sebastian. It is a difficult time for all of us. This is the hardest time for followers of the Lord to have faith—but that's exactly what He expects of us. God makes all things work together for our good."

"You really think this is for my good? You must be joking."

"Seba, the ways of God may be inscrutable, but He never for a second stops loving us."

"Like He loved Thaddeus? Remember those coffee grounds? I saw them myself, and they foretold good things for Thaddeus. Those coffee grounds were wrong! God abandoned Thaddeus when he was in need."

Brother Tim shook his head vigorously. "God never abandons us, Seba. *Never*. Don't let the form of the message or your own limitations distract you from the beautiful mystery of our Creator. Tell me, exactly what did you see that night in the square?"

"The grounds showed that Thaddeus would find love."

"What was the symbol?"

"A volcano."

"The volcano usually means that the person will *feel* love."

"That's what Phillip said."

"And do you think Thaddeus felt love?"

Seba knew where Brother Tim was going, but he wasn't ready to follow. "Yes, we all know he felt love for Demetria. But that volcano was wrong, because he never got to marry her."

"Feeling love does not always lead to marriage."

"You know what I mean."

"Yes, I do. You were adding *your* wishes to the symbols instead of taking God at His word. We do it all the time, putting God in a box that fits our expectations. But God is infinite love. His thoughts are much bigger than ours."

Seba may have lost this argument, but he had many other complaints to make. "God allowed Nikos to torment Thaddeus since we were little, and look what happened—it led to Thaddeus's death!"

Brother Tim stood up from the bench and put his hand

on Seba' shoulder. "We all know it was Thaddeus's choice to swim the channel. Let us not accuse someone of murder when there were two willing participants in this tragedy."

Seba hated that Brother Tim had an answer for everything, but he knew the monk wouldn't be able to defend the coffee grounds' final prediction.

"The last thing the grounds showed was that Thaddeus's fortunes were going to change. His family was one of the poorest in Sessera, so a change in fortunes meant that he was going to be freed from poverty."

"What was the symbol?"

"It was a wheel."

Brother Tim nodded. "The symbol of change."

"That's what Phillip said as well. Thaddeus deserved a change in fortune—he always worked so hard. The wheel should have foretold good news and an easier life for him, but instead it was death."

"The wheel also represents the circle of life, Seba. Tell me, where do you think Thaddeus is right now?"

Seba envisioned Thaddeus in heaven, in a beautiful garden beside a clear running stream, surrounded by angels. "He was the best person I knew. He has to be in heaven. What does that have to do with the wheel?"

"Everything, Sebastian. In showing the circle of life, the wheel could have represented Thaddeus crossing earth's threshold to the promised land."

Seba was flummoxed. "The coffee grounds knew that Thaddeus was going to die? How?"

Brother Tim leaned forward. "Never underestimate the power of the mysteries of God, Seba. We don't always know what is going to happen, but God has a much better idea than we do."

"Then I need to ask the coffee grounds why the

Ottomans are so evil. Thaddeus only wanted to provide for his brothers and sisters, to marry Demetria, and support a family of his own." Seba's voice caught in his throat. "And why did the Ottomans take my father away? He gave his best for them his whole life, and in return, they stole him from us."

Brother Tim said nothing. Seba's rage bubbled up and would not be quelled. "Why do we have to slave all day under the skinos trees without getting to enjoy the fruits of our labor? And why does Xenia hound me like I'm some kind of prey? And why has Nikos never been punished for Thaddeus's death? And why does Phillip hoard—"

Brother Tim's eyes went wide. "Hush, Seba! Not here," he whispered urgently. Brother Tim looked over his shoulder, but they were alone in the courtyard.

Seba continued in a whisper, "I can't stand it here. Everything is all wrong. You have to help me escape this prison. I need to find my father."

Brother Tim looked thoughtful. Then he turned in the direction of the refectory. "I promise you that we will talk about God's plan and purpose for your life, Sebastian. I think the time has come, and you need to hear it. But first, help me bring this milk to Brother Stephen. Then we can speak privately."

Seba was surprised that Brother Tim didn't try to argue with him. His mother would have argued that Seba's feelings were improper in some way, or that he wasn't grateful for what he had been given. The fact that Brother Tim accepted him at his word and allowed him to display his rage caused it to dissipate, if only a little bit.

They walked past the refectory and took the goat's milk to the kitchen, where several monks were preparing the midday meal. Seba and Brother Tim dumped the goat's milk into a large earthenware amphora.

"Ah, perfect! We were getting low on cheese," said the fat monk who was kneading bread dough. Seba could smell the mastiha mixing with the dough's yeast. Immediately Seba's thoughts fled to the storage tower, and he felt like he was choking. He coughed.

"Brother Timotheos, do we have a hungry visitor? Young man, would you like some mastic bread and cheese? I've certainly had my share, don't you know?" The fat monk patted his belly, which was bulbous and hung over his belt.

Brother Tim noticed the queasy look on Seba's face and answered for him. "That's very kind of you, Brother Stephen." He turned to Seba. "Let me warn you that there is no refusing Brother Stephen when he wants to feed a guest. Come, let's sit in the kitchen garden. I'll get the water, and we will talk."

Seba stared at Brother Stephen, whose hair and beard were mostly white with a few gray and black strands running throughout. It looked like a sea sponge was encircling his head and another was hanging from his chin.

"Are you—" Seba began, but was interrupted by Brother Stephen.

"Are you related to Vaios Georgelous? By God and Saint Peter, you certainly look like him."

Seba nodded the affirmative.

"The stories I could tell you about him when he was a boy. Troublemaker doesn't even do him justice! Oh, but he could sing and tell a story. How are you related?"

"I'm his grandson."

"And how is that comedian? I haven't seen him at the monastery for ages."

"He's just as you say, and he's still the best storyteller in Sessera."

"Brother Timotheos will tell you that I am the best storyteller of Nea Moni." Brother Stephen winked conspiratorially.

Brother Tim smiled. "We monks aren't given to boasting, but we are charged with telling the truth, and it is true that Brother Stephen is quite gifted—maybe even to rival your grandfather."

Seba nodded and believed that this jolly fat monk would probably have the men of Sessera laughing in the village square just like Papouli.

"You have your grandfather's good looks—do you have his jaunty singing voice? If so, you can join us for vespers."

Seba stared at the sea sponge in fear—Seba could sing, but he did not want to be on display at vespers.

"Brother Stephen, please give Sebastian a moment to breathe before you draft him into the choir. He's mourning the death of his dear friend Thaddeus—the young man who was tragically drowned not more than a week ago."

Brother Stephen's sea sponge beard looked contrite. "The Lord bless and keep you, Sebastian. I am sorry for your loss. I hope you can find comfort in the words of Psalm 34: *The Lord is near to the brokenhearted and saves the crushed in spirit.*"

"Thank you, Brother Stephen."

Seba followed Brother Tim into the kitchen garden, a walled enclosure filled with plantings of herbs, edible flowers, and citrus trees. The garden was surrounded by mosaics on every wall, and there was a small wooden table near the far end of the garden, in the shade. Birds chirped and sang, calling to one another and flitting among the tree branches, and a sweet breeze swept across the patio. A fountain gurgled happily, providing water for the birds. *This must be what the Garden of Eden was like,* Seba thought.

Seba felt the tightness in his chest release ever so slightly as Brother Tim explained the nature of God, hope, joy, and the importance of refraining from judgment of our brothers and sisters. Seba wasn't sure he believed or understood all that was said, but he couldn't deny that he felt a little lighter as he listened to Brother Tim's words.

Then Seba's eye caught sight of something that sent a frisson of electricity from his feet to his fingers.

The mosaic on the wall behind the fountain was of an ornate cross that almost looked like a ship's anchor with two dolphins wrapped around it, as if they were jumping out of the fountain.

Brother Tim followed Seba's gaze. "An especially popular symbol of early Christianity was a dolphin, or sometimes two, twisted around an anchor. This is a powerful message of the hope of eternal life. And the anchor—well, the anchor represents endurance, and the ability to persevere in difficult circumstances."

Seba was astonished. His father never told him that an anchor represented endurance. He also never expected to see dolphins inside Nea Moni.

"Seba, there are signs of hope everywhere, even in our humble kitchen garden."

Seba sat up a little taller. "My father always told me to watch the dolphins. He was obsessed with them."

Brother Tim leaned in and his face turned serious.

"God may be using these dolphins to show you a path that is different than the one you are currently on—one that comes with great personal risk."

"The path I'm on right now leads nowhere. I thought Phillip was an important man who protected us. But now I think he's just the Ottomans' number one slave, helping them to keep us in our place."

Brother Tim nodded, as if he knew about Phillip and his secret.

"He works for the people who took my father from me and from everything he loved. Phillip might as well have taken my father away from me himself. It's not fair—my father never did anything to hurt anyone! Why couldn't something bad happen to someone who deserved it, like Nikos or—"

Brother Tim spoke sharply. "Sebastian, do not curse Nikos. Anything that we curse, we set apart from God, and *nothing* can be set apart from God. We are all children of God. Some may hide the light better than others, but they are no less divine—and no less loved by our Creator." Brother Tim put his finger on Seba's breastbone. "This is where God resides in you. He will never mislead you. Your father knows this, both your earthly father and your Heavenly Father. God has been sending you signs all your life, to help you find your way."

"What kind of signs? The only thing He's been sending me is misery."

"Can't you think of something in your life that is not misery?" Seba could tell that Brother Tim was trying to help him, but he simply didn't understand. Then Brother Tim held his hand over his head and pointed to himself, a sheepish smile breaking out from his curly beard.

Just for a second, Seba's brain stopped its diatribe on misery, and he was able to hear the beating of his heart. "Oh, I see." Brother Tim had been a blessing in his life, someone who always tried to lift his spirits and teach him about the world. At least God hadn't taken Brother Tim away from him, so that was something.

"Remember that day when we learned about the clepsydra? Your face was beaming like I had never seen it before. You loved hearing about the mariners and how they could use the stars to navigate in clear weather and the clepsydra to navigate in poor weather. I had a brief vision of you on a ship, sailing west, that day, and it was as real to me as the water in this fountain."

Seba felt excitement rising in him—the same excitement he felt that day on the school's roof.

"What do you know of Smyrna?" Brother Tim still wore the sheepish smile from earlier.

"You mean the City of Silks? What about it?"

"I have told you about my brother, Stavros, haven't I?"

Seba vaguely remembered the conversation at the school, many years ago, when Brother Tim told him that he had a brother named Stavros. He nodded.

"Actually, I have two brothers and three sisters. They all live in Anatolia. My oldest brother, Stavros, owns a textile workshop in Smyrna. He's quite wealthy. He has many connections, trading his silks and velvets with merchants all over the world."

"Can he help me find my father?"

"It's possible. However, as I said, this venture may place you in danger. I'm not sure how Phillip would react, and there could be no indication that I had assisted you. You would have to leave the village in secret, and travel north in the dark until you reach Mount Aeon. Are you sure you have the courage?"

Seba could still feel his heart beating, and it was as if he was feeling it for the first time. "Of course."

"I have an idea that might take you to Smyrna, where my brother can help you."

"Nea Moni's sailing ship?"

"Possibly. The journey would be difficult. You would not be able to return to Chios. You would be leaving Sessera without permission—and if my assumptions are correct, you would be taking with you a secret that your uncle shared with you. One that you almost blurted out in the courtyard just now."

Did Brother Tim already know about the secret?

"He's not really my uncle," Seba said defiantly.

"Regardless, Seba, it is clear that Phillip and I disagree about what level of information should be shared with the people of Sessera. I think they should know the truth, but Phillip does not concur with my sentiment."

"I know! It's all wrong—those Ottoman vipers stockpile the mastiha, and the rest of us are scraping around in the dirt to find every last tear from the harvest. I knew we worked for the Ottomans, but I didn't know that our own council helped the slave drivers to keep us under control."

"And that has changed your mind about working for the council?"

"Absolutely—I could never work for them. Phillip and the rest are puppets of the Ottoman Empire. The same empire that took away my father and my future."

Brother Tim wagged his finger at Seba, correcting him for the first time today. "They cannot take away your future, Seba. It has been gifted to you by God. Remember the words of Jeremiah: *For I know the plans I have for you, declares the Lord, plans to prosper you and not to harm you, plans to give you hope and a future.*"

"And you're going to help me escape? So I can find my father and reclaim my legacy?"

"I believe the Lord intends me to do just that, Seba." Brother Tim leaned back in his chair. "Many years ago, when I was a young monk studying here at Nea Moni, Brother Stephen told us a story about the Israelites' liberation from slavery in Egypt, when the Lord worked through Moses to part the Red Sea." Seba remembered that story—he loved envisioning the line of Israelites escaping captivity via the dry sea floor, flanked on either side by walls of water many fathoms high. "In Brother Stephen's version of Exodus, the dolphins of the Red Sea were waiting for the Israelites, jumping out and back through the walls of water, showing God's people the way to freedom with their happy chirps and clicks, and clapping congratulations with their flat tails splashing the waves."

Seba had never heard that version of the story before, but as soon as the words left Brother Tim's mouth, Seba knew it was true. Hope welled up from deep inside him. As Brother Tim leaned further back in his chair, Seba looked past the monk's unruly hair to the mosaic beyond him. What he saw was two dolphins; they seemed to be in motion, leaping from the confines of the fountain.

20 PHILLIP

On the long journey back from Nea Moni, the world seemed brighter and the colors of the Chian landscape appeared more vivid than Seba remembered. The sun was setting as they neared Sessera, an enormous pulsing orb of burnt orange dipping between Mount Phaneros and Mount Aeon. The willow warblers were singing their twilight ballads, and the first butterflies of spring had appeared, their blue and gold wings outlined in velvet black.

Brother Tim's plan was dangerous, but to Seba it was far more palatable than being an Ottoman slave. He had a short time to prepare, and then he would be gone.

"I see that your prayers at Nea Moni have given you solace, Sebastian. You look happier than I've seen you in years." Mama took Seba's hand in hers, something she hadn't done since he was a young boy. "Nea Moni is a thin place, as my mother used to say—a place where the veil between heaven and earth nearly disappears, as does the distance between God and man. I felt it, too."

Seba had heard the concept of "thin places" before—those locations where God came so close that His presence was palpable. Nea Moni felt like such a place, but Seba now believed that in addition to predetermined thin places, there were also people, like Brother Tim, who could pull back the veil and collapse the distance between heaven and earth, no matter where they were.

"Tell me, Sebastian, did Brother Tim share any scripture with you that has helped to ease your pain?"

Seba nodded. Everything Brother Tim said eased his pain and gave him hope.

"Tell me."

Seba quoted Isaiah 43:19: "*See, I am doing a new thing! Now it springs up; do you not perceive it? I am making a way in the wilderness and streams in the wasteland.*"

Mama squeezed Seba's hand. "The prophet Isaiah brought a promise of salvation to people who thought the Lord had forsaken them. I know these times have been difficult for you. You've lost your father and your best friend at such a young age, but I am pleased that you have found hope in the words of the Lord."

Seba was silent. The words of Isaiah meant one thing to his mother, but something entirely different to him. He felt a pang of guilt as he thought of leaving her behind. When he found his father, he would come back for her.

Seba and Agnete returned just as the guards were closing the gates to the village. One of the guards said to Seba, "Your uncle has requested your presence at his home immediately."

The guards didn't usually speak to the villagers; they were Ottomans, and lived apart from the villagers when not guarding the gates. Seba guessed it must be something important. He was not looking forward to seeing Phillip.

They had spoken only a few words to each other since the incident at the storage tower.

"Go on, Sebastian. I need to rest from our trip—I'll make a fire in the hearth and be asleep before long. Give my regards to your Uncle Phillip."

Seba wondered if Phillip had heard of Brother Tim's plan. He couldn't have, could he? Seba and his mother had just arrived in Sessera, and Brother Tim was still at Nea Moni. There was no way that he could have been discovered.

When Seba arrived at Phillip's house, he found the dining table full of delicious food. A feast fit for a king—or for the chief Ottoman slave of Sessera: roasted lamb stuffed with artichoke hearts, feta, rosemary, oregano, sun-dried tomatoes, and olive oil. There were several olivewood bowls filled with *spanakorizo*, a blissful combination of rice and spinach, slowly simmered over the fire for hours until it became a creamy and delicious ragout. It was generously seasoned with olive oil, lemon juice, leeks, chickpeas, and large bunches of basil and thyme.

Papouli was sitting at the table with Phillip, whistling his favorite *tripatos* tune. His feet were tapping under the table and he lifted them to click his heels together at the end. Seba loved seeing Papouli like this, but it was bittersweet. What would he do without his beloved grandfather?

"My grandson, just back from the sacred ground of Nea Moni. My, but you look like your father today!"

"Thank you, Papouli."

"Phillip is getting some wine from his cellar. He'll join us in a moment. Have I told you how very proud I am of you, Seba? You will do great things, and everyone will know the name Krizomatis when you make your mark on this world!"

He stood and gave Seba a big bear hug. Seba thought of all the wonderful times they had together, playing music and telling stories, and felt his throat constrict. He gulped down the emotion that was welling up, but hugged his grandfather as if he might never see him again.

Phillip walked into the dining area holding two bottles of wine.

"My two favorite people, Vaios and Sebastian!"

"God is good, my friend, God is good. How could He not be, when He sent me this precious grandson?"

"Well said, Vaios. And Sebastian, you have just come from Nea Moni? How is our favorite monk, Brother Tim?"

"He's well. Also, Brother Stephen sends his regards."

"Brother Stephen! He helped Vaios save my life, or so I've been told."

Papouli laughed. "How is my old friend? He must be getting up in age. Is he doing well?"

"His hair is completely white, but he's full of life. Actually, he reminds me of you—just much fatter."

Phillip laughed. "Your *papou* and I, we just never could gain the weight. Not like my dear departed apprentice, Thaddeus, who was made of muscle. Everything he ate went straight to his biceps, that beautiful boy."

Seba frowned. It was too soon to be commenting on his friend. It felt wrong. Like so many things that he had learned about Phillip in the last few months. Wrong.

Papouli laughed. "I don't know what you're talking about, Phillip—this is pure muscle right here, and I'm happy to test your skinny bones by arm-wrestling, if you dare."

"You are a force to be reckoned with, my friend, and I wouldn't like to compete with you for who tells the best story, or for who has the strongest biceps. I'll stick to leading and negotiating. That seems to be my strength these days."

Seba used all his willpower not to roll his eyes. Then Nikos strolled into the dining area and Seba had an excuse for his eyeroll.

"And you're very good at leading and negotiating, Phillip. This village couldn't survive without you."

Seba bristled. He couldn't stand to be in the same room with Nikos, especially if the latter was heaping praise on the Ottomans' number one co-conspirator.

Papouli stood and reached for the wine bottles in Phillip's hand. "*Kalispera*, Nikos. I'm afraid we cannot speak of business yet this evening. First, we must drink this wine and enjoy our delicious meal—which will taste even better when you hear the news I have to share!"

"Vaios, I invited you and my apprentices to dinner to discuss council business. I need advice based on your years of wisdom as well as input from fresh young minds regarding Sessera's ahdname with the Ottomans."

"That can wait. Lord knows the Ottomans aren't going anywhere. This is more important—it's about love! The heart of a Greek man beats strong in here." He thumped his chest. "As Plato said, *Love is the joy of the good, the wonder of the wise, the amazement of the gods.*"

Phillip could never say no to his best friend. "What do you have to tell us about love, *filo mou*?" Phillip reached into his large wooden cabinet and his hand emerged with four green blown-glass goblets. No one else in the village was wealthy enough to drink from glass like this, and the blood began to race behind Seba's temples. What other benefits did Phillip enjoy for being the Ottoman's number one pawn?

"I'm getting married."

Seba's head swiveled around. "What?"

As Phillip removed the cork and poured the local retsina into Seba's glass, Papouli said, "Barbara Lampros, who is soon to be Mrs. Vaios Georgelous, has accepted my offer of marriage."

He told the story of their courtship; Seba was genuinely happy for him, but also sad, because he knew he would not be attending the wedding.

Several glasses of wine later, Papouli was channeling Dionysus as if he were entertaining the Olympians long into the night. In some ways, Seba never wanted this night to end. Papouli and Phillip could have been two schoolboys shooting marbles in the square, for all of their mirth. They never got to the business of the day; those schoolboys too lost in their merrymaking.

Then Seba remembered what was stored in the central tower and realized that this night was just a dream. The reality was slavery; and just like Moses, he would be escaping with the help of God.

Nikos was laughing and joking with the older men, joining in their revelry. Seba slipped out unnoticed and went to the only place in the village where he felt like himself: the roof.

It was Phillip's roof, much larger than his own and adjacent to the village's outside wall. Could he really go through with Brother Tim's plan? Phillip gave no indication of being suspicious, and Seba couldn't live like a donkey for another day. The spring breeze blowing from the Aegean down through the valley reminded Seba of what was waiting for him: the sea.

Seba hoped he had the courage to follow through with the arrangement. As he breathed in the scent of orchids and sage wafting up from the valley to the rooftops of Sessera, he remembered everything that brought him to this moment:

His father taken by the Ottomans.

His best friend betrayed and led to his death by Nikos.

His mother, pushing him to make a name for himself with the mastic council.

Xenia, planning his life without his consent.

And now, the final straw, the man he trusted to keep them all safe, was simply a hand-puppet for the Ottoman Empire. He had believed Phillip on Mount Phaneros when he said the Greeks in the mastic villages were on a level playing field with the Ottomans. They had an ahdname—something that no other Greeks on Chios or any other island could boast. Special privileges, small allotments of mastiha, lower taxes, and the protection of the guards. All of these were provided in exchange for the villagers' prowess with skinos trees.

But it was all a sham. Phillip and the villagers had no real power. The sultan set the prices, and apparently the sultan determined how much mastiha could be released to the world. The scarcer the commodity, the higher the price the sultan could extract from buyers across the globe. That there were hundreds of pounds of mastiha in the storage tower of Sessera—all of which could have been sold by the villagers to improve their circumstances and actually put them on an equal footing with the Ottomans—was a crime; a crime of which Phillip was not only aware, but a willing participant. Did the other members of the council know? They must. They hid the mastiha, guarding it with a cache of weapons that could annihilate every mastic village on Chios in a matter of hours. Seba pounded the rooftop's stone chimney with his fist.

If Thaddeus's family had been able to sell just a handful of the tower's tears at the port of Chora, or even to some of the merchants who visited the shipyard, he would not have taken Nikos's dare. Thaddeus would still be alive.

They were all slaves, every single one of them, regardless of their legacy and their expertise with the translucent drops of resin from the skinos trees.

He said out loud, though no one was there, "God help me." It became a mantra—so strong and solid that there was no question that the promise he made to himself would be fulfilled.

After the moon was high and small in the sky, Seba stood up, ran across the rooftops of Sessera for what would be the last time, and arrived at his own home. Mama had washed and hung his clothes on a rope across their roof, making it easy for him to take them. He knew Mama was a light sleeper, so he took care not to make a sound when he climbed down into the living area. He could hear her breathing, deep and slow. She really was exhausted from their long walk from the sacred mountain. He tiptoed over to the place where he had hidden the tiny pouch of mastiha Phillip had given him. He took a few tears from the pouch and stuffed them into his trousers pockets, along with the coin he had discovered in the Saint Vasilios cake and the ring he had stolen from the *Dame*. Then he tiptoed over to Papouli's bed and placed the pouch under the pillow. That would be his wedding present for Papouli and Mrs. Lampros. They deserved it.

Seba realized that he might never again see his grandfather tapping his toes or whistling a *tripatos*. He might never hear the familiar story of Socrates's three rules, or taste Mrs. Lampros's orange-cured olive bread. He might never sing with Papouli or dance with Mama again. It was the Ottomans' fault: If they hadn't captured his father, Seba would not have to leave the rest of his family to go find him.

He squeezed his eyelids shut and tried to put the visions of Papouli, Mrs. Lampros, and his mother out of his mind.

Silently, he climbed down to the ground floor and said goodbye to Myra and Sheba, patting them between their little horns and giving them each a kiss. Artemis, as keen as ever, must have known that Seba was leaving; she appeared in the open window next to the goats' pen and began weaving between Seba's legs as he said goodbye to the donkey, Matilde. Artemis was meowing loudly, expressing her displeasure, protesting as if she knew the exact details of Brother Tim's plan.

"Shhh, you're going to get me in trouble." He picked her up and scratched under her chin and neck while she purred, temporarily mollified. He carried her up the steps to the hearth, stroking her silky fur. His mother was sleeping peacefully. What would she do when she woke up and found out that her only son was gone? His chest began to tighten.

"Bye, Mama," Seba whispered, his voice catching.

"I love you, Sebastian," Mama replied.

Seba froze. Was his plan thwarted before it began?

Then Mama turned over and Seba heaved a sigh of relief. She had been dreaming. In that moment, Seba understood that despite her prickly exterior, his mother loved him. His throat constricted as he realized how much he would miss her.

Artemis followed Seba up the stairs to the roof and continued to meow, pacing between his legs as he grabbed two shirts and a pair of trousers from the line and put them on over his clothes.

"Bye, girl. I hope you find someone to share your catches with." Then a large insect caught Artemis's eye, and she was off, leaping gracefully across the rooftops. Seba smiled sadly.

He walked over the rooftops back to Phillip's house. It was late; no one was about in the village. Phillip's house was on the perimeter of the village, and its outside wall was the village wall. Unlike Seba's house and some of the other smaller ones that were interior dwellings, Uncle Phillip's house was enormous, taking up a large area on the north side of the village. Because of its location, Phillip's house was the best place to make an exit; the guards never expected any activity around the council leader's home. Phillip made sure of that.

From Phillip's rooftop on the edge of the village, Seba could see the watchtower in the center of the village. There was no movement. Seba guessed that the guards were probably sleeping after all those extra shifts they worked while trying to prevent further spoilage of the precious mastiha. All for the sultan.

Phillip could take his Ottoman privileges and shove them up his ass, Seba thought. He was a donkey and a slave, and Seba had decided he would have none of it.

He put one leg over the outer wall, prepared to jump from imprisonment to freedom, and heard a voice.

Seba looked back toward the door to the roof and saw Nikos's head appear through the door leading to the roof. "Going somewhere?"

Seba froze, one leg still hanging on the outside of the wall.

"Yes, and you're not going to stop me."

"Who said I wanted to stop you?"

Seba pulled his leg in and squatted down, so as not to be seen by the guards. They both hunched against the outer wall, in a face off. Seba wondered what game Nikos was playing this time, mimicking his actions.

"Then what are you doing here, Nikos? Shouldn't you be kissing Phillip's ass right now?"

"I know you think I killed Thaddeus, Seba." His words were a bit slurred. Phillip must have plied him with more retsina than he was used to. Then Seba noticed a half-full bottle of retsina in his hand. "You don't have to say anything, I just wanted to let you know that I haven't been able to sleep since the day he died. Everyone in the village hates me, except maybe Phillip, and he probably only appreciates the fact that I have a quick mind so he can use me to scheme against the Ottomans."

Seba held his breath. This must be a ploy to delay him. Had Nikos already called the guards? Was he going to reveal Seba's plans and have him sent to jail for abandoning the village? Seba's brain raced to think of a way out.

"You probably don't believe this, but I miss him, too. I never wanted him to die. I just liked to push him—and to tell you the truth, I think he liked being pushed."

"No, he didn't. He thought your father was responsible for his father's accident."

"What? That's not true!"

"I don't know whether it's true or not, but I know that's why he could never back down from your taunts."

"Seba, I'm sorry. I don't want to fight with you. My father had nothing to do with that accident. And I truly wish I had never dared Thaddeus to swim the channel."

Seba had an idea. "Fine. Give me some of that wine." Nikos raised his eyebrows and handed over the bottle. Seba pretended to take a long draught, so long that Nikos said, "Hey, that's mine!"

Seba handed it back to him and Nikos took a long draught himself as Seba said, "You may regret your actions now, but it can't be undone. There's nothing we can do to bring Thaddeus back." He stretched out his hand toward the bottle. As Nikos handed it to him, there was only a finger's worth of wine left. Seba pretended to drink again.

Nikos's shoulders sagged, and he slumped down on the roof as Seba handed him the bottle.

"I know ish all m' fault. Sometimes I wish th' Lord wou' punsh me." Nikos's voice cracked with real emotion, and his slurring made his sentences almost unintelligible.

Seba said, "The best thing for you to do tonight is drown your sorrows."

Nikos was still holding the wine bottle, but he hadn't taken the last drink. "Where y' gon?"

"None of your business."

Nikos's mouth was gaping open, and a bit of saliva dripped from the side of his lower lip. He leaned his head back against the outer wall.

"Ish a secret? Phillip?"

"Maybe. Look, Nikos, I don't trust you, and I'm not going to tell you anything. I think it's time for you to step up and become Phillip's special apprentice here in Sessera."

Nikos closed his gaping mouth, stunned. He looked like he had hoped for something like this, but he also was very drunk. He finished the retsina that was left in the bottle and let it fall from his slack fingers.

"I dun d'serve it."

Seba thought of Phillip and his pact with the Ottomans.

"I think you do."

Nikos was on the verge of passing out, but he seemed heartened by Seba's apparent forgiveness.

"Thank you, Seba. I won' mesh up dis tum."

"Go to sleep, Nikos. You'll need all your energy to be Phillip's special apprentice."

"Mm-hmmm." Nikos eyes rolled back in their sockets

and he passed out. He wouldn't be giving Seba any problems tonight.

Seba looked up at the eastern horizon and saw the constellation of Astraea, with her scales of justice.

Seba knew in that moment that Jeremiah 29:11 might apply to Nikos as well. Maybe the Lord was going to give Nikos the opportunity to redeem himself—once he sobered up.

Seba threw his leg over the wall again and looked over the edge. It was three stories down, but he didn't care. He found a few footholds where the rainwater drained into the village cisterns, but it was still a long way up. He knew from the many times he had jumped the ravines by the mastic groves that the best way to land was to bend his knees as soon as his feet hit the ground, and roll until his momentum ceased. He held his hand over his heart and jumped.

He hit the ground and his knees buckled. He felt a twinge in his ankle, as if he had not landed solidly, but he made it. Running faster than he thought possible, he took the road toward the shipyard. It was the only road he had traveled that had ever made him really happy.

Running east, he could only hear the heaving of his own lungs. The birds were silent this time of night. As each foot struck the ground, a new mantra popped into his head, matching the rhythm of his steps: *This better work.* Was he crazy? Maybe so; but the tiniest sliver of hope was growing inside him, just as the distance from his village grew. He was taking action of his own choice for the first time in his young life. That fact, joined by the unexpected assistance of a former enemy, buoyed his legs and his spirits. He felt like Hermes, the god of roads, travel, and luck. He knew that he would not be bothered by robbers, wild animals, or Ottoman guards. He had escaped his prison; nothing would stop him.

Just as Brother Tim had instructed, he turned north when he reached the coast. What felt like an eternity later, when the pale moon had moved westward in the sky, he spied the promontory where Thaddeus had begun his deadly swim. In the magic of the moonlight, Seba expected Thaddeus to miraculously appear like Jesus at the transfiguration, with words of hope and direction. It was a crazy thought, but the adrenaline was flooding Seba's brain, and he could no longer remember exactly what Brother Tim had told him.

The moon gave the impression of daylight over the water. Seba could see the tide moving and feel the night air across his face. Just as on the day of Thaddeus's funeral, Seba whispered, "Thaddeus, what do you have to tell me?"

Just then someone grabbed him from behind and covered his mouth. Seba struggled, thinking that this was where Thaddeus had drowned and this was where he would be murdered by robbers.

Then he noticed that the hands were sweaty and smelled like mastiha, chickens, and incense. He knew those hands. He stopped struggling and turned.

Brother Tim held his finger up to his lips. Seba knew not to speak. The wind carried up on this promontory, and raiders could hear the shuffle of a sandal on dirt from miles away.

"Brother Tim! You're here. Are we in the right place?"

"Led by the Holy Spirit, yes."

"Where is the ship?"

Brother Tim shook his head. "First, let me ask you a question. If for some reason there is no ship, do you still want to leave? I told you this venture would be a great personal risk for you. If things don't work out as planned, will you return to Sessera?"

"Never. And now that I'm leaving Phillip, carrying his secret with me, I can't turn back. If he finds me, he'll have me handed over to the Ottomans."

Brother Tim's unruly beard partially obscured his grim expression. "I'm afraid you're right, Seba. When you told me about the cache of mastiha, I knew that your life was taking a dangerous turn."

"More dangerous than this?" Seba looked at the waves crashing on the rocks below. What happened to Brother Tim's ship? What if Phillip already knew that he had run away? Were the guards gathering their weapons to come after him as they spoke?

"Yes. Listen carefully, because what I am about to say will shake you to your core."

Seba had always trusted Brother Tim, the smartest person he knew. He nodded in agreement.

"Seba, you are going to have to swim the channel tonight."

Seba jumped back, terrified. A spine-chilling vision of Thaddeus, cut and bleeding in the middle of the Strait of Chios, appeared in his mind.

"What? Are you crazy? No one has ever made it across the channel, and Thaddeus, the strongest boy in the village just died trying! Right here in this very spot!" Seba stomped his foot in anger. "You said you felt bad for him, and maybe he shouldn't have done it. And now you want me to do the same thing?"

"Yes, I do. You are right about Thaddeus—I thought he shouldn't have tried to come back across right away. I think he would have made it back if he had waited long enough to regain his strength." Brother Tim pointed toward the water, his arm shaking with excitement. "It was Thaddeus who showed me that it could be done."

Seba thought Brother Tim might be losing his mind. "What are you talking about?"

Brother Tim continued to stretch his arm out toward the water, which was visible in the glinting moonlight. "Thaddeus swam the channel—and probably as fast as a boat could have made it."

"But he died!"

Brother Tim grabbed Seba's shoulders as they both kneeled behind a rock. His hands were still shaking with emotion. "Seba, I know it was a tragedy, but Thaddeus's downfall was not the swim across the Strait of Chios. It was his decision to swim back before he had regained his strength. Do you remember what Xenia said?"

Seba remembered Xenia's description. She did say that Thaddeus was thrilled with his accomplishment of swimming the channel. Then something seemed to snap, and he went crazy. However, Seba was not Thaddeus and he was still confused. "I thought you had a ship, and it was going to take me to my father!"

"I don't have access to the ship right now, Seba."

"Then why did you tell me to leave today? Couldn't we have waited for the ship?"

"I'm sorry, but circumstances have changed. The English merchants are involved in an altercation with the Ottomans, and my brothers at Nea Moni are attempting to keep the peace. The ship will not be back to Chios for some time. There is no other way. You'll have to swim."

Seba wanted to scream. Brother Tim had promised to get him to Anatolia, but it seemed like he was telling him to commit suicide.

"If you're afraid to swim, you could go and live with Brother Stephen and the monks at Nea Moni. But in light of Phillip's secret, I'm not sure that the monks could keep you safe there either."

Seba balled up his fists and pressed them to his forehead. "I thought I was supposed to find my father. I thought you were helping me."

"Seba, listen to me. I am helping you—and Thaddeus was helping you, by showing you the way. He made it across! It was his anger that betrayed him and caused him to jump back in the water too soon."

The moon cast a silvery glow on Brother Tim's face; his eyes were shimmering with emotion. "Do you remember our conversation about the Holy Spirit? And Brother Stephen's recounting of Exodus, complete with dolphins assisting the Israelites' escape from slavery? Well, I think Our Heavenly Father has been prompting me to assist you in your search for your earthly father."

"You call this help?" Seba was disgusted. He had put his trust in Brother Tim, and all it got him was to the place where Thaddeus died.

"I understand your frustration. I'm frustrated too. But what do you remember most about that day at Nea Moni?"

"The dolphins in the fountain."

"Exactly! Ever since our conversation at school, about the clepsydra, water, and the sea, the Holy Spirit has been showing me dolphins everywhere I go. I couldn't figure out the connection, but every time I saw you, the Holy Spirit showed me dolphins. Seba and dolphins, Seba and dolphins. It didn't make sense because you were Phillip's apprentice, and he doesn't have anything to do with dolphins. So I prayed for guidance and waited for God to reveal the message in His time. He revealed it to me in the garden at Nea Moni. You were grieving the death of your friend—the same friend who showed us that swimming the channel was possible. I think you are supposed to swim the channel. It is your destiny."

Seba remembered the sun glinting off the dolphins in the gurgling fountain, the smell of Brother Stephen's mastiha bread, and Brother Tim's offer of hope.

"It was my father who first told me to watch the dolphins. We used to see them playing out in the sea, across from the shipyard. They were so free and happy."

"Yes. They're a symbol of Christianity, of the hope that Jesus brings."

Seba considered Brother Tim's words, and thought of his father. "Papa told me the dolphins were so smart that they helped recover a net for a fisherman who had lost it in the sea. He said they showed compassion to humans. Do you think they will help me?"

"Yes, Seba. I truly believe you were meant to swim the Strait of Chios."

"How can you be sure?"

"I've watched you, Seba. You come alive when you speak about the sea. It's in your blood, passed down to you from your father. He had the same look in his eyes when he spoke of the ocean. I didn't know him well, but we both shared a love of science, and often sat on these very rocks overlooking the Aegean, talking about the wind and tides. I saw that same look when you were at Nea Moni, looking out over the monks' quarters, mesmerized by the movement of the water."

Seba shivered, imagining the shocking cold water enveloping him. "If I do manage to make it across, then what will I do?"

Brother Tim pulled a bag from beneath his robes and held it up in the moonlight. "This pack is leather, and I have a glass jar of wool grease. I didn't want to open it until I was sure you were coming, because it smells awful." He opened the jar and the stench of putrid wool grease overtook them both. Brother Tim dipped his fingers into the jar and slathered the wool grease over the outside of the pack with both hands. He opened the flap and Seba peered into the bag.

Brother Tim pushed his glasses up with the back of his grease-covered hand. "There are coins in here for food and lodging. Not many, or it will be too heavy for your swim." He held up a leather envelope and took out a folded piece of paper. Seba had only ever seen paper at the monastery. He knew it was valuable.

"You must go to the port city of Smyrna and find my brother Stavros. This is a letter of introduction. Stavros can help you. I don't know if he knows where you father is, but in this letter I've asked him to help you as a favor to me."

"But I don't even know the way to Smyrna. This is crazy. How long will it take? What will I do?"

"Seba, we don't have much time. I'm must return to Nea Moni before sunrise. And if Phillip finds out you've run away, there could be guards on the road looking for you this very minute. I don't even know if the guards in the watchtower can see our movements from here. It's possible that we've already been spotted."

Seba instinctively crouched lower behind the big rock. Brother Tim handed him a pair of canvas trousers. "There are coins sewn into the lining of these trousers as well." He rubbed the rest of the disgusting wool grease on the carrying strap of the leather pack and handed the bag to Seba. "Wear this on your back, under your shirt, and protect this letter at all costs."

Seba changed into the trousers that Brother Tim had given him, and Brother Tim began to tear up Seba's old trousers. He chuckled. "Brother Stephen will love these new dishcloths I've brought him."

Seba took the pack and looked down at the water, his stomach and his head churning. His whole body buzzed with electricity. "Do you really think I'm meant to do this?"

"Seba, listen to your heart, and you tell me."

Seba didn't expect that answer, but he could tell from the excitement rising within him that Brother Tim was right. It was his destiny to go east. He would swim.

Brother Tim hugged him and made the sign of the cross on Seba's forehead. "Godspeed, and may the grace of our Lord and Savior be with you."

21 THE SWIM

If anyone had been watching that chilly May evening, they would have seen a boy—really, a young man—with thick dark hair and eyes the color of a turbulent winter sea standing at the precipice of a life-changing event. They would not have known he was declining one of the most prestigious commissions a young man could be granted on Chios, in exchange for an icy battle against Poseidon himself. How could they know that this was the only way to escape the deadly Ottoman vipers?

Seba had been an excellent swimmer when he was a young boy. On the rare days when the villagers of Sessera had free time to enjoy frolicking in the sea, Seba would swim for hours, ducking in and out of the dark blue waves, diving for shells, and feeling the tickle of tiny fish on his feet. He would not leave the water on his own accord, so it was left to Mama to drag him onto dry land while he kicked and screamed. Unfortunately, when the Ottomans stole his father That Day, they also stole Seba's confidence in the water. He had almost drowned after being thrown overboard, and probably would have sunk to the bottom of the sea if Papa's friend Mesich had not been there to pluck him from the water. As he stood atop Mount Aeon, Seba tried to push that thought from his mind. He also tried to push away the vision of his friend Thaddeus being drawn to his death by the current. Seba knew his Greek ancestors were the best sailors on earth, but very few inhabitants of Chios attempted this narrow chute with their boats, much less with their arms and legs. As Papouli often said, it was a fool's gambit, and only an idiot would attempt such a swim. *Either that or someone desperate, with nothing to lose,* Seba thought to himself.

His arms and chest were bare; he had stuffed two shirts into the smelly wool-greased leather pack slung across his shoulder. He wore canvas trousers with coins sewn into the linings of his pockets, a gift from Brother Tim. He carefully picked his way down through the uneven rocks, then looked back at Brother Tim and waved goodbye. Brother Tim was still crouched behind a boulder, hidden from the guards of the mastic villages, just in case they were awake and watching for enemies to attack by sea.

Seba slowly stepped into the churning water. It was freezing. Just for a second he considered turning around, but the thought of becoming another puppet for the empire gave him enough energy to propel himself forward. He took a deep breath, and thought of Thaddeus. "I'll do this for both of us, my friend," he said aloud, and he did something he had never done outside of church: he made the sign of the cross, as he had seen Mama do every day of her life. This time, it felt right. If ever he needed to feel the presence of God in his life, it was at this moment.

He submerged his whole body; the water was biting

cold. All those days that Mama had pulled him from the water when he was just a boy had come in the heat of summer. Seba had only swum in the Aegean Sea when the sun was strong and hot. The sun now was still below the horizon and it was not yet summer. In his memories of swimming with his father as a child, the water felt refreshing. This time, the water was a shock, as frigid as if he were bathing in a snowstorm.

To keep warm, he started off strong, arms and legs slicing through the water like a sharp knife at butchering time. He advanced quickly, but the water got even colder as he progressed. He was approaching a deeper part of the channel now, and the waves were pushing him southward. Xenia had said that Thaddeus was pulled northward by the current—and now Seba was terrified. Why was the current pulling him in a different direction? He wished he had remembered more of what his father had taught him about the winds and tides.

He felt the tugging of an undercurrent and kicked even harder. Didn't Papouli tell him never to struggle with Poseidon? And where were the dolphins? For all of Brother Tim's encouragement, he thought he'd at least see one dolphin as he set out across the sea. This was much more difficult than he imagined. He was exerting all his energy just to move forward by inches. The undercurrent grabbed him and slowly pushed him toward the jagged cluster of rocks jutting up near the center of the channel. The moonset was near, and a faint change in the eastern sky lightened the darkness ever so slightly. As the dawn approached, the wind over the open water picked up.

Seba hadn't looked up all this time, but he thought he heard the sound of shouting coming from the north; as he turned his head to breathe between strokes, he saw an

Ottoman merchant ship passing to the north, maybe on its way to the port of Chora. The wake that would be coming in Seba's direction was going to thrust him into the strongest part of the current. Damn those Ottomans! If any other ships were nearby, Seba would be plucked out of the water like a prized fish and handed over to the sultan as a slave. He would not survive that ordeal. Why was there a ship out in the sea so early anyway?

Seba ducked under the water and held his breath for so long that blackness invaded his vision. Sputtering, he came up for air, even farther from his intended line, too dazed to fight the strengthening wind and tide. He struggled to catch his breath, unable to continue the swim. Fear began to grip him—fear of failure, fear of the cold water, fear of being torn to pieces by whatever creatures lurked in the deepest parts of these waters. He started to imagine all of the monsters of Poseidon that Papouli had cataloged for him since he was a child. Why did he have to think about them now? As the frigid water stung his arms and legs, he couldn't help but envision the Ketea, the serpent-like sea monsters with long rows of sharp teeth. Would Poseidon send them to punish Seba for attempting to conquer his watery domain?

Seba knew he had to stop thinking this way or he would not succeed. He flipped onto his back, chest heaving, kicking against the pull of the water with his muscular legs and trying to quiet his mind. His brain was telling him that he should have reconsidered the opportunity of a secure life in the village. What he was attempting was an adventure fit only for the ancient Greeks of Papouli's stories. What made him think he could succeed? He was just a boy from Chios who no longer had a future there or a father who could help him fulfill his legacy. His emotions swung wildly from feeling sorry for himself to feeling angry for thinking these defeating thoughts. He made a fist and stabbed at the water. *No, I won't go back!*

In a rage, he twisted over, put his face in the water, and started kicking with a vengeance. He kept his head down and began to make progress again. It seemed like hours, and given the tide, it may have been an hour, but Seba finally reached the submerged limestone of the tiny unnamed island that sprung up from the Strait of Chios's midsection. It was treacherous, with sharp rocks spiking up out of the water, and even sharper rocks hidden just below the surface. Seba tried to defend himself from the force of the current smashing him against the saw-toothed mass of granite and limestone. As he neared the rocks, he swiveled around to put his feet in front of him, and swimming backward he attempted to slow the thrashing. This didn't dampen the force of the sea against the rocks, but it did protect his head, so that it was his feet and legs that were shaved and scraped against the sharp rocks instead of his skull. Each surge of the tide that catapulted him against the knife-like rocks felt like the heavy slash of a many-headed monster. Bloody, bruised, and exhausted after being tossed about like a broken seashell, Seba gave one last thrust and was able to wrap his arms around a rock.

Finding strength that he didn't know he had, he pulled himself out of the water. Heart pounding out of his chest, he slowly crawled over the jagged rocks to a dry spot, where he attempted to catch his breath. The salt water pricked the bloody scrapes that covered his body; he felt as if he was under attack by a hive of angry bees. His eyes were burning from the salt water. He began to stagger eastward across the tiny island.

Seba knew from Xenia's story that Thaddeus had easily made it this far, but the most difficult part of the swim awaited. He was tired; the salt water stung his open skin. He kept blinking, trying to wipe the salt out of his eyes with the back of his hand. He thought of Brother Tim, who did the same with his spectacles. Was Brother Tim watching over him? He could use all the help he could get. Seba looked back to see if Brother Tim was still there. He was gone, probably on his way back to Nea Moni. Seba was all alone with the sea.

Seba slowly and gingerly climbed by hands and feet like a crab as the wind whipped across his shivering body. He looked back and saw that he was leaving drops of blood in his wake. He thought to himself, *I beat you, Scylla,* as if the island were the many-headed hungry monster Odysseus faced. When Seba reached the eastern edge of the little island, he looked at the shore of Anatolia. It still seemed impossibly far away.

He didn't want to get in the cold water again, but he had no choice. He had already come this far, already suffered so much pain. He couldn't go back now. He had nowhere to go anyway. For all he knew, there were Ottoman guards on their way to his home to arrest him right now.

Seba dove in again; the water was even more shockingly cold than before, because he was already trembling from the freezing water and the wind was blowing more strongly, as it often did when daybreak arrived. It was at least four more miles to the Anatolian coast, and that was if Seba remained on course, unhindered by the current. Why was the water so much colder now? It felt like the angry hive of bees stinging him was made of ice. He was afraid his limbs would go numb, but he kept swimming, repeating "συνεχίστε να κολυμπάτε, συνεχίστε να κολυμπάτε." *Keep swimming. Keep swimming.* The sounds became nonsense in his head. He couldn't feel his arms.

The current was stronger on the eastern side of Scylla; his head and lungs both felt as if they would burst as he fought the pull of the flow. The tide began to suck him away from the coast, southward into the wide Aegean Sea. Unlike Çeşme to the north, there were no cities or towns on the south coast of Anatolia here. If the current pulled him southward, there would be no chance of Seba being pushed onto a southern shore. Instead, he would be left all alone in the Aegean with no land in sight. Seba's limbs were leaden weight and his head was a thick fog, so much so that he could no longer remember why he was swimming.

He opened his eyes and saw his father at the bottom of the sea, covered in seaweed, hammering away at the hull of a ship with a group of other men, like an undersea shipyard chain gang. Seba stopped kicking. His father saw him and began gesturing wildly and shouting at him to keep moving. He called to his father to follow him and kicked his legs with strength he didn't know he had. Seba looked again; the chain gang was cheering him on. He called for everyone to follow him to the coast. He would save them all!

A loud noise shocked him from this vision and he raised his head. It was a passing fishing trawler to the north, probably leaving the port of Chora to begin the day's work. A jolt of electricity zinged him from head to toe: If he was caught, all his hard work would be wasted. His adrenaline surged and he redoubled his efforts, hoping the fishermen had not seen him, and hoping the strength of the current would not overpower him.

He kept his head down; if he looked up and realized the distance left to go, the fear of exhaustion would overtake him, thwarting all his efforts. He had barely survived Scylla. Now the tugging current was the sea-monster Charybdis, sucking him into a watery grave. But he would not let his father down, no matter how difficult his circumstances. He had seen his father, and his father was cheering for him to prevail against the sea. His muscles were screaming, and the numbness in his limbs suddenly turned to fire.

Just when he thought his body could take no more, two young dolphins appeared on either side of him, clicking at him as if they were trying to communicate. The dolphins darted up and back in the water, then dove under. Seba could feel them pushing his body forward with their noses. He could hear the voice of his father whispering *Watch the dolphins*. He remembered the dolphins leaping from the fountain's mosaic at Nea Moni. With the dolphins to guide and support him, he looked up to see the sun rising over the Anatolian coast. The rocky outcroppings were closer than he had imagined.

The dolphin on his left was bobbing her head up and down. Seba thought, *She's telling me I'm going to make it!* This joyful realization thrust him forward the final half mile.

Reaching the coast, he heaved himself up on the shore and rolled his battered body onto the dry sand, coughing up water—and part of his lungs, or so it felt. He looked around, but the dolphins were gone; he wondered if they had ever been there at all. The fishing trawler, too, was out of sight. Seba was completely alone. The wind blew over the water, raising the gooseflesh on his arms. It smelled of freedom—and opportunity. Lying on his back, looking up at the wide blue sky, he yelled, "Ζήτω!"

22 EARTHQUAKE

As the thrill of victory slowly wore off, the pain in Seba's body surfaced. His limbs felt like giant boulders, too heavy to lift. He allowed his body to sink into the ground; he had an otherworldly feeling of becoming one with the earth, heavy and immovable, like the stones that jutted up along the coastline. This was no sandy beach, no beautiful Eden. It was desolate, with isolated clumps of wild chora springing out from between the dagger-like rocks. Seba's breath was still fast and labored, as if Poseidon was sitting on his bare chest, his lungs shriveled up under the sheer weight of what he had accomplished.

He felt for Brother Tim's leather pack, which was still hanging from his shoulders. Everything inside was dry—the wool grease had done its job. Another one of Brother Tim's scientific miracles, used to bring blessings to others. Seba wondered if his father knew about the water-repellent properties of wool grease. He would ask him when he saw him. Seba's long-buried hope of seeing his father alive was now closer to becoming a reality.

His mind raced through the myriad of things Papa, Papouli, and Brother Tim had told him about the world. There were Ottoman raiders on the roads and other opportunistic predators of the wild animal variety as well— wolves, snakes, scorpions, and a myriad of other natural dangers. Seba knew he had to get out of the open, but his body would not move. It was as if his mind and body were two separate entities, and one could not persuade the other to join the cause.

He didn't know how long he lay there, mind alternatively racing, then too exhausted to hold a coherent thought. He may have fallen asleep, or fallen unconscious— he wasn't sure of the difference right now. He dreamed he was on a ship, crossing a vast ocean, his father beside the captain, explaining the new improvements to the ship which made it faster than any vessel on earth. The captain's back was to Seba, hands on the helm, listening intently to everything Papa said. Seba was proud of his Papa, and was happy that they were together on this ship, traveling toward the sunset.

As Seba basked in the glow of this happy dream, the ship rumbled and everyone on board shook—not from the roll of a wave, but something quicker and more ferocious, like a monster in the hold was tearing the ship apart from the inside out. The crew ran around, trying to find the cause of the problem; but the shaking of the ship would not stop.

Seba's eyes snapped open to find that the ground was shaking below him. He had felt the earth's little tremors throughout his life—Papouli attributed it to Poseidon, the god of thunder, who controlled the sea and the shaking of the earth—but this was not a minor tremor. It felt as if Poseidon was ripping the mountains from their foundations and throwing them around like dice. The entire rocky coastline—all the rocks, plants, dirt, and scrubby little trees—were moving back and forth like butter in a churn.

Seba sat up and looked around. Rocks were tumbling into the sea, and Seba looked across the channel to see the entire island of Chios moving and twitching violently. He knew this was an earthquake—but far more violent than anything he had ever encountered.

Seba feared that the entire Anatolian coast would crack open and swallow him whole. Was God punishing him for leaving his mastic family? Were his eyes, the gray-green color of a churning winter sea, a curse? What if Brother Tim and the dolphins were wrong? He prayed to God to forgive him for his refusal to accept the mastic life. As he prayed, he wondered if God would be sending a whale to eat him, like Jonah, who refused to go to Nineveh.

The rocks were sliding underneath him toward the sea. He tried to stand up, but could not gain his balance. He knew that sometimes an earthquake would send a wall of water toward the shore; he had heard the men at the shipyard speak of it, their voices grave and somber. No one knew why that happened, but some had seen the enormous rogue waves hit land from aboard ships anchored well off the coast. According to their accounts, an earthquake under the sea caused a benign swell like any other wave as long as the ship was far offshore. That same swell, however, turned into an enormous fifty-foot wall of water when it reached the shallow waters of a harbor or coastline. The force of the wall of water could devastate any buildings near the shore, annihilating an entire harbor in a matter of seconds. Seba did not want to be swallowed by a whale or a wall of water, so he scrambled painfully on all fours, like a startled Chian crab, climbing straight up the rocky hill and away from the water's edge.

Time slowed as Seba crawled away from the shore, and he felt as tired as if he had run up the steep slopes of Mount Phaneros. In reality, it was only a few minutes; the earthquake continued, becoming slightly less violent as the seconds passed. The tremors had loosened the rocks, so Seba advanced only a few feet before falling down and trying to start again. The ground continued to sway beneath him.

To make things worse, the salty sea water was beginning to dry and sting his bloody cuts and scrapes so much that he thought his skin was on fire. If a whale did swallow him now, it would feel the fire of blood burning out of his skin and vomit him up just like Jonah.

He reached the top of the cliff where the land was level, high above the water; just as he put his back foot on flat ground, the shaking stopped. It felt strange. He was unsteady, as he had been walking on land after being on one of the ships with Papa. His body was expecting the land to keep moving. He lost his balance and fell face-first to the ground, stretching his arms in front of him to break his fall. As he hit the ground, a shooting pain fanned from his hand all the way through his chest to a place behind his eyes. Instinctively, he rolled over, grabbed his left wrist with his right hand and held it close to his body. The pain in his wrist felt like a hot iron; he knew it was injured. Now there was no going back. Even if he wanted to swim back to Chios and accept his fate as a donkey for the Ottoman Empire, he would be unable to make it with a broken wrist. He looked closely, as Mama had done whenever he hurt himself as a child. He saw no bones sticking out of place, but his wrist was beginning to swell, making it hard to see if any smaller bones in his hand were broken.

He pulled a shirt from his leather pack. Stepping on it, he grabbed a corner with his teeth and ripped a strip from the bottom of the shirt with his right hand, then tied the strip tightly around his wrist and thumb to keep the swelling down, as Mama had taught him. He gingerly donned the shirt, trying not to rub it against his cuts and scrapes. He hoped the blood had dried enough not to seep through his shirt, or he would be a prime target for thieves and raiders on the road.

Next, he surveyed what he had brought with him. He still had the coins that Brother Tim had given him, sewn into the pocket linings of his canvas trousers, the silver coin from the Saint Vasilios cake, and the gold ring. He had Brother Tim's letter to show Stavros, who might be able to help Seba find his father. He had a few tears from the pouch of mastiha that Uncle Phillip had given him. Seba knew those little white nuggets were valuable, but also extremely dangerous. If the Ottomans caught him carrying the tears of Chios, he would be accused of stealing from the sultan. He shuddered, feeling the throbbing in his left wrist and thinking of the punishment of having that wrist cut off for the crime of mastiha theft.

If that happened, he would be much worse off than a donkey in the *mastichochoria*. He shook his head, dismissing the thought. He also had a skin to hold water that Xenia had given him as a Christmas gift. She had simply left it on his doorstep in a basket; Seba wouldn't have known who it came from if Papouli hadn't seen her leaving it there on Christmas day. Seba had wanted to return it, but Papouli convinced him to keep the skin, saying that she had given him a thoughtful gift without making a scene. Papouli had said maybe Xenia was learning that actions speak louder than words; and in any case, the gesture showed that Xenia was being considerate of Seba's feelings.

His face felt hot as he thought of the last words he had said to her: so thoughtless, so cruel. She had never tried to hurt him or embarrass him; she just wanted to be with him. Just like Artemis couldn't help but be a huntress, Xenia couldn't help but be a talking ball of energy. And what had he done to Xenia in the face of her confession of vulnerability? He crushed her feelings like a bug beneath his boot. Seba's head was now pounding as painfully as his wrist. What an ass he had been, hurting her when she needed kindness. She had been right—she didn't deserve to be treated so poorly by Seba, or anyone else. He wondered if he would ever have the chance to apologize. Seba held the water skin to his chest. It was filled with fresh water from the village, which was almost as valuable as the mastic tears; he didn't know when he would find fresh water to drink.

He recognized the weakness of his position at this moment; he was a victim-in-waiting for robbers, raiders, or wild animals on the road. He hoped there weren't any Anatolian predators who stalked their prey by the scent of blood. He didn't want to find out. Papa had told him about the sharks in the water who got themselves into a frenzy at the scent of blood, so he was glad to be out of the water.

As he lumbered away from the shore, holding his injured wrist close to his body, he noticed a path that wound to the north, toward Çeşme; he could see Çeşme Castle in the distance. The fortress was a remnant of the time when Genoa ruled the area, before the rise of the Ottoman Empire. Seba thought the Genoese must have really liked building with rocks, as Papouli said they were the ones who built Sessera and all the other mastic villages. Unlike Sessera, however, Çeşme Castle could be seen from miles around, on land or on sea. Ahead of Çeşme Castle, the road split. The path to the east was the way to Smyrna, to Stavros's textile workshop, to finding his father—and keeping his freedom. Seba hoped that Brother Tim had already contacted Stavros to secure his cooperation. He had not swum the Strait of Chios just to trade one form of slavery for another.

He hobbled his way onto the wide dirt path, on high alert and ready at the snap of a finger to jump off the road and hide.

23 TRIPATOS

Staggering slowly eastward toward Smyrna, Seba could feel his arms hanging like dead tree limbs from his shoulders. The left hand, Seba's dominant, was still wrapped in the makeshift bandage, and was very swollen. Papouli would have said that he looked like he was hiding a small chicken under the strips of cloth. He didn't think he could move either one of his arms very well if he were attacked. He felt defenseless, and was more scared than he had been since That Day.

Then he looked westward, back toward the Aegean Sea. He had done it! He had conquered the Strait of Chios, just as Brother Tim had said he would. It was one of the greatest heroic feats ever accomplished by anyone from Sessera, or all of Chios for that matter. It was even greater than Thaddeus's success with the Firewood Challenge. But every person who might celebrate his victory was on the other side of the channel. He considered whether he had just made the biggest mistake of his life. His emotions jumbled and swirled around him—pride at his accomplishment, sadness for leaving everything he had known behind, exhaustion from the stress of the last forty-eight hours, and fear of being robbed while he was in no condition to defend himself.

But there was one other emotion, buried so deep that it was almost imperceptible: a tiny glimmer of hope that he might soon reunite with his father.

Seba's legs felt immovable; each step was a challenge. He was still breathing heavily from climbing up the rocks, but he would not stop moving forward. If he were caught alone on the road, the Ottomans would take him and put him to work in a slave camp in a heartbeat. If they found the few mastic tears in his pocket, his hand would be cut off at the wrist.

If the Ottomans forced him to disclose Phillip's secret, it would spell even more trouble. They would kill Seba to protect that secret. If the villagers found out what was in the storage tower, what would stop them from rising up and taking control of their livelihoods? And if the pirates knew how much mastiha was stored in the towers of each mastic village, they would double their efforts to raid the coffers. It could create an all-out war on the island of Chios, and Seba could not allow that to happen. Unfortunately, the villagers did not know that the answers to their prayers were rotting in a stone tower in the middle of every village in the *mastichochoria*. He had to keep moving.

He looked back as the island of Chios and thought of his family and friends. "I wonder if I'll ever see any of you again," he whispered.

Seba shuffled toward the sun all morning, too afraid to stop. Without a hat, his head pounded as the hot sun baked him from above. By midday, his mouth was dry and his eyes felt like they were being pinched and squeezed by a pair of invisible claws. His teeth were clenched tightly together and the back of his neck ached from carrying the pack. The Aegean Sea to the left was in view, and he knew from Brother Tim that if he kept the sea to his left, he would find Smyrna. He had never walked this far in his life, not even to Nea Moni.

As the overhead sun moved behind him, preparing to end its journey for the day, Seba thought of his family. The villagers would be packing up their farming tools and walking back toward Sessera, laughing and planning the evening meal. "I haven't eaten since yesterday," Seba thought to himself, and as if by his thinking it, his stomach began to grumble. This was also the longest he had ever gone without eating a meal, and possibly the longest time he had ever gone without seeing another human being. He knew that he would likely have nothing to eat until he reached Smyrna. He also knew he should save the mastic tears to trade or use to buy food, but his throbbing wrist was calling out for the magical healing of mastiha. He reached into his trousers pocket with his right hand and extracted a tiny tear, white and glistening in the fading light. He popped it in his mouth and immediately felt better. The glimmer of hope increased just a bit as he chewed the mastic gum. He would find his father and together they would find a way to free his family from the Ottomans. Renewed by the burst of minty, herbal flavor in his mouth, he looked for a place to sleep for the night. He needed to be off the road and out of sight before the constellation Hydra appeared in the night sky.

He remembered his conversation with Brother Tim just before he jumped into the Strait of Chios: "If you are on the road to Smyrna at nightfall, you must be very careful. The road is dangerous, even deadly. The Ottomans patrol the road to the port of Çeşme. Yet there are also thieves and desperate men on those roads. Stay off the road at nightfall in all circumstances. Remember the story of the Good Samaritan? Well, there was a reason why the Samaritan's help was necessary—a man had been attacked and beaten on the road between Jerusalem and Jericho. That road, called the Way of Blood, was full of thieves and murderers. Unfortunately, there are many such roads in our world."

Seba was glad for the advice and moved as quickly as his weary legs allowed.

Seba stepped gingerly through the scrub brush beside the road, which led him to a small knoll dotted with rocks and boulders. As the sun dipped below the mountains behind him, he wedged himself under a rock that jutted out laterally, leaving just enough room under its ledge for one human body to squeeze out of sight. The rocky ground was uncomfortable, and the scabs beginning to form on his arms and legs were filled with dirt. Not knowing what else to do, he silently recited Psalm 23:

The Lord is my shepherd, I shall not want. He makes me lie down in green pastures; He leads me beside still waters; He restores my soul. He leads me in paths of righteousness for His name's sake. Yea, though I walk through the valley of the shadow of death, I fear no evil; for Thou art with me; Thy rod and Thy staff, they comfort me. Thou preparest a table before me in the presence of my enemies; Thou anointest my head with oil, my cup overflows. Surely goodness and mercy shall follow me all the days of my life; and I shall dwell in the house of the Lord forever.

Those familiar words made these bizarre circumstances more bearable. For the first time, he felt as if he understood what it meant to walk through the valley of the shadow of death, because he was doing it right now.

Why was Psalm 23 one of comfort? He understood the part about the anointing with oil: outside the village, they sometimes poured oil on the heads of sheep, letting it drip into their noses to keep the flies from laying eggs in their nostrils. This was because when the fly larvae hatched inside the sheep's noses, the buzzing flies drove the sheep insane. Seba had seen many a sheep bang their muzzles on the ground, sneezing incessantly, and stamping their feet to expel hatching fly larvae. That's why the shepherds anointed their flocks' heads with oil—it was one of the many ways that shepherds cared for their sheep. Seba also knew from Brother Tim that kings and queens were anointed with oil to show that they were meant for a higher purpose. Seba's skin was so dry and crispy that he would welcome a shepherd pouring oil on his head.

As for some of the other verses of Psalm 23, however, Seba was perplexed. Why a shepherd would make a meal for his sheep right in front of his enemies was something that Seba had pondered. He resolved to ask Brother Tim if he ever saw him again. He knew that Brother Tim would know the answer, and he hoped that even if they never met in person again, they might be able to correspond through his brother Stavros. Seba's true hope, however, was that Brother Tim would pull into the port of Smyrna aboard Nea Moni's sailing ship and invite him to sail to Constantinople, where Papa was slaving away for the Ottomans.

He put his bag under his head and lay down, thinking about why God made the Ottomans his enemies, and why certain people were born into slavery while others were born into royalty. He drifted into an exhausted sleep to the calm clucking of the nightjars—small brown birds who made their nests on the ground They called back and forth to each other from the scrub brush, their evening discourse rising like the muffled tap of a small drum. Their bark-colored plumage was impossible to spot in the darkness, but Seba felt comforted by their sounds. He remembered a story Papouli had told him about the nightjars, one evening as they sat around the hearth:

"I'm so old that Aristotle himself personally shared this wisdom with me, Seba. You think the nightjars are just harmless brown birds hopping around the scrub brush, but don't believe it! They might be the size of my hand, but goatherds all over Chios must protect their goats from these nightjars—they are goatsuckers and can ruin an entire herd!"

"But Papouli, we don't have a herd of goats. We only have Myra and Sheba."

"I know, Seba, but maybe one day you will have more goats than anyone in Sessera, and then you will need this important information! I for one will not question the wisdom of Aristotle, who wrote about the goatsuckers, and I quote, 'Flying upon the goat, it sucks them, whence it has its name. When it has sucked the teat it becomes dry, and the goat becomes blind.'"

Seba had thought at first that this was one of Papouli's made-up stories; but on reflection, Seba decided that Papouli would never misquote Aristotle, so it must be true. Seba had seen many birds riding on the backs of goats and sheep, eating insects from their fur and from around their eyes. Seba thought the goats were probably grateful for the nightjars' service, and he had never seen any goats killed by small brown birds.

In any case, the memory of Papouli's story brought Seba comfort rather than fear as he lay in the sheltered dark. These low-churring nightjars nesting around Seba tonight felt harmless. Seba was as safe as could be expected, given his circumstances. If there were any thieves or murderers who were traveling the road to Smyrna, Seba hoped they were afraid of nightjars, just like Papouli. Maybe that would keep them away from these bushes and Seba's hideout.

At that moment Seba's stomach gurgled; he was so hungry that if Artemis appeared with one of her furry victims right now, he'd gratefully eat it. His heart lurched as he thought of his feline friend, the beautiful silver huntress. He would probably never see her again. At that moment, he would have given anything for her to noiselessly emerge from the rocks with a mouse hanging between her teeth. She had always offered to share her spoils with him. *I hope you catch something good tonight, Artemis*, Seba said to himself.

He slept fitfully; every time he tried to turn over onto his injured wrist, bolts of pain fired all the way from his fingertips to his temples, and he had to turn back the other way. He wanted to cry. This was not what he had imagined of his escape from slavery—one arm useless, the other cut and bruised. The early morning darkness offered some protection to him, and he wondered if he should stay under the rock ledge until he had a chance to recuperate from his ordeal.

But he had no food, and the sparse scrubby landscape of western Anatolia did not offer any fruits or plants that Seba could eat. This was a far cry from Sessera, where there was no end to wild fennel, fig trees, chora, olives, and citrus. How could he have known that the land did not yield the same fruits on this side of the Strait of Chios?

He drifted in and out of consciousness as the sun rose over the hills. At some point later in the morning, he thought he heard voices passing by the road, and he squeezed into the rock ledge so closely that he felt he would become part of it. He knew his circumstances were grim. He heard the derisive laughs of a group of men passing by him on the road. He understood how Phillip felt the day he was saved by Papouli. At this moment, Seba felt just as Phillip had described — crucified, dead, and buried.

He didn't know how long he lay there, but he could feel the energy draining out of him. His empty stomach was making noises and bunching up, twisting around itself. He had eaten nothing for two days and had very little water left in his skin. He was glad the night air was not too cold. He was accustomed to sleeping outside on the roof, and it served him well on the road where he had little protection from the elements.

The whole day passed with Seba slipping in and out of consciousness, alternately dreaming of his past and trying to focus on his current circumstances. His arms and legs were stiff, and he wondered if he tried to move them whether they would comply. He decided not to try.

As night began to fall, he hallucinated that he was in the tomb with the Savior. The rock ledge hanging over Seba's head served as the stone blocking the tomb. A voice inside his head warned him that he was giving up, and he mustn't do that; but he told that voice to be quiet and let him sleep.

He heard the nightjars again, and this time they sounded like the thrumming of a large and happy cat. He imagined Artemis sitting beside him, purring contentedly as she often had on his roof in Sessera.

He felt his lifeforce dissipating, and thought that he might be on his way to see the sister he had never met. He was so tired. He simply didn't want to fight any more.

Then he heard someone whistling a *tripatos*.

He felt a slight movement of energy from his spine to his toes. He vaguely remembered a story about someone being saved by Jesus singing the *tripatos*, but now he couldn't remember if that really happened or if he was imagining it. Seba was confused, because someone told him that Jesus didn't know the tune to the *tripatos*. Or did he? Seba was so exhausted that he couldn't remember; but if Jesus was going to save him, he was going to try to stay awake for it.

He said out loud, "Jesus, did you come to save me? Do you know the *tripatos*?"

Jesus responded, "Of course I know the *tripatos*. It's a Greek folk tune, and I'm Greek."

Seba said, "No, you're Hebrew. Your whole lineage is in the Bible. Mama made me memorize it."

"If my lineage is in the Bible, then why am I over seventeen hundred years old and still walking to Smyrna on my own two feet? Shouldn't I be in a temple in the heavens with someone feeding me grapes?"

Seba sat up and opened his eyes, which were crusted with sleep. It was morning, but Seba didn't know what day it was. He didn't care, though, because Jesus was talking to him. He wondered why Mama had never mentioned how sarcastic Jesus was.

Seba couldn't see more than a few feet in front of him, and Jesus was a fuzzy outline in the dark.

The voice of Jesus said, "Are you hurt?"

Now that was the Jesus that Seba was used to.

"Yes, my Lord. I think my wrist is broken and my arms and legs are cut and bruised. You must have seen me swim the Strait of Chios."

"You swam the Strait of Chios! Are you insane? And I am *not* your Lord—my name's Paolo."

"What?" Seba tried to sit up, but banged his head on the rocky ledge and fell back down. "Ouch!"

"Are you all right?"

"No, I just told you I'm hurt—and that was before I just cracked my head on this rock! What's happening to me?"

Paolo said, "I was walking along this road to Smyrna, minding my own business, and I heard a ghost whispering 'beware the goatsuckers.' My grandmother told me that evil spirits cannot abide the sound of happy whistling, so I tried to whistle the happiest song I know to scare the ghost away. The *tripatos* reminds me of dancing with my sisters when I was a little boy. It's a happy memory. Then I heard someone ask Jesus for salvation, and I thought someone possessed by demons might be calling for help."

Seba squinted into the gray, misty morning, trying to focus his eyes on the *tripatos* whistler. "You have some imagination, sir."

"Well, you can't be too careful." Paolo reached out his hand. It was calloused and rough, like a laborer's. "Can I help you up? You smell like dried blood. That's not safe."

Seba grabbed it with his good hand. "Yes, I think I broke my wrist during that earthquake. Did you feel it?"

"Oh, yes. The day before yesterday. It was a strong one."

Seba realized that he had been delirious, or asleep, for two whole days since he had swum the channel. All of a sudden, he was starving again. He clutched at his stomach.

Paolo reached into a small pack he was carrying and brought out a few dried dates and a big hunk of hard cheese. He offered them to Seba.

"You look like you haven't eaten in a while. Demons prey on the weak, and you don't want to be food for them."

Seba thought that Paolo was overly concerned with evil spirits and demons, but he wasn't going to criticize someone who was offering him food. "Thank you."

With a bit of food in his stomach, Seba felt like a new person. He was able to tell his story to Paolo, who was particularly impressed with the part about the vision of Seba's father and the other Ottoman slaves helping him cross the Strait of Chios.

"Could you look right through them, like ghosts?"

"I don't really remember. I just knew that they worked together and they were encouraging me to keep going."

"Ah, so they were helpful ghosts! Those are the best kind."

"I guess so." Seba had never known anyone in Sessera to talk about ghosts, other than the Holy Ghost. Paolo was altogether different than anyone he had ever met.

"You must be a pretty special person to get undersea ghosts, water spirits, and dolphins to help you. What's your name?"

"Sebastian Krizomatis." Seba liked saying his whole name—it made him feel close to his father. "But most people call me Seba."

Paolo nodded. "Where are you going, Seba?"

"I'm going to find my father."

"How are you going to do that? I thought your father was a ghost."

"No! The Ottomans took him away, but I'm going to Smyrna and a businessman there is going to help me find him."

"Smyrna? That's where I'm going!"

Seba couldn't believe his luck. As long as Paolo didn't scare him to death with talk of demons and ghosts, he would be the perfect traveling companion.

Paolo continued, "I was working on the barges that carry goods between Smyrna and Çeşme all winter and spring, but now it's time for me to go back home. Smyrna is exploding with ships and merchant trade. The work there is much better during the warm season—and so is the food."

"You traveled back and forth on barges? What about your family? Did they mind that you were gone all these months?"

Paolo's face darkened. "I don't have a family anymore." He waved his hand, as if dismissing a thought. "I don't want to talk about it. C'mon, let's get going."

Seba wanted to ask him why he was walking to Smyrna instead of traveling by barge, but after seeing Paolo's reaction to the question about family, he decided not to pry. Paolo was thick and muscular, not as tall or Heraclean as Thaddeus, but with a similar build, indicating that he could beat Seba to a pulp if he wanted to, especially in light of Seba's injured wrist and battered body. Seba was worried that he had offended his new friend by asking about his family, but as they walked and talked, it became evident that Paolo was more interested in ghosts, spirits, and being mistaken for Jesus. Paolo gestured demonstratively as he spoke, and at one point, even made the sign of the cross just like Mama, saying, "The evil spirits won't come near me now that I've been mistaken for Jesus. I feel like He's with us right now."

Seba agreed. "My mother says that Jesus is always on our side. It's just that we forget it sometimes when we get scared."

Paolo nodded approvingly, and Seba marveled at his luck in finding the perfect travel partner. He thanked God and every saint, apostle, and divine being he could think of for sending him a guide who was familiar with Smyrna.

After a few miles on the road, they were fast friends, laughing and joking as if they had known each other for years. That night, they found a spot off the road where they could sleep for a few hours under cover of the scrubby bushes. As they heard the nightjars clucking in their nests on the ground, Seba considered whether he should tell Paolo the story of the goatsuckers. Paolo was highly suggestible when it came to anything dark or scary, but Seba thought he could spin the story as a comical old tale to ensure that the village children would bring their goats into the pens at night rather than leaving them out to be eaten by wild animals.

By the time he was finished with the story, Paolo was holding his stomach, laughing as he rolled back and forth on the ground. Maybe Seba had inherited a little bit of Papouli's storytelling talent after all. He liked the feeling of lifting Paolo's spirits through the act of sharing a story, and Paolo seemed happy to have his mind off his usual dark and dire thoughts.

The next day, still hungry and with newly blistered feet, Seba and Paolo walked nearly fifteen miles east along the coast of the Gulf of Smyrna. The sunlight sparkled off the blue sea, and they could see the mountains that encircled Smyrna rise up in the distance. The road widened as they neared the bustling city and they encountered more people and animals, passing local traders who went about their daily routines on the coastal road. There were small farms clustered across the hillsides, complete with herds of sheep and goats dotting the landscape. Paolo spoke to some of the travelers and Seba saw that Brother Tim had been correct—cotton and silk were the topics of the day, and merchants were taking their raw materials to various markets for sale.

Seba and Paolo fell in with a group of farmers bringing their raw cotton to Smyrna to sell to the textile shops. The farmers were familiar with Stavros, and seemed impressed that Seba had such a wealthy connection. Emboldened by his newly found storytelling abilities, he had the farmers' rapt attention.

For some reason that Seba could not fathom, though, Paolo kept interrupting him. Finally, Paolo cried, "Seba, we need to stop for a moment! I've got something in my shoe and I need some shade. You fair merchants go on ahead—it was nice talking with you."

Seba reluctantly stopped by the roadside. As the farmers continued ahead of them, Seba said to Paolo, "What's wrong with you? I thought you were a seasoned traveler, and we need to keep moving. Are you really that tired? We're almost there."

Paolo waited until the farmers were completely out of earshot, then he stood his full height and put both hands on Seba's shoulders. He narrowed his eyes: "You need to keep your mouth shut. We don't want everyone to know our business. Besides, there are pickpockets everywhere on this road, and no matter how innocent you think those farmers were, no one can be trusted."

Seba involuntarily tapped his trousers where his coins were sewn into the lining.

Paolo stepped back and frowned. "You have coins in your trousers?"

Seba's face turned crimson. "What?"

"I just saw you tap your trousers when I mentioned pickpockets, and that means that you were checking to make sure that your money was safe."

Seba let his hands hang by his sides as he stared at Paolo. "You figured that out just because I tapped my trousers?"

Paolo sighed and rolled his eyes. "You have a lot to learn about the world. How old are you, anyway?"

"I'm fifteen. And I don't need you to treat me like a child. I just swam the Strait of Chios, and I can take care of myself."

Paolo held his hands up in mock defense. "Calm down,

I'm just trying to offer some friendly advice. Especially since I'm seventeen, which means I have two more years of experience than you on this earth. Plus, I'm traveling with you, and when you talk too much you endanger us both."

Seba, still smarting from being reprimanded, snapped, "I don't care how old you are and I don't need your protection. You should mind your own business, or this is going to be a short trip to Smyrna. I just hope I can trust you."

Paolo threw his head back and laughed, a truly musical sound that defused all the tension between them. "Yes, of course you can trust me! I'm in Jesus's inner circle, singing the *tripatos* wherever I go." He did a little dance step and tapped his toe on the dusty road. "Can you just let me do the talking until we get to Smyrna, please?"

Now that Seba had established his authority and independence, he nodded in agreement. He imagined that this is what Papouli was like when he was a young man. It was comforting, but also made his heart ache. He wondered whether he would ever see his grandfather's twinkling eyes and dancing feet again.

Paolo's voice pulled Seba from his musings. "Are you listening to me? Will you please promise me that you won't tap your trousers anymore? Smyrna is a big city, probably full of sights and sounds you've never experienced. I think it would be best if you let me take the lead."

Seba stepped in front of Paolo and said, "Not a chance. I just escaped the Ottomans and swam the Strait of Chios, so I think I've earned the right to take the lead."

"Have it your way." Paolo laughed, shaking his head and extending his arm to invite Seba to walk ahead. They picked up the pace as they neared the city, smelling the salty air off the coast mixed with exotic spices being loaded for export. The road rose to a thousand feet above sea level, and they could see the billowing white sails of ships moving in and out of Smyrna's harbor. The merchant vessels looked like toy ships bobbing up and down in a basin, illuminated by golden beams of sunlight. Seba's heart skipped a beat as he thought of his father. He was closer to him now than he had been in the last six years.

Between the water and the mountains, the port of Smyrna was spread out in front of them. The boys stopped to take in the view, their hearts beating with anticipation. The city stretched in a semicircle around the inner bay like a coronet on the water's edge, its streets teeming with shops, factories, churches, kafenions, homes, taverns, animals, and more people than Seba had ever seen in one place. It reminded him of the colonies of ants that were everywhere on Chios. Seba couldn't believe that he had actually made it this far. This day felt like a new beginning, one of the best days of his young life. As he took a deep breath of ocean air and felt the sun on his shoulders, he realized that the golden city before him was the next step in the journey to find his father and reclaim his legacy. A verse from the *Odyssey* came to his mind as he set his sights on Smyrna: "You will be brave and thoughtful if your own father's forcefulness runs through you. How capable he was, in word and deed! Your journey will succeed, if you are his."

AUTHOR'S NOTE

The idea for this book came from my friend Tony, whose grandparents were first generation Greek immigrants in America. He told me a family legend about an ancestor from Chios who had escaped the Ottoman Empire in extraordinary fashion. Although I'm not of Greek descent (at least not that I know of), the more I learned about the people of Chios, the more I wanted to know. Tony generously allowed me to use his ancestor's escape as a jumping off point for this fictional story, and didn't balk when I told him he was the inspiration for the beloved character of Vaios Georgelous. I can't thank him enough for his help in making this story come to life.

I traveled to Chios to research the book and fell in love with the warmth and graciousness of the Chian people. The Chios Mastic Museum in Pyrgi provided a wealth of information, from clothing styles to musical instruments to ancient mastic production tools. The writings of Professor Dimitris Ierapetritis regarding the mastic trade in the 18th century were invaluable. I stayed in a medieval mastic village just like Sessera and spent many evenings on the stone roof watching the stars appear, just like Seba. It was magical.

Thank you for reading this book. I hope you enjoyed reading it as much as I enjoyed writing it. If you liked it, please consider leaving a review. Honest reviews help authors find their readers and enable authors to continue writing what they love. If you would like to read more about Sebastian's adventures, sign up for my mailing list at www.kpearsonbradley.com and receive updates on upcoming books in the Merchant Tides series.

ABOUT THE AUTHOR

K. Pearson Bradley is an American writer. Tears of Chios is her debut novel and the first book in her Merchant Tides series. She lives in Saint Augustine with her husband.